BETTER THE DEVIL

WES MARKIN

CONTENTS

ABOUT THE AUTHOR

Wes Markin is the bestselling author of the DCI Yorke crime novels set in Salisbury. His latest series, The Yorkshire Murders, stars the compassionate and relentless DCI Emma Gardner. He is also the author of the Jake Pettman thrillers set in New England. Wes lives in Harrogate with his wife and two children, close to the crime scenes in The Yorkshire Murders.

You can find out more at:

www.wesmarkinauthor.com

facebook.com/wesmarkinauthor

BY WES MARKIN

The Lonely Lake Killings

The Crying Cave Killings

~

Details of how to claim your **FREE** DCI Michael Yorke quick read, **A lesson in Crime**, can be found at the end of this book.

Text copyright © 2023 Wes Markin

First published 2023

ISBN: 798397782470

Edited by: Brian Peone

Published by: WFM Publishing Ltd

For Donna Morfett

THE PEARLY GATES

*T*he child, Matthew Brace, had been left by Salisbury's High Street gate.

To die?

It certainly appeared that way to Detective Chief Inspector Michael Yorke.

Matthew, just shy of his seventh birthday, had been placed in a sitting position against the northside of the locked gate, almost directly beneath the Stuart royal coat of arms, which crowned the coursed stone archway.

The ashen-faced boy had been placed here at three in the morning, four hours after the gate into the grounds of the iconic Salisbury Cathedral had been locked, as it was at the same time every night.

'Brazen.' Yorke looked at Detective Constable Sonia Jones, an ambitious young widow with three children, who'd gone all out to become a detective despite her challenging personal circumstances. Yorke hadn't thought this highly of someone since Emma Gardner. He kept her close. Under his wing. 'Brazen and cold.'

Sonia, who was still taping up the scene, nodded at him.

Yorke eyed the still stationary ambulance behind him, then returned to his thoughts, trying to establish a clear chain of events:

One of Matthew's kidnappers had parked around the corner on New Street at the precise moment Brenda Loomes, an elderly insomniac, had opened her door to Cindy, a cat which had, in recent months, become too overweight to fit through the flap.

'He took that old Skoda right up on the pavement,' she'd told the emergency services. 'Cindy barely got out of the way ... bless her. I'd have given him a piece of my mind if ... well, if ...'

She hadn't given the man a piece of her mind, because he'd emerged from his vehicle, hoodie up, carrying a limp child in his arms.

And then you swung a left onto High Street, Yorke thought. And bold as brass, you displayed Matthew here. For us. Brazen and cold.

Evil too.

He looked behind himself at the ambulance. The child had been gently lifted in a minute or so ago. Why are you not tearing a route to Salisbury Hospital?

It was starting to bug him. Was everything all right in there?

Had the paramedics, God forbid, lost the boy?

Too soon ... don't assume anything ...

You know better than to assume ...

The boy had appeared out of it, but he'd shown no visible injuries. To Yorke, he'd looked drugged, but that was a good while away from confirmation.

Beside him stood another officer, fresh-faced Detective Constable Rob Wood. Rob reminded Yorke of his own adopted son, Ewan.

The thought of Ewan in this job?

Over my dead body.

He watched Rob ready the logbook for the impending arrival of the full team.

Yorke recalled meeting Rob's parents. They'd glowed with pride.

'I'll keep an eye on him,' Yorke had said. At the time, he'd smiled to keep the comment light; he didn't want to ruin their big day. However, deep down, Yorke had been deadly serious. Everyone needed someone to look after them in a job like this.

One day, the Woods' pride would be gone, replaced with the bitterness over the fact that their beloved son, Rob, had ever taken the job.

Yorke, Sonia and Rob ... the paramedics and Matthew in the ambulance. That was it. Far too quiet for a crime scene. He checked his watch for the umpteenth time. *Where the bloody hell were his people?*

Yorke wasn't used to this. When he arrived at crime scenes, they were bustling. And he certainly never got a personal invitation from the criminals involved!

Something was wrong.

He shouldn't be first to the party.

His mobile rang. Recently promoted Detective Sergeant Sean Tyler. A good lad if not a little dim-witted sometimes. 'Yes, Sean?'

'The Skoda's still here, sir.'

Shit. Yorke had expected the kidnapper to be long gone. 'You sure? You got the right one?'

'Yep, directly outside Brenda's house. Right up on the pavement like she said. The car seen better days, too. Been swerving its MOTs, that's for—'

'Don't touch it, and ensure no one else touches it until the SOCOs arrive.'

He sneezed. 'Sorry ...'

'Just guard it—'

He sneezed again.

'Are you okay?'

'Yes, sir. Brenda's fat cat was rubbing itself against my legs. Allergy has flared—'

Shaking his head, Yorke hung up and pocketed his phone.

'Sir?' Sonia asked.

'Skoda is still outside Brenda's house ...' He shook his head. 'Our man is on foot.'

'Or in another car,' Sonia said. 'Do you think one of the other kidnappers came to collect him?'

'Possible, yes ...' *But I've got an awful feeling ...* He looked around. *He's still here, I'll bet.*

He'd met others like this before—others who liked to watch.

His neck was cold. He reached for it, relieved when his fingers fell on material. People would think him mad to have a jacket on during the heatwave on so balmy a night. But no one ever understood. Didn't matter the temperature, the nape of his neck always grew cold in the presence of death.

Yet, no one was dead, were they?

He looked at the ambulance and thought of the child inside.

Are they?

He shook his head, hating that cold sensation. It wasn't really a warning; it was just a damned inconvenience.

A hangover from discovering his first body—his best friend at university. Brendon ...

A hangover? Behave. A hangover passes, you stupid man!

Your sensitive neck is just another of your scars. One of many. Physically, mentally ...

Morally.

He stared up at the stone archway and the windows on

either side of the Stuart royal coat of arms. Two blackened eyes, looking down. *Others who liked to watch.*

Curious, he went to try the door in the archway. It rattled but wouldn't open, locked. The police had a key to the gate but not to the office inside. He suspected that key would be with the council—or, at least, should be. Had the kidnapper got in somehow?

'Sonia, keep your eyes on the door and those windows,' Yorke said.

Sonia nodded. 'Yes, sir.'

Through the archway, Yorke watched concerned residents emerge from their homes on the southside, no doubt drawn like moths by the flashing lights of the ambulance and intrigued that the gate was open at such a late hour.

For now, the residents were content to stare. If the rubber-neckers approached, Yorke would have to move quickly to shut them down. Yorke hoisted the phone from his pocket and rewatched the short video sent to his personal phone fifteen minutes earlier.

A closeup of ashen-faced Matthew Brace, coughing and moaning for his mother. A zoom-out to reveal his location. The closed High Street gate. North side. Recognisable by the Stuart royal coat of arms.

Fifteen minutes earlier, Yorke had been the kidnappers' first point of contact; they'd acquired his personal number. It didn't take a genius to work out how. Giving out his personal number to someone involved in the case had been an unpro-fessional lapse from Yorke and it'd come back to bite him. Still, on receiving that message, there'd been no time to despair over his stupidity. No. There'd only been time to get into his electric Volkswagen, put his foot to the floor, and call in the cavalry.

'This really doesn't make sense. They could have asked for

whatever they wanted,' Sonia said. 'Why return him without a payday?'

Indeed, money would have been no object to the Brace family. Landowners, monied up to the eyeballs.

Sonia continued, 'Maybe these bastards got spooked, sir? There didn't seem to be any physical wounds on Matthew. Maybe he fell ill, and the kidnappers panicked?'

Yorke took a deep breath and stared at the cathedral through the open gate. He exhaled slowly. The tallest spire in Britain remained proud and dominant on the horizon, overseeing all. Right now, the Christian symbol irritated him. The cathedral seemed decadent. Revelling in self-indulgence while injustices had ravaged the grounds beneath it for a fair number of centuries.

He gritted his teeth and shook his head again. *Think ... think ...* He turned to the ambulance. 'That should be halfway to the bloody hospital by now.'

'Shall I check, sir?' Sonia asked.

Yorke was about to tell her to hold back, that he'd do it, when he heard the footsteps of one of the bloody rubber-neckers creeping closer. Yorke spun, held up his badge, and marched forward. 'This is a crime scene, sir. Can you stay back? We'll be taping off the other side in the next minute or—'

'The back doors are locked, sir,' Sonia called out from behind him.

Yorke turned. She was trying to open the rear door of the ambulance.

Shit! He didn't want either of his two youngsters out of his reach. He opened his mouth to holler for her to come back over when she knocked on the rear doors. 'Open the doors, please!'

Yorke shook his head, his thoughts racing.

The sudden return of the boy? The message directly to him? The presence of the kidnapper's car? And this location, a significant location, below the eye of the cathedral ...

What a place for fireworks.

Sonia called out to him, 'No one is answering. It doesn't make sense.'

But it does make sense, Sonia. Unfortunately, it does.

'It's a bloody trap! Get away from that ambulance and over here.'

He spun and shouted at the gathering crowd on the south-side of the gate. 'Back to your homes. Now!' He sprinted towards Sonia, who was slipping around the side of the ambulance. *Stubborn as usual!* 'Sonia, I told you to get back!'

Rob, who was already trying to play the hero, marched after her.

'*You're* making it worse,' Yorke shouted at him.

Rob stopped midway alongside the ambulance by the side door, allowing Yorke to draw level. Yorke was about to tear him to pieces when he saw the confused, vague look on his face.

He thought of his adopted son, Ewan, again. A child. Naïve. In need of guidance.

'Get your arse back to the gate and get on the phone. We need armed response,' Yorke insisted.

Rob obeyed.

Heart thrashing in his chest, Yorke continued towards Sonia, who was now level with the passenger side at the front of the ambulance. She stared in, her eyes widening. After putting her hand to her mouth, she stepped backwards.

Yorke drew level and looked through the passenger window.

The side of the paramedic's neck was a bloody mess, and their head was on the steering wheel.

A bullet wound ... yet not a sound.

A silencer?

Blood running cold, Yorke glanced in both directions, then held his breath and listened. He heard the loud chatter of the residents by the gate.

Chances of hearing the killer's footfalls over that were close to zero.

He fell to his knees and looked beneath the ambulance. No feet, at least.

Yorke took a deep breath and stood. *Was he in the van, perhaps?*

He turned and glared at Sonia. She seemed to get the message and headed towards the gate.

Turning back, with his stomach doing somersaults, he shimmied to the side door and reached for the doorhandle.

Was the killer in here?

Could Yorke be the next dead public servant?

The next firework?

The internal questions steadied his hand until images of his daughter, Beatrice, entered his mind.

Almost the same age as Matthew Brace—the pale, suffering child they'd wheeled into the back of this ambulance.

Someone else in his shoes, with his daughter in the back— wouldn't he want them going in? Expect it?

He opened the side door and sighted Matthew on the gurney.

Before, against the gate, the six-year-old had been still, now he was writhing, coughing, and wheezing. Whatever they'd drugged him with must have worn off.

If it wasn't for another quick flashback to the paramedic at the front, whose neck gaped, the sight of Matthew would have sent him pouncing in. But the killer could easily be hunkered down near the rear doors of the ambulance, out of Yorke's line of sight. *Caution, Mike.*

'Matthew, can you hear me?'

The child was suffering too much to respond.

Shit. 'Is anyone else in there?'

He caught the sound of someone else moaning, an adult female. The other paramedic perhaps? 'Help ...' The words were faint. 'He's gone ...'

Taking a deep breath, he lifted a foot to the step to get himself in—

A hand landed on his shoulder.

He reached, gripped the hand, and twisted as he sharply turned. He drew back his fist to deliver a blow but stopped himself just in time.

He released Sonia, and she backed away, shaking her now sore hand.

'Do you not listen?' Yorke hissed.

'I couldn't just let you go in there.' Tears welled in her eyes. The sight of the dead paramedic had taken it out of her.

'You can. I need you over there, taking control of the situation, please—'

Sonia's head turned slightly; she'd seen something. He didn't wait for her to gasp. He spun, ensuring his body was completely blocking Sonia should the gunman be about to shoot—

'For God's sake,' Yorke spat at Rob coming around the back again. 'I swear if this prick with a gun doesn't cut all of our lives short, I'm going to start cutting careers short instead!'

'Armed response and other emergency services are coming. Sorry, sir. I thought you'd like to know.'

Yorke sighed. 'Listen. There's another paramedic down in there, injured, with Matthew. I don't think the gunman is in there. While I unlock the rear doors from the inside and get the child out, you get to the gate and organise. If I come out again and see you anywhere else, so help me!'

Yorke turned, mounted the first step, and entered the ambulance.

Beside him, a female paramedic lay on her back, clutching her stomach. Blood saturated the front of her uniform. The floor around her was a red swamp. Her eyes rolled back in her head. 'Help ... me ...'

Avoiding the spreading pool of blood on the ambulance floor was a no-go. It made moving difficult, and he was suddenly glad of the running trainers he'd thrown on in a hurry. Work shoes would have seen him on his arse. He manoeuvred slowly to Matthew, steadying himself against oxygen tanks, the roof, and anything else he could lay his hands on.

When he reached the writhing boy, his heart sank further. Matthew's small hands were tensed into claws, and as he squirmed, he pounded and scratched the ambulance walls.

What've they done to you?

Yorke gulped, unable to keep the innocent, vulnerable face of Beatrice from his mind. He gritted his teeth. *Hold on, Mike.* If he lost composure, everything else would quickly follow.

'I'm getting you out of here, Matthew.'

He glanced down at the paramedic. Her eyes were now closed, and she was no longer making a sound. Looking at all the blood, he could only think the worse.

Okay. Two paramedics, a tortured child ... is this enough? Is your point made?

God, he hoped so.

He moved for the ambulance door, but Matthew grabbed his arm. The poor boy's face was completely contorted now. Yorke let one of his own hands settle over Matthew's and noticed he now bounced his other hand off his stomach rather than the wall.

Yorke yanked down the bedsheet to see what was bothering the child so much.

He gasped at the sight of large blood-stained square bandage taped over his abdomen.

'What've they—' He bit back the words in time.

The child was terrified. In agony. *Give him only reassurance.* He stroked the child's face. His skin was like his daughter's. Unblemished. Soft.

He stared at the bandage again.

An appendicitis?

No. The dressing was too central.

In the distance, he heard sirens.

Good. But what's taken you so bloody long?

Matthew's hand slipped free of his while his other hand swatted the bandage.

A knock on the back door made him flinch.

'It's Sonia! It's all under control back here, but you're taking too long, sir!'

She certainly was persistent. He couldn't blame her, really. Roles reversed, he'd have been the same.

'Coming,' he shouted at the doors.

He regarded Matthew again. The boy bashed his head from side to side, at war with the painful damage caused by these kidnappers.

'I'm going to open the doors, Matthew. Help is here.' He was about to turn away but noticed Matthew had pulled away part of the mysterious bandage.

Yorke tasted bile in the back of his throat.

Ah Jesus ...

What's that?

He steadied himself against the gurney, which was locked

in and unmoving; yet he still felt as if he would fall and disappear through the floor.

Matthew had unearthed some crude stitching, which started just below his chest.

Yorke eased off the bandage.

Oh God above ...

The stitching ran the length of his stomach.

Yorke turned from him, holding his mouth, his composure again at risk.

Move it, Mike. Move it now.

Sucking in a deep breath, he moved for the ambulance door and unlocked it, then heard another long guttural moan from Matthew.

Focus ... focus ...

He opened the right side, jumped onto the street, and went to his haunches.

Sonia came close. 'Sir, are you—'

He held up his hand, willing himself not to vomit. He gulped at the air. 'Bastards ...'

'Sir?'

'They've taken something from Matthew.' He broke off again, retching. *Hold it together, hold it together.* 'From his stomach.'

He took another deep breath, felt momentarily steadier, and rose. He stared into Sonia's creased face.

'I don't understand,' she said, slowly shaking her head.

'Neither do I. I've never seen anything like it.'

Matthew screamed in agony. Both Yorke and Sonia looked into the open ambulance.

The sirens grew louder.

'Thank God,' she said, her voice wavering. 'Shall we bring him out?' The emotion was breaking out of her now.

'I don't think we should move him. Where's Rob?'

He recalled, then, the gunman on the loose. The imminent danger. The fact that two paramedics and a child might not be enough for whatever the hell all this was.

'*Hello?*'

Yorke looked over Sonia's shoulder.

A middle-aged man had worked his way from the residential area on the cathedral side to the archway, his hand raised in greeting. 'Hello?' he repeated loudly.

Yorke marched forward, waving him back; he was now, of course, in no mood for etiquette. 'Weren't you asked to stay back there?'

The man paused, considered, then had the audacity to continue.

Blood boiling, Yorke quickened his pace. 'This is a crime scene, man! Can you not see the tape? Are you blind?"

'No. I'm on the town council, and so I demand—'

'I couldn't give a fuck if you're the prime minister,' Yorke said, clenching his fists. 'Get back off the bloody crime scene.' He was close now. If he reached him, he couldn't be responsible for his actions.

'Inappropriate, Officer. Can I take your—' He broke off when Yorke was a metre from him.

Yorke wondered if it was the anger in his eyes or his large, intimidating scar that divided his right cheek into two separate chunks. It was probably a combination of both.

The man knew Yorke was on the edge. He backed away.

Yorke continued, enjoying watching this idiot's retreat. He neared the archway where this whole shitshow had started—

A loud scream came from the residential area ahead.

Yorke looked but couldn't identify the source.

Then came more screams.

Yorke ran, barging past the town council imbecile and sending him into a spin.

Ahead, the arrogant residents, who should have already been inside after Yorke's earlier instructions, scattered, a fair few of them screaming.

Chaos.

Fireworks.

Some residents dove into their homes while a few high-tailed into Choristers Square.

Yorke, watching them all disperse, increased his speed, until it became patently obvious that only one unmoving individual remained.

Is this who they were running from?

The man stood near the Blumenfeld's Angels Harmony sculpture—a four-metre statue of three abstract angels in a harmonious dance. Fluid, graceful movements, a nod towards joy and unity.

Fear whipped the DCI's stomach when he sighted the gun in the man's left hand.

Joy and unity were the furthest thing from this nutcase's mind.

The gunman started towards Yorke. He was wearing dark clothing and kept his head lowered slightly to shroud most of his face with a hood.

And now what?

Yorke had no weapon.

If he ran, he'd be offering his back as a target.

All he had now was reason.

However, thinking of what these bastards had done to Matthew, he wondered if reason was, in this instance, of any use.

The gunman approached until he was a few metres away. The Salisbury Cathedral rose behind him, an emperor staring down on its gladiators. Although, unarmed, Yorke felt more like a sacrifice.

'It's over,' Yorke said. The sirens were loud now. 'They're moments away.'

The man didn't raise his gun, instead he raised the other hand. For a ridiculous moment, Yorke wondered if he was simply greeting him.

But when he saw what was in the bastard's hand, the world spun around him.

He desperately needed something to hold onto. To steady himself. He fought to keep himself on his feet.

The gunman's thumb was poised above a black explosive's trigger.

Yorke didn't know much about the blast radiuses of suicide vests, but he took a deep breath and consoled himself over the fact that most people had retreated. Those in the houses should keep their heads down from shattered glass. Loss of life could be kept at a minimum. Still, any loss of life was far from insignificant. 'Why? You'll only kill the two of us.'

The man shook his head from side to side. 'I'm not going to die today.'

'Then, what ... how ...?' *Oh God, no.*

Matthew.

In his mind's eye, he saw those stitches on the boy's stomach again.

You didn't take anything out of that child, did you?

No.

'You put something inside him. Oh Jesus, no. Why?' Yorke lurched towards him, but he was too late.

The gunman stepped aside as he pressed the trigger.

Having missed his target, Yorke fell to his knees.

There was a deafening explosion, and a rush of air.

Already the cathedral and his surroundings glowed as the flames at the gate licked at the darkness and shadows. As car alarms, shop alarms, and screams drowned out everything else, Yorke rose and turned.

He held out some hope that Rob and Sonia were there, having followed him. He wanted so desperately to see them, restraining the terrorist on the ground.

As irritating as it sometimes was, at least they always showed initiative.

But Rob and Sonia weren't there. His incessant bollocking had finally steadied them.

And the consequence?

Ahead, he glimpsed the fires that were surely consuming them.

He felt the gun press against the back of his head. The bastard must have circled around him.

He closed his eyes. He couldn't feel fear. Only despair.

Images flew through his mind.

Sonia's three young children. Rob's proud parents.

Matthew, in pain.

His own family.

'At least tell me why,' Yorke said. 'At least give me that.'

The gunman didn't oblige.

THE LONG GAME

*P*rinceholm Hospital was a funny old place.

And not because a hulking meat sack called Stan Burns raped Lacey Ray every night—because rape was anything but funny—but rather because Princeholm called their prison cells *convalescence rooms*.

The late-night screaming, the number of suicides, and the fact that no one ever really saw the light of freedom again suggested that recovery and rehabilitation were the furthest things from Dr Stewart Holden's mind.

Yet he continued to run the institution on the taxpayer's purse. Lacey wondered if he was held to account for the lack of success in his management of the mentally ill or praised by sleazy politicians for having thrown away the key on the insane under the false promise of rehabilitation?

She'd plump for the latter.

After all, it was probably cheaper to keep the crazies locked away here for the rest of their days than support them outside in a welfare state. Plus, reoffenders were a pain in the arse and could cause a haemorrhage at the ballot box.

Dr Stewart Holden was quite the card.

He'd diagnosed himself as a malignant narcissist. Off the books, of course. Symptoms of grandiosity, extremely low empathy, and a wicked sadistic streak wouldn't look good on a job application, after all. He shared his nature with Lacey Ray though, due to her possessing the same diagnosis, then proceeded to toy with her. One malignant narcissistic seeking power over the other.

The first time she noticed him observing her through the slot in the door of her convalescence room—or rather *heard* him breathing through a bent septum—she'd determined not to play a one-sided game of chess with the prick. So she made her first move in one of their therapy sessions, which, until that day, had really just been hour-long opportunities for the narcissist to tease and provoke.

She'd told him straight that she'd spent almost seven weeks taking him into the Blue Room—a place accessible to her through meditation, a place where she rehearsed her kills. She promised that when the day finally came when he lost control of his impulses, moved away from the slot, and actually entered the convalescence room, she'd show him who truly had the power.

He was irritated, especially when she added that he was little more than a rat that was misjudging its own importance. That scurrying around in the dirt, preying on vulnerability, was a poor excuse for power.

So, Lacey's opening gambit had worked. He'd taken the bait. The irritated rat would seek retaliation. Make his own move.

He was a predictable old bastard.

And sure enough, one night she'd woken up paralysed.

Paralysed!

Yes! He did have a taste for the sadistic.

It'd been easy for Holden. He'd access to all sorts of chemicals, which included a neuromuscular-blocking agent. It prevented all nerve impulse transmission and left her to the mercy of him when he did finally emerge from behind the door.

She'd be lying if she said she hadn't been a bit disappointed with the paralysis. But only a little, mind. The game had been prolonged, not finished. There was nothing wrong with a long game if you kept up with the pace.

Or the lack of pace, if you considered her inability to move.

Still, protracted wars brought sweeter victory and more memorable rewards, so she got a handle on her disappointment and embarked on the long game.

Holden's play was to give her the *same* diabolical choice every night.

Blink once if you want me to resign. Then you'll never have to see me again.

Blink twice if you want to endure what I've brought with me tonight.

Him, resigning? Before she'd had her move again? *Unthinkable.* But he'd known that.

So, that night, and every night since, she'd blinked twice.

And then Stan, the doctor's minion, pumped on Viagra, would enter the room and rape her.

Every time it'd happened, Lacey had fought the urge to retreat inside herself to the Blue Room. She *needed* the experience, in all its horrendous magnitude, to feed her, to strengthen her.

Every night, Holden had made the same promise to her after Stan had fulfilled his duties.

'*Tomorrow I'll come back to your room with Stan and offer you the same choice I gave you today. One day, I'm certain, you'll beg me for death.*'

Over my dead body, Lacey had thought. *Or rather yours?*

~

DR HOLDEN LATE?

This wasn't like him at all. The doctor was like clockwork.

Suddenly distrustful of his Casio watch—he'd been wearing it since his late teens, after all, and he was now into his forties—Stan flicked the screen with his finger.

The digital time remained unchanged.

He patted the pockets on his scrubs. Lubricant, condoms, and jangling keys in one side. His old mobile phone in the other. He hoisted out the mobile for a second opinion on what time it was.

Seems his trusty Casio was bang on. He almost felt ashamed for doubting it.

So, it was true, then. Dr Holden was, for the first time in years, missing *party time.*

Party time wasn't Stan's crude expression. It was what Dr Holden himself called it. And only in front of Lacey. His strange boss really did enjoy antagonising her.

Whereas Stan, himself, wasn't much into torture. Honestly, at first, the whole setup had horrified him, and he hadn't wanted to play ball. Not at all. He'd simply complied. Stan knew *exactly* where he was in the pecking order. He was a grunt, paid very little, organising himself using a twenty-year-old Casio, while the good doctor moved gracefully to the sweeping second hand of a twenty-k Rolex.

However, over the last year, his stance had softened towards the whole thing, and he had, of late, started to look forward to it throughout the course of the day.

Some of his friends would be grateful for the opportunity to have sex every day with a decent-looking woman, even if she couldn't move. Although, he hadn't confirmed this because, as per Dr Holden's instructions, he'd not breathed a word to anyone.

So, many months back, he'd shrugged off the bitterness of being forced into doing something his long-dead parents would have been horrified by and moved more into the territory of never looking a gift horse in the mouth. That, and the fact he'd developed some feelings for Lacey. Yes, there it was. He'd started to actually like her. *More than like?* He shrugged. *Possibly ...*

He nodded and peered through the slot into the convalescence room.

It was dark inside, but he could see her bed at the far side, in the shadows.

Lacey Ray had been big news before her incarceration, and afterwards, to some extent. Stan often wondered how Frank and Jim would react if he ever dropped the bombshell on them during cards on a Friday.

'Guess who I'm fucking, guys?'

They wouldn't believe it. At least, they wouldn't believe it *there and then*. After he was found murdered for spilling the beans, which was as sure as night turns into day if you broke Dr Holden's trust, they would exchange a few knowing looks at the funeral.

One of Stan's predecessors, another security guard, had disappeared in mysterious circumstances. Dr Holden had been sure to take the mystery out of it for Stan with a photograph of his victim.

No, Dr Holden was the boss here. Stan was a grunt, and the dangerous babe on the other side of the door had had her wings clipped.

In a way, Stan and Lacey were alike. Both Dr Holden's prisoners. It was almost romantic.

He felt the Viagra kicking in, and the blood rushed to his cheeks. Closing his eyes, he visualised pushing back her lengthening hair, so he could gaze at that large jaguar tattoo that rose up her neck. He felt a stirring below.

He liked that tattoo; he really did.

It made him feel like he was coupling with a wild animal.

Considering Lacey Ray's reputation, that kind of made sense.

He checked his Casio again. Ten minutes late!

Unbelievable!

Every night, for years, the doctor had been here before him.

Every *single* night.

His first words always the same: '*Have you taken it?*'

The Viagra.

Holden didn't trust Stan's nerves. Seeing anything go wrong in there would be inconceivable.

Before Stan would go in, Holden would enter the room first to give Lacey that same choice. *Blink once and I'm gone from your life. Blink twice and endure.*

Stan had once looked up the word *endure* on his computer. It had saddened him for a few days. Was he, Stan Burns, really something to endure?

He wondered if, one day, both he and Lacey would finally speak, and she'd reassure him that this had never really been the case, that she'd seen him as a pleasant distraction from her mundane incarceration.

Wishful thinking, yes, but hey, his parents had always taught him to be positive.

Anyway, onto present day. What about right now?

Stan was torn.

If he walked away, Dr Holden mightn't be best pleased about Stan giving Lacey a night off. After all, this endurance

—he scrunched his face up over the mere thought of the word—was some kind of daily punishment that he was administering to Lacey. Once, Dr Holden had referred to it as a *treatment programme*. You'd be forgiven for thinking he was being sarcastic, but there'd been something about the look in Dr Holden's eyes as he said this which made you wonder if he did in fact believe it to be a treatment—at least on some level. A level probably not accessible to grunts such as Stan.

So, walking away felt like a bad move. A *dangerous* move.

But, if Stan went in and delivered what he delivered every night without Dr Holden's introduction—his *ultimatum*, as he liked to call it—wouldn't this cause outrage too?

Dangerous outrage?

He sighed. A rock and a hard place.

He plucked his keys from his pocket. He held them by the keyring, and they jangled in his shaking hand.

Despite knowing he was the only guard on duty in this wing, he did what any panicked individual would do; he threw glances both ways. It was a waste of time, but it did give him some sense of security.

Due to the trembling, it took him a moment to get his key in the lock. He didn't turn it immediately. Instead, he looked through the slot. Lacey hadn't changed position. But why would she? The drug had been injected barely an hour ago, as it was every night.

The nurse on duty would administer the drug while several guards restrained her. Dr Holden would give the syringe directly to the nurse, who believed the medication was for Lacey's condition. The excuse was that she was being delivered the drug in this manner due to her refusal to take it orally. The nurse would have no reason to suspect otherwise. At first, Stan had been stunned and had quizzed Dr Holden over the reason for Lacey keeping schtum. *'Couldn't she just tell the nurse? Another guard?'*

'Yes,' Dr Holden had replied. *'But she wants to win. Desperately. Winning for her isn't my incarceration or yours. She tells anyone the truth, she loses. At least in the way that she views our contest.'*

By his own admission, Stan wasn't the brightest, but he knew what constituted a victory for Lacey Ray; one only had to consult the press archives for that information. Also, during their closer moments, Lacey had sometimes managed to hiss something into Stan's ear as the drugs lifted their grip slightly.

At first, he thought it was just a peculiar sound emerging from someone drunk on Holden's cocktail, but in time, as he heard it over and over, it dawned on Stan that it was an actual word. One he'd never heard before.

'Lingchi.'

He Googled it.

And immediately regretted doing so.

Death by a thousand cuts.

Wow! *Really?* Surely this was just his imagination? Besides, even if she had threatened it, what could she do? She was practically catatonic whenever he saw her. He was rarely on day shifts, so seldom saw her outside her room, but even if he did, she'd be restrained and chaperoned by two guards.

He was still to turn the key, and his hand shook incessantly.

What do you want me to do, Dr Holden?

Turn the key, do my duty? Hold fire, wait for your order?

I'm bloody drowning here!

His phone beeped. He hoisted it out and read the message: *Running late. Get on with it.*

Having never received a message from Dr Holden before,

Stan was at first surprised, then gave a heavy sigh of relief. He turned the key and entered.

The only light in this convalescence room slithered through a strip above the door, so after Stan had closed it, his vision became limited, making Lacey merely a silhouette.

As he stalked towards her at the side of the room, his eyes quickly adjusted. Then he paused at her bed and breathed another heavy sigh.

You're as beautiful as ever.

Admittedly, the light was limited, but Stan was certain that she just didn't age. Apart from her longer hair, Lacey hadn't changed. She looked as fresh-faced as the first day he'd been with her.

He often wished to talk to her about such things. Compliment her on her beauty. Flatter her like his father had always flattered his mother. Make their coupling more delightful to her and less of a test of her endurance.

Of course, he'd never been able to do that. Dr Holden's regular presence in the corner of the room, sitting, arms folded, had taken that option off the table.

He thought of the doctor's message again: *Running late. Get on with it.*

Stan smiled. Was this his one chance to treat her like an angel?

He looked over his shoulder just in case his boss had made a quiet entrance. Seeing that this wasn't the case, he turned back and leaned over Lacey's face, close enough for his breath to settle on her skin. 'We've known each other for so long.' He paused, hoping she'd open her eyes and acknowledge him. 'I can't tell you what it means to me that we're finally alone.'

Stan straightened, slipping the Vaseline from his pocket. He'd used to wear a condom, but Dr Holden had recently instructed him to stop, having introduced a contraceptive into Lacey's once-a-night cocktail. *'I want her to feel ... soiled.'*

The word *soiled* had bit deep into Stan, because he couldn't marry up how his act of love could result in something so base. He hoped on some level, Lacey would agree with him.

Stan removed his scrubs and underwear and applied the lubrication. He leaned in again, stroking her face with one hand while stroking his erection with the other. 'I'll tell you the truth. Usually, when we're together, I block him out completely. Yes, I know he's here in that corner, watching, but I try to forget he's there. This isn't really the first time I've been alone with you. I wanted to tell you that. In here'—he drew his hand from her face to touch his forehead—'I'm always alone with you.' He closed his eyes and kissed her forehead, and when he pulled back, he saw that her eyes were open. He felt his heart beating faster.

'There're so many questions I want to ask.' Stan continued to massage himself. 'First, am I gentle enough? Dr Holden tells me to be forceful, but I try, I really try, to hold back. It could be worse; it really could.'

He looked into Lacey's eyes, now fixed firmly on his. 'But if you want, I could be gentler, you know? Fuck him. Who died and made him God, right? Besides, the egomaniac isn't even here tonight, so we could even kiss? You deserve that. That care and attention. That appreciation. Shall we kiss?'

Had he really just said that? Stupid question! She couldn't kiss; she was practically paralysed.

He felt his face reddening, 'Sorry. I meant I could kiss you. On the lips. That's what I meant. I'm sorry, I'm just rambling now. I just want to, you know, make it nice for you, perhaps?'

She blinked.

Stan's eyes widened. Blinks are answers! One blink is a yes! *Wait. Don't get ahead of yourself.*

'Can I kiss you?'

Blink.

Stan's heart raced faster still. Before the courage left him, he swooped in and pressed his lips to Lacey's.

She didn't move a muscle, but the pleasure and excitement that rushed through him seem to shake his entire world at the core.

Afterwards, breathless and speechless, he glanced behind himself to confirm Dr Holden was still absent, before realising he'd never known desire like this. Excitement coursed through him, and it would be easy to give in, to take what he wanted. Consume. But he didn't want to rush it, not this time. Didn't want it to be over before it ever really started. And he'd already promised not to be too frenetic and forceful with her. So, trying his utmost, he slowly slipped off Lacey's blanket and rested his hand on her stomach. After a tentative moment, he drew his hand down her nightie until he reached the warmth of her upper legs. He gradually worked his fingers upwards beneath the material to trace the flesh on her inner thigh. He looked for pleasure in her expression but saw nothing, but that didn't mean there wasn't any. The drugs in use were powerful.

'I don't want you to endure tonight. I want it to be natural. A coming together of two like-minded individuals.'

Blink.

He restrained himself from whooping with delight. She was unable to give a pleasurable expression, but she'd been able to give a clear indication that she felt the same way.

'We're both his puppets.'

He lay his hand over her underwear but didn't apply pressure. 'May I?'

Blink.

He moved his fingers over her, caressing her, then eased

the underwear down her legs and climbed on top of her. This moment always felt clumsy and awkward, but tonight, without the added pressure of Dr Holden's eyes on his back, Stan believed it felt natural, almost graceful.

He had his elbows on either side of Lacey's head, so he was no longer touching himself. Not that he needed to. He was so hard, he practically ached. He was unsure of whether to move in now or extend the anticipation they both felt. His heart sank slightly when he considered that their time together hadn't really developed him sexually. It'd been too manufactured, too structured, too forced. Pressing his erection against her, he gazed into her still face, trying to delay the next moment as long as his willpower would allow. And then he felt, inside his head, a greying shadow of guilt, and he realised what would be the next and most natural of moves.

'I want to say I'm sorry. I should always have treated you this way. Things will be different. I don't know how, I really don't, but I'll say something to him. I promise.'

For a while, he stared into her eyes, willing her to accept his apology, while his erection throbbed demandingly.

So focused was he that he ignored the saliva that dribbled from the corner of his mouth. Although, he did see it settle on her cheek.

His face flushed again. Rather than make an excuse, he put his weight on one elbow and rubbed the spit off her face. 'You're the only woman I've been with.' He righted himself on both elbows and beheld her once more. 'Is that okay? Me telling you that?'

Blink.

The grey shadow of guilt dissipated, and the need to be inside her increased. It was time. But first, one last kiss.

'I'm going to kiss you again.'

Blink.

He pressed his lips to hers and let a glorious warmth run through his entire body. This time the kiss lingered, and he flicked at her paralysed lips with his tongue. He pulled back. He wondered if he was glowing in the darkness. He certainly felt like he was. 'I wish you could touch me. I wish you could guide me inside you—'

Her hand closed around his erection.

Eyes shut, he groaned.

This was wrong ...

... but right. Yes, *so* right.

As she manipulated him towards her, he wondered if his eyes might completely roll back into his head. The sensation of her hand on his erection, the way she massaged him as she guided him, it was unbearable ... wrong ... without reason. It shouldn't be happening, yet nothing had ever felt so right.

'How?' he asked as she pressed him against her warmth. 'How?'

'Abra-fucking-cadabra,' Lacey said.

Stan winced and yelped. The stinging sensation below was sudden and painful. Recoiling from Lacey, he stared down and saw the needle protruding from the end of his cock. He grabbed it and yanked it free as he fell backwards from the bed and onto the floor. 'Shit ... shit ... that fucking hurts!'

He stared up at Lacey as she swung her feet from the bed. She outstretched her arms and waved her hands through the air. 'Yes. That's magic.'

'My dick. Fuck. My dick!'

Lacey laughed. 'Dicks, dicks, dicks! Always about dicks with you guys!'

Stan felt nausea rushing over him. 'What've you done to me? What've you done?'

'I stuck a needle in your cock. Are you blind as well as thick?'

'Help me ... I feel *strange*.'

'Well, you would. I pumped you full of the same shite you've been pumping me full of for time immemorial. You know, listening to those sweet nothings before ...' She paused and pulled a stupid expression, then used a monotone voice. 'Can I kiss you? You're the only woman I've ever been with?' Her voice returned to normal. 'I almost wondered if there was another side to you. A soft core, perhaps.' She retrieved a hunting knife from under her pillow, which she showed Stan. 'But no. It's all about the dick. As per usual. You men. You crack me up! Try thinking with something else.' She regarded him for a moment with a raised eyebrow, then patted her lip with the tip of the blade, thinking. 'Unless ... could I be wrong? Maybe you do have a soft core. Perhaps, I should carve you open to find out. There's no truer way to find out how soft someone is inside!'

The pain had disappeared, and Stan felt the numbness, the *spreading* numbness. 'I can't move. I can't fucking move.'

'Your voice is also turning to shit,' Lacey said, stretching out. 'Won't be long before the only person you'll make any sense to is yourself.'

Stan was well and truly freezing over. 'You ... I ... what ...?' As she'd warned, his words now emerged as little more than an incomprehensible drone.

Lacey placed a foot on either side of his stomach. She twirled the hunting knife in one hand and then sat on his stomach. She then laid the knife on his chest and again donned a stupid expression and used a monotone voice. 'I want to say sorry.' She reverted to herself. 'For treating me like a blow-up doll? About time.' Back to an impression of him: 'I wish you could touch me.' And back to herself: 'I'm going to touch you, all right, Stan ... many, many times.'

He tried desperately to reach the knife on his chest, but his arms wouldn't obey. They twitched, came off the floor slightly, but got nowhere near.

'I'd laugh, at you fighting it, but it's rather pathetic, isn't it? Welcome to my world.'

'Dr ... Hol ...'

She sighed. 'Really? Save your energy. You're going to need it, every last drop. But speaking of the good doctor. No. I'm afraid he isn't coming. One at a time. What do you think I am? Impatient? I've been lying under you for years! No, I'm going to take my sweet time with both of you. Sweet, quality time.'

Stan was completely immobile now. He wondered if he was crying. He certainly felt like he was, although he could sense no tears on his skin.

Inside was a different matter. Inside, dread was alive and kicking.

He was going to die. Nothing could be clearer.

How had she done it? How?

Fooling Dr Holden was almost worthy of respect.

But all such thoughts drained from his head when she grabbed the knife off his chest and twirled it. 'Please don't worry. I was only joking before about carving you open. Frankly, I couldn't give a shit what you look like inside—probably like any other dead animal, I expect. However'—Lacey smiled—'I did make you a promise, didn't I?'

A promise?

What?

She'd only ever said one thing to him.

Oh God, not that ...

'Lingchi.' She took a deep breath and said it slower. 'Lingchi. It took every ounce of my being to squeeze that word out for you! Lingchi. And now it just kind of rolls off the tongue.' She picked up one of his limp hands and pressed the serrated edge next to the palm. 'You ready?'

Please ... please ... don't ... I was only doing what I was told.

He wondered if she could see the pleading in his eyes and hear the screaming deep inside his soul. Would it have mattered if she could?

'A thousand cuts, and'—she held up her finger—'after each and every cut, I expect you to blink once. That blink is everything to you. That blink is your plea for forgiveness. Yes, I know you've already apologised in your own way.' She mimicked him again: 'I want to say sorry.' And back to herself: 'Hardly cuts the mustard, eh? So, do you understand the rules of the game?'

No ... please ... it wasn't me. I was made to do it.

Lacey raised her voice. 'Do. You. Understand?'

Yes ... but ... I—

'We can do this with or without your eyeballs.'

God, no. Without eyeballs, there would be nothing. No sight. Paralysis in the dark.

He blinked.

'So, if you survive nine hundred and ninety-nine cuts, and you've begged for my forgiveness nine hundred and ninety-nine times, you'll live to fight another day, albeit in a rather messy state, but still, another day is a day to find that one special person. That one special person worthy of all those sweet nothings you wasted on me. *May I kiss you? You're the only person I've been with.* Blah, blah.' Lacey put her fingers down her throat and made a vomiting gesture. 'If you're into all that. But I know what you're thinking, Stan the man, with your ginormous heart and massive pot of lube.' She wagged her finger in the air and tutted. 'You're thinking, how the hell will I find love with my face hanging off?' She lifted her eyebrows. 'Huh?' She punched his arm. 'Am I right? You big sensitive soul, you. So, here's the deal. And I'll need to get a quick blink for this one, because nine hundred and ninety-nine cuts will take a long time, and I really must get going. I won't cut your face. Not once.' She pinched his fat cheek and flapped it. 'You iccle cutie-pie. So, think about that, Stan the man. You can cover up all nine hundred and ninety-nine little scars and get yourself out there. Tinder, a wine bar. A brothel? The world's your oyster. Do I have a blink about giving me this blink every time I cut you so I can get on with this?'

Inside, Stan was crying.

The despair was such that her words were moulding together.

But still, he heard that faint promise bubbling along in the background.

Fight another day?

I won't cut your face.

Find love.

Such words sounded almost ridiculous coming from this person, whose atrocities would be written into the annals of history.

He blinked.

Once.

Not the face. I'll take another day. Find love? Well, let's play it by ear.

'But with every cut, you must blink. I must have that apology.'

Blink.

She took a deep breath through her nose and looked up, exhaling. 'You know, I'd forgotten what it was like to feel alive.' She eyed his limp hand and the knife pressed against it. 'Don't forget to blink, or with the thousandth sweep of this blade, I'll split your face in two and only stop cutting when I've opened your jugular. First cut. Ready?'

She cut into his hand. He felt the pressure but not the pain. He blinked.

I can make this, he thought. *I really can.*

It was particularly hard to count himself, especially when they hit three figures, but she kept him informed.

I'm going to do this, you just watch, you bitch. I've got this. I've fucking got this.

'I like the Casio, by the way. Rather retro. Shit. Sorry. I lost count ... ah, I remember now. Three hundred and six.'

Stan blinked. *Bring it on, psycho, you won't win.*

'Have to say, Stan the man, I don't usually get queasy, but you're looking rather messed up. Four hundred and two.'

I'm going to beat you. I'm going to beat you and then laugh when Dr Holden kills you.

By the time Lacey got to nine hundred and ninety-nine times, Stan wished he was dead already.

～

MANY, many moons ago, Lacey Ray was lucky enough to find her one.

On their first day together in bed, after making love countless times, Lacey placed her finger on her one's suprasternal notch, the visible dip in the neck between the clavicles, and said, 'I've never told anyone what's in the Blue Room.' She traced her finger gently over her one's sternal head and smiled. 'Well, no, that's a lie. I've told many.' When her finger came to rest on the sternum between her one's breasts, she felt her heartbeat. 'But all those people are now dead.'

'Does that mean I have to die?'

Lacey leaned in and kissed her one gently on the lips, moving her hand onto her breast.

Her one moaned, and Lacey saw it as an invitation to press in harder with her lips.

Her one's second moan was louder, more intense, and

Lacey drank this pleasure. Her eyes rolled, but she locked away her own pleasurable sounds. For now.

Lacey pulled back from her one. 'Apart from the colour, the Blue Room isn't unlike this room. Or many other rooms in this world, for that matter.' She pointed at the mirror over on the dressing table. 'Look into our reflection and tell me what you see.'

Her one's eyes found the mirror. 'I see us. I see us here, now ... but ...' She broke off.

'But?'

'But, right this second, all I want to do is, well ... fuck, like we did this morning, like last night, like—'

Lacey put a finger to her lips. 'Still, when we've started such a conversation, we must finish.' She withdrew her finger.

'Yes, but—'

'You just asked me if you're going to die in the Blue Room. Do you not want a response?'

Her one's face fell. 'You think I was being serious?'

'No. But there's a time to be humorous and a time to be serious. Now we must lean towards the latter. Look towards the mirror again, and imagine now, if you will, that everything you see in it is coloured by the deepest hue of blue.'

Her one's hand settled on her thigh. Lacey let it stay for now, but she did find it unfortunate. She wanted her one fully tuned in. So, if her one's hand was to move during this process, Lacey would be further disappointed. And disappointment never sat well with her. 'It's also cold. Do you feel that?'

'Yes.'

'Good. It should also feel more real to you than the world you're physically sitting in. Does it, my one?'

'Yes.'

Are you humouring me, my one?

Still, her one's hand hadn't moved farther up her thigh as she'd first feared. Maybe the Blue Room did have her undivided attention now. It was how it should be.

'Welcome to my place of judgement,' Lacey said.

Her one nodded.

Lacey took a lungful of air and exhaled slowly. In the reflection, she saw her breath as a plume of icy air.

'And now?' her one asked.

'And now what?'

'What's next?'

Lacey smiled. 'There's no next. You're there. And that's all.'

Her one stopped gazing into the mirror and glanced at Lacey. 'But how do you kill them?'

Lacey, too, moved her gaze from the mirror to her one. 'In whichever way I see fit. The Blue Room allows you so much creativity. It allows me to find the sweet spot for each and every one of them.'

'But you kill them. Not just in there but here too, don't you?'

'Yes. In exactly the same way.'

Her one nodded, grasping the concept. 'I guess a predator will always rehearse their kills in their head.'

'I like to think that the Blue Room is more than just a symbol for my head, but yes, you touch on the premise.'

'And that's what you did with my father? You took him there? First?' Her one regarded the mirror, as if indicating it was the real route into the Blue Room—which, of course, it really wasn't.

Lacey nodded. 'Although he bled a lot more in this world than the Blue Room. But remember the connection between any two things cannot be perfect. Just as a single speck of dust or a stray beam of light on that mirror will distort the reflection. Not always perceptibly, mind. But it will be distorted, nonetheless. The connection between my two realms can't be an *exact* replication.' She ran the tip of her tongue over her upper teeth. 'But it's close enough.'

'I see.' Her one looked ceilingward, thinking.

'Penny for your thoughts.'

'Just processing.' She tightened her grip on Lacey's thigh. 'So, you took me into that realm first to watch him die, then you let me watch in this realm too?'

Lacey nodded. 'In a nutshell.'

'I'm so grateful to you for letting me be there when you killed him.'

'You don't need to be.'

'Seeing him bleed, with the light fading from his eyes, changed me. In ways, I never expected to change. Even when he asked my forgiveness, I couldn't help but feel the ... the ...'

'The pleasure?'

'Yes.'

'The man was a monster.' She laughed again. 'And as a hawk will feed on vermin, we will feed on monsters. In time, they'll call you a monster. It's nonsense—used flippantly—a label that's so crudely broad. We aren't the monsters; we're born from them. The way they've acted, for so very long, has evolved their victims.'

'We're the effect. Not the cause.'

'Bravo.'

'I wish now I'd killed my father myself.'

Lacey laughed. 'There're always others. So, so many others.'

'Daunting.'

'Try exhilarating.'

Her one nodded. 'Yes.'

'So?'

Her one creased her face, confused. 'So?'

'Back to your question. The one about whether you must die?'

'Yes.'

'It all depends, I guess.' Lacey smiled. 'Do you need to stand in judgement for anything?'

Her one's hand drifted from Lacey's thigh to her crotch. 'How about this?'

'No, my one. That's perfectly fine.'

~

PAUL FLEGG WAS HUNGOVER.

He'd been out all night with his best friends. All of them in the public sector, bar Jimmy. Jimmy the smug bastard, who drove a brand-new Tesla and didn't sweat over mortgage repayments and parking tickets like the rest of them did.

Still, credit where credit was due, Jimmy loved to flaunt his money by spending it and was happy to keep buying the rounds. He was also happy to listen to the rest of them moan about decades of depressed pay in the public sector.

Not because he was their mate but because he loved the elevation in status such chats afforded him. 'No, lads, I'll grab the next one. You guys have got your strikes coming up.' A quick wink. Off to the bar.

'The cost of doing business. Drinking the bar dry while that prick shouts his mouth off. I can live with that!' Jason said.

They all agreed.

And they had, indeed, drunk that bar dry.

He knocked on the door to Lacey Ray's convalescence room. 'Rise and shine.'

No reply.

Another knock. 'Lacey?'

Still nothing. *Odd.*

Queen Psycho was usually prompt with her salutations, if not always polite.

He knocked a third time. *Come on, princess. It's a beautiful day. Sooner you're up, sooner we can get you outside in your shackles.* There'd been a time when he could get away with saying such things. Now, if the administration overheard him using such a tone, he'd be out of work.

He missed the good old days, days when he could get away with anything and get paid reasonably well for it.

What're you playing at, woman? I'm in no mood. Got a right bastard behind the eyes.

He glanced through the slot in the door. The direct sunlight through her window came at him laser-like, and he looked away. After blinking several times, he tried again. This time, he fought through the burning light, but it was hard with the hangover, and it was taking some time for his vision to—

Blood ... a body!

He recoiled, sucking in a deep breath.

Thinking suicide, he thrust in the key and, with shaking hands, unlocked the door, opened it, and peered inside.

His hand flew to his mouth, and his stomach turned. 'Oh fuck, fuck ...'

Not suicide.

Murder.

Stan Burns.

What was most unusual about this corpse was how his exposed torso and arms were a bloody mess of raised welts, while his face was perfectly preserved, like he'd been whipped to death. No wounds were on his legs, but someone had gone to work on his genitalia. The copious amount of blood on the floor must have spewed from the opening made here.

He lifted his gaze to the bed where Lacey lay with her back to him, bloody and curled up, shaking in her underwear.

Heart now thrashing, and ever so grateful that he could put himself back on the other side of the door before she turned and got to him, he looked between the corpse and Lacey, trying to interpret what was happening.

Stan had always been an odd bloke. Eyes-down kind of bloke. Quiet. Unresponsive to banter.

Had he come into the psychopath's room late at night to play ... *Wow ... Really?*

Getting close to Lacey Ray, Stan?

That took some balls! Stupid though, because she's now taken them from you. Literally.

He fled the room before she could even think about turning on her bed and eyeing him like prey.

Then he called in the cavalry.

∾

PAUL TOLD the other guards what the animal had done to Stan.

No one believed him, of course.

'Be my guest,' Paul told them, offering up the slot in the door. Maybe the sun had moved, and they didn't have raging hangovers, giving them a better chance of seeing exactly what'd happened before entering.

They did.

Their faces paled, and they spewed profanities—no vomit though. This surprised Paul. He'd thought at least one of them would buckle.

Dave, the religious one among them, went into a full-on prayer.

Paul rolled his eyes.

'His fucking balls,' Dave said, which sounded ridiculous immediately following his interaction with God.

'So, who's first in to restrain her?' Paul asked, smirking.

No one. Not until they were suited up at least.

However, by the time they'd donned their riot gear—because the fastenings could be a right ball-ache with trembling hands—the emergency services had arrived.

~

U*N-FUCKING-BELIEVABLE*, Paul thought.

In his twenty-five years of service here, no one had ever managed to escape! *No one!*

And the fact that it was Lacey Ray ... well ...

He saw Dave mumbling to himself and wondered if he was praying.

I hope there's a God because this is one almighty shit show.

He gave Dave the thumbs up and stopped himself short of saying, *'Crack on. Intervention needed.'*

He removed his helmet as they pushed Nurse Amelia Banks out on a gurney. Poor girl. In complete shock. They'd want to know how she got into that chamber of horrors, but they'd get nothing from her yet. All he could see was a gibbering child. How old was she? Mid-twenties at a push. Had she been in that abattoir all night? It was a godsend she wasn't Lacey's preferred gender, or she'd be in pieces, too.

Paul looked at the CCTV camera. The answer to what had gone down here last night would come soon enough. Still, he had his suspicions, and he told Dave them when he'd given up on divine intervention.

'Dirty bastard paid Lacey a visit, I bet you.'

'A booty call? Nah, who'd be that stupid?'

'Come on, mate. You said it yourself the other day. He was an eyes-down mute!'

'You think Lacey tempted him in? Really?'

'That, or he went in to get what he wanted.'

'Bollocks.'

'Think about it. How else would the knife have gotten in there? He took it in with him, to threaten her,' Paul insisted. 'Bastard was raping her, bet you.'

'And the girl, smart arse? Amelia?'

'Poor Amelia may've noticed the door ajar.'

'I think Stan would have closed the door; don't you?'

'Unless he was in a rush. Wanted to be in and out, made a mistake. Hardly the sharpest tool in the box.'

They both watched the paramedics wheel Amelia down the corridor.

'Lord have mercy on her!' Dave said, shaking his head. 'First week here, too.'

'Yeah, seemed nice enough. And look at the state of her. Wouldn't have been too hard for Lacey to convince her to hand over her uniform, identification, and key card. Walk straight out.'

'If you're right ...'

'I know. Heads will roll, right? Not ours, as we weren't on duty. And Stan can't be executed twice. Where's Dr Holden anyway?'

Dave shrugged. 'I don't know. Odd though, isn't it? He's always here.'

'Yeah. Like my fucking shadow.'

~

EARLIER ...

.   .   .

AFTER BEING INFORMED that his wife and child were in serious condition following a traffic accident, Dr Holden locked his office door at Princeholm, wondering what it would feel like to be someone neurotypical receiving that phone call. To the average person, such a phone call would trigger panic of the highest order—a stomach-churning, heart-wrenching panic attack.

Not to him, of course.

He didn't love his wife and son. Not their fault, of course. He didn't love anyone, except himself. Part of his condition. He didn't even care for them. If anything, they simply irritated him for not being particularly interesting.

However, Holden cared about their continued presence in this world.

They existed as subterfuge. They provided the dour but necessary appearance of normality.

Without them, without the mirage, someone might truly see him one day.

Yes, the odds were still against it. After all, he'd operated well in this world in his own manner before their arrival.

But still ...

He'd worked hard, *suffered* a lot, to ensure this extra blanket of security, and it'd be better if they lived.

Regardless, live or die, he was under obligation to show concern and be present.

So he left Princeholm and drove to the hospital. En route, he planned to speak, tearfully, to their fractured bodies to inspire healing or, at the very least, give weight to his pretence of being bereaved.

When he discovered at the hospital reception that his wife and child weren't there, he phoned home.

His wife answered, and he cursed himself for not making this call before leaving Princeholm. After all, he was always so cautious and methodical. Such a drastic turn of events should have inspired some suspicion, should it not?

Well, looking back never solved anything, so he gave the present situation careful thought.

Someone wanted him on a merry goose chase and out of Princeholm, but now he was on his way back, which meant one of two things. Whatever was going to happen had happened already or was in the process of happening. The second option was that someone wanted him where they could see him. So, two potential solutions. He could contact Princeholm, but that could be dangerous, considering his many activities there and not knowing exactly what'd gone off or was going off. Solution two: he could surprise those who wanted eyes on him.

He opted for the second, the unpredictable, and when he took the back exit out the hospital, his watch beeped, reminding him of his nightly meet with Stan outside Lacey's room. Missing this was rather unfortunate, but there was little he could do about it now. He paused mid-flight to send a text message to Stan: *Running late. Get on with it.*

Then he smirked as he wondered.

Lacey?

Are we playing?

He directed himself to a queue for a taxi, but seeing it was far too long, he changed direction again, heading over a patch of grass that bordered the hospital grounds. He wound himself around a row of planted trees.

Lacey lingered in his mind, smiling at him from the corner of her convalescence room.

You, of all people, would know I'd have to respond to that call.

You're very aware of the need to keep up appearances.

Of course, if he was playing with Lacey, and he was

becoming more and more convinced that he was, she'd be anticipating his move.

She'd predict his different exit from the hospital, his impatience in waiting for the taxi, his chosen shortcut across the hospital grounds to the main road and the bus stop—

He heard a buzz.

Clever girl.

He experienced convulsions and passed out.

He woke in darkness, disorientated. It was stuffy and enclosed. He reached out to ascertain how tightly he was closed in. Buried alive?

No, he sensed movement and heard a moving vehicle.

A bump and a sudden jolt confirmed it. He was in the boot of a car.

He closed his eyes, imagined her again, as he'd done before the ambush, smiling at her from the corner of his mind.

He smiled back. 'Stan?'

She nodded.

'How? You can't beat the drugs.'

She chewed her bottom lip.

'But you don't need to beat if it was never administered, do you?'

She tapped her nose.

'Nurse Amelia Banks.'

Lacey widened her eyes.

'I checked her thoroughly. I always do. Background and references. Newly qualified, too. Certainly, no relative of yours.'

Lacey shrugged.

'A lover. Yes, a lover.'

Lacey flicked her finger in his direction, as if to say, *You got it!*

'She was already in your life, wasn't she? Years before me.'

Lacey was laughing now.

'And then you used her for your long game. How did you stay in touch with her? One of my greasy guards, perhaps. Paid? You had her train to be a nurse; you waited all this time, all this time ... so patient. And who, apart from you, would be so sure I'd select her from all those many candidates? Congratulations, Lacey, you read me like a book on this one. You'd knew I'd take to Amelia, didn't you? Her eccentricities, her knowing smiles, her edginess—you told her not to repress her narcissism in that interview. If she'd have done that, I wouldn't have given her a second look! I'd have gone for experience. How clever ... how very clever. You knew I'd be interested, that I'd take her on, start to watch her. Just not close enough, it seems!'

Lacey was in hysterics now, banging her fists on the floorboard.

'I'm impressed. I really am.'

The car stopped, but Holden stayed inside his mind for now with his muse.

'Amelia, eh? At least I was right. She's like us, isn't she? Just like us. Did she leave a weapon beneath your pillow? But, of course, she did! And what did she do with the *real* syringe that she surely replaced with a water-filled one? Left it for you to use on poor Stan, I expect.' He snorted. 'Are you taking your time over him, right now? But, of course, you are! I mean, what's the rush? No one will come until morning, and I'm here ... who knows where. And you're simply going to walk out, aren't you? Walk out *wearing* Amelia's uniform while she pretends to be a poor terrified girl.'

Lacey looked ecstatic now. She'd risen to her feet, twirling to non-existent music.

'Exceptional,' Holden said. 'What a move!'

Lacey nodded as she danced.

'Unique, breath-taking, I stand in awe. But also some sadness. Why? Because such a move does deserve victory, and it almost pains me to say that you won't get it.'

She paused and regarded him, looking confused.

'You only win when you get to kill me in all the ways you described.'

The boot opened. Holden opened his eyes.

A man with a balaclava, holding a gun, stared down at him.

'No need for that, my good man,' Dr Holden said. 'I'll come willingly. I don't fear death. I only fear losing. Besides, if you kill me, I win. She did warn you of that, I hope. You won't want to meet your employer if she loses.' He laughed. 'You really don't.'

∽

HAND IN HAND, Lacey and her one entered the house on Sycamore Street in Southampton. Her one was renting it under the alias Carrie Birkham. Having slipped from her hospital room while being treated for shock, Nurse Amelia Banks had ceased to exist.

Lacey closed the door behind her and faced her one. They admired each other for a moment before passionately embracing and kissing.

When it became clear from her one's wandering hands that she was ready for more, Lacey broke away.

Her one furrowed her brows and tapped a foot. 'I've wanted—sorry, strike that—*needed* you every single day since I first saw you again at Princeholm.'

Lacey smiled. 'It's not healthy to need. Only to want. So, *want* this reunion, my one, and it will come, but first'—she

looked down the decrepit hallway at the two closed doors—
'the spoils. Where are they?'

Her one pointed at the first closed door on their right. 'In
there, but I've yet to receive a confirmation from the person I
used to grab Dr Holden.' She moved towards a pile of newspa-
pers at the bottom of the stairs and retrieved a knife from
underneath them.

'Handy,' Lacey said.

'Best to be sure.'

Lacey nodded.

Together they stepped over unopened mail and takeaway
menus. The house stank of stale smoke, and the threadbare
carpet beneath their feet was stained. Her one stopped them
halfway down the hallway. 'I haven't thanked you yet,' she
whispered, 'for letting me make the final cut.'

'I took your father. I owed you one. I thought it fitting you
take Stan.'

'I'm surprised you could stop yourself.'

'I promised him I wouldn't kill him if he blinked. It kept
me focused. Honestly I didn't think he'd survive the cuts. But
he did. Good on the meat sack. However'—she smiled—'I
never thought you'd get his bollocks off with that knife once
I'd finished with it.'

'Yes, it wasn't the sharpest. And it was knottier than you'd
think down there.'

'Anyway, isn't it me who should be thanking you? For my
freedom? Still, my one, be warned; this monster is all mine.
I've rehearsed this to perfection for years in the Blue Room,
and now I must release.'

They turned at the open door to the lounge, which had
been recently inhabited by squatters, and the yellowing seven-
ties' floral wallpaper glowed with spray-painted tags. Aside
from that, the room was bare, apart from the man in a single

chair, facing away from them at the lounge window, with a burlap sack over his head. Net curtains allowed the sunlight to stream in and around the prisoner, while keeping him hidden from the eyes of the outside world.

'The spoils,' Lacey said and smiled.

'The man I paid delivered him,' her one said, sounding relieved. 'Still, why didn't he let me know?'

'Dr Holden?' Lacey said. She paused and took a deep breath through her nostrils. She tilted back her head, allowing every horrendous moment of the past few years to resurface to the front of her mind and bubble there in an acidic frenzy. She slowly blew it out through her mouth. 'Nothing to say?'

She waited.

Seems not.

'No congratulations before we begin?'

Nothing.

Seeing that he was unmoving, she refused to consider the option that Holden may be dead already, that the duress of the kidnapping had stopped his heart. He was still with them. She could feel his cancerous presence in the same world as her. Maybe he slept, or maybe he was just toying with her.

She approached him, cautiously. 'This is a suitable place for you. A place perfect for rats! Dirty, stinking rats that scurry around in the darkness, waiting, and then prey on vulnerability. Except, bad news, there's no vulnerability around you. Not anymore.' She paused two metres from him. 'You remember that time when I told you about the Blue Room? What to expect there? But of course, you remember, because you tried to mirror it yourself in the convalescence room every single night! I gave you freewill in my Blue Room —the ability to make choices—and what did you do? Exactly the same! Couldn't even come up with your own idea! But I never folded in your world. Never asked for your resignation despite your desperate attempts to break me. And now, here we are.'

She took a large step, closing the gap to almost a metre. She reached her hand out. 'My one, the knife, please.'

Lacey felt the handle pressed against her palm and closed her fingers around it.

'Today, Doctor, I'll ask you to choose between a finger and an eye. Freewill. If, as you did in the Blue Room, you opt for a finger, I'll give you the same choice tomorrow. Don't worry; I've readied the painkillers. I need you to have a clear head to really consider your choices. It's nice to have freedom.' She passed him without glancing at him and stood before him, gazing onto the sunny road. 'Then, in ten days, you won't have a choice anymore, and I'll take both your eyes on a single day. Then I'll take another piece of you daily, until you beg me for death, but I won't give it you. No. Not until ... not until ... How long did you torture me for?' She turned and pulled the sack off his head. 'How long?'

You clever boy.

You clever, clever boy.

The dead man in the chair was unknown to her.

His shirt had been torn open. A bullet could have made the dark hole in his chest. The twisted red flesh around it suggested the doctor had cauterised it.

Dr Holden had carved a message into the stomach of the hired kidnapper: *Let's play.*

JAKE PETTMAN AND THE DEVIL

*M*ossbark County Deputy Scott Derby had done Jake Pettman a fair number of solids in his last month in New England.

Special mention should go to the fact that Scott had nursed him back to health from a gut wound that really should've killed him.

But reporting Jake's death in the blaze at the small community which had called itself the Nucleus shouldn't go uncredited either. *A true masterstroke, Scott!* Having become a mass grave of charred bodies, the Nucleus was no more. It would take the authorities a reasonable amount of time to determine whether Jake was among the bodies.

Not that they'd bother. Jake's experience of Maine law enforcement gave him confidence that the incompetent fools would give up quickly. The Nucleus had been full of peculiar outsiders. Many of them without a registered identity.

Whatever happened, it was certain that Scott's masterstroke had bought Jake time. The insidious UK-based organisation Article SE wanted him dead. So if they thought him a charred corpse, due to their connections in the states, they may've reined in their feelers, buying Jake a free pass home.

Blind hope?

Yes!

If Article SE knew he was on this plane, you could bet your bottom dollar that he'd be lucky to make it from Heathrow to Salisbury with no holes in him.

However, he had to take the chance. He needed to put an end to their vendetta against him, once and for all, before they struck against his family again.

He had an idea of how to do this.

A flaky one. Or, as Scott had put it, *'A very fucking flaky one.'*

Still, flaky or very fucking flaky, it was all he had, and Scott delivered once again by acquiring Lacey Ray's contact details.

While Jake had been laid up, waiting for his gut to glue itself back together, Scott had discovered that a nurse called Amelia Banks had assisted Lacey with an escape from Princeholm Hospital. At first, it'd looked like a dead end. Amelia Banks had been a false identity, effectively shutting that down as a route to Lacey.

Unless you were the Scott Derby, of course. Canny fella that he was.

Good old Scott set up a new email account and e-mailed AmeliaB@Princeholm.org.uk, a work account you'd expect to have been killed long ago.

Seems that Princeholm's admin department was slow on the update or, more than likely, preoccupied with donuts, coffee, and idle gossip.

Scott was blunt. He'd told the woman formally known as Amelia that Lacey had an old friend, desperate to get in touch with her.

Fortunately, the woman had kept an eye on this email. A mobile number, presumably for a burner, came through less than a day later. Jake had contacted Lacey and arranged to meet her when he landed at Heathrow.

Scott had been in disbelief, especially when Jake had given him a potted history of the vicious and dangerous entity that was Lacey Ray. Jake's reply hadn't really reassured him. *'Without at least one vicious and dangerous entity in my corner, I'm fucked.'*

Jake considered Deputy Scott Derby's final favour less of a solid—ridiculously powerful sleeping pills to see him through a night on the plane, because they stopped Jake from waking when the dreams turned awry.

Dreams that focused on his downward *spiral*—the downward spiral that was best forgotten but the most potent predator there was in your sleep.

The dream from which there was no waking took him on a whistlestop tour of the worse parts of his life. A stop at the breakdown of his marriage and a detour to the moment he had taken his first life to protect Lacey Ray. He had struck down the CEO of Young Properties, a Southampton-based company that was connected to Article SE.

On this detour, he surveyed his handiwork. Simon Young. Axe in his back. Lacey prodding the corpse with her foot, smiling at Jake. *'I always knew you had it in you.'*

She hadn't been wrong. The list of bodies strewn across New England would lay testament to that.

He then journeyed onto a bedsit in Salisbury, where he lay on a bed clutching a picture of his son to his chest. Frank. His own voice echoed through his head. *This is who you are now, Jake. You're no different from all those monsters you put away.*

Including Lacey Ray.

His dream swerved him into his contract with Article SE. Good money for surveillance and intel. Money to give his son the best life he could have.

Spiralling.

Not the end of the journey, but one of the worse places to disembark. Alexander Antonovich, ex-soviet military intelligence officer, hiding in Salisbury with a new identity and with his daughter Nina. Article SE had asked him to watch them, to provide patterns of their movements; the reasons had been obvious. They were marked for assassination.

Jake's cold feet had come too late. When he went to warn them about what was planned for them, Article SE had already made their move. A car bomb ended the lives of the defector and his daughter, but the cost was staggering. The debris from the vehicle had struck a young boy from the house next door, Paul Conway.

A child.

Jake knelt in the centre of the road, drenched from rain, clutching the broken boy in his arms.

Spiralling.

You're no different from all those monsters you put away.

Jake did what he thought best. He ran.

His dream twisted and turned like a rollercoaster through his experiences in Blue Falls and Mossbark. The losses he'd experiences, the atrocities he'd witnessed, the crimes he'd committed, and the love he'd found.

An angel. Piper Goodwin. Watching her grow smaller in his rear-view mirror, knowing he'd never see her again.

Then that phone call from DCI Michael Yorke. *'It was a gas explosion. Sheila was there. I'm so sorry. But your son was with her mother. He's alive.'*

A flight attendant shook his arm to wake him. 'We're coming into land, sir. We need you to fasten your seatbelt.'

Even though he was disoriented, Jake managed to force back the words on his lips.

I'm not letting Frank pick up the tab for what I've done.

∾

BLEARY EYED FOLLOWING a bloody long flight and plenty of fucked-up nightmares, Jake entered Heathrow's arrival lounge. The noise of excited friends and relatives greeted him, as well as insistent taxi drivers thrusting name boards above their heads.

When someone brushed against him, he swung to one side, ready to defend himself. He quickly regained control of himself after realising it was just an enthusiastic elderly woman increasing her pace towards a loved one.

He inwardly sighed over his paranoia but knew he could do little about it.

Now that he was back in the UK, paranoia would be par for the course. He'd be continually looking over his shoulder whenever anyone drew close. After all, powerful people wanted him dead. And if Jake knew anything about powerful people the world over, it was they nearly always got what they wanted.

Jake perused the names held up on boards.

There it was. Farthest right. A name born from the names of two late colleagues. A tribute, if you like.

Mark Brookes.

His gaze followed the long, slender arms down from the board, until it settled on a woman wearing a headscarf over long hair and shades, as if avoiding the paparazzi. Well, after her escape, she was certainly famous.

He could hear Scott's voice in his head, telling him that hooking up with Lacey was a gross misjudgement.

Probably.

But he was through running.

And, although she was most certainly bad news, Lacey Ray possessed a rather unique skillset.

One he'd most certainly need.

He approached her, and she lowered the board, eying his backpack, surprised maybe that he wasn't wheeling a trolley filled with luggage, like nearly everyone else on the long-haul flight. 'Hello, Mark. Or do you still prefer *Jake*? You're a person of many identities.'

'As are you, Lacey.'

They didn't look at one another, just stared ahead, as more passengers swarmed through customs and into the departure lounge.

'With so many people about, I guess we're safe,' Lacey said.

'You and I will never be safe.'

'No. I don't suppose we will. I, though, wouldn't have it any other way.' She faced him, and he caught her smirk from corner of his eye. 'How about you? Do you like it this way?'

Swerving the question, Jake said, 'What? Your hair? Yes, I do like it long. It suits you.'

She laughed. 'I've missed you, lover.'

'Being your lover isn't one of my identities.'

'A shame. I guess the feeling isn't mutual, then?'

You've never loved anyone, Lacey. 'Sex isn't the reason I contacted you. You know that.'

'A girl can hope.'

Jake guffawed. *Do you hope? Do you really feel such things?* 'How the hell did you get out of that hospital, anyway?'

'With difficulty. It wasn't my easiest challenge. I had to *endure* discomfort first. A lot of discomfort. But it was necessary. Without it, I may not have built the strength to leave.'

'That hasn't really answered my question.'

'A magician never reveals their secrets.'

'You're not a magician; you're a killer.'

'As are you, Jakey.'

Jake looked down. 'Maybe, but I'm certainly not as efficient as you.'

'At least you've accepted who you are now. It makes it easier.'

'It hasn't been. It hasn't been easy at all.'

'You just need more practise. Nothing's easier than doing what you know. And with my help, I'm sure you'll be just fine.'

Jake sighed. *This really was a mistake, wasn't it? Okay, Scott, if I live to see you again, you dare start up with the 'told you so's.'*

'I wasn't sure you'd ever come back,' Lacey said.

'I had to. Sheila's dead. They killed her.' He felt a tear in his eye. They'd been happy once, him and his ex-wife. And they'd created something truly beautiful together in Frank.

Lacey shrugged. 'She was a bitch.'

'She was the mother of my son!'

'Yes ... but she was still a bitch.'

Jake shook his head. 'You really have no fucking empathy.'

'Maybe you don't know me as well as you think you do?'

'Whatever. We've been standing around here for long enough. We need to get out of sight, and we need to get ready.'

'Sounds good. My place or yours?' Lacey asked.

'Well, I don't have one—'

'Thought so! My place it is!'

'Before we go, I need you to assure me that you're going to help. That you don't have an agenda.'

'I'll help if ...'

Shit. Here it comes.

'You answer me one question. And answer it truthfully.'

'I'll try.'

She faced him, removed her sunglasses, and looked into his eyes. 'Why did you call me?'

Jake shrugged. 'Better the devil.'

∽

STEERING THE WHEEL ONE-HANDED, she reached for Jake's face with the other. 'Many new scars, Jakey.'

He recoiled when her fingertips brushed his face.

'Are there anymore? Scars? Inside, perhaps?' Her hand hovered close to his face, waiting for him to come near again.

Scars?

He recalled his good friend Peter in Blue Falls, killed by an Article SE assassin. Then there was Piper, the woman he'd loved and left alone, with no real promise to return. 'We all have scars. Still, I'd like to avoid getting any more, so please put both hands on the wheel.'

She laughed. 'Still hate being in a car?'

He shrugged.

'Anyway, listen, I know how we enjoy a good flirt.'

He stared at her incredulously.

'But we must cut out the affectionate terms. Jakey has to go.'

Thank fuck for that. 'Agreed.'

'And I have to insist nothing can happen between us.'

Believe me, nothing could be further from my mind. 'Okay.'

'I've met someone. Well, I met her a long time ago, but recent circumstances have brought us even closer together.'

'You have to be kidding me.'

'Why would I be kidding you?'

'Well ... you know ...'

'No, I don't.'

'Okay, so tell me how you *feel* about her, then.'

Lacey cocked her head from side to side, clearly mulling that over. 'I find her fascinating. Everchanging. Adaptable. To any situation and need.'

'Is she a chameleon?'

'Tone, Jake, *tone*. And yes, why not? It's a good analogy.'

'Okay, so you admire her. Anything else?'

'Like what *exactly*?'

Jake contemplated it and changed his mind. 'Doesn't matter.'

'No, go on. Say what's on your mind.'

'Okay. Do you love her?'

'In my way.'

Jake snorted.

She indicated onto the fast lane of the motorway and accelerated. Jake watched her grip tighten on the wheel.

Jake felt a cold sensation in his stomach. He'd antagonised her.

'There's desire,' Lacey said.

'That's good,' Jake said, determined to appease her now.

She hit eighty mph.

His heart raced.

'And she has strong feelings for me. But I hear the point you're trying to make. I *hear* it loud and clear.'

Eighty-five mph.

'Okay, good. Slow down.'

'I seemed to remember you asking for my help, remember?' Lacey said.

Ninety mph.

'Slow down!'

Ninety-five mph.

Jake closed his eyes, fighting back a panic attack.

'A single, simple little word could end this frustration.'

'Okay. Sorry.'

He felt the vehicle slow.

'Good,' Lacey said. 'I mean, it wouldn't do us any good to get pulled over now, would it?'

Or die in a fireball either, Jake thought, taking deep breaths.

He was pleased to see the speedometer settle around seventy again.

'So, let's not discuss my love life anymore.'

'Fine by me.'

'Because I think I'm going to surprise you one day.'

You constantly surprise me. He simply nodded.

'I believe I'm capable of love and compassion.'

Bollocks. He looked at her and started to open his mouth, but after recalling her attempt at F1 racing, he quickly closed it again.

'I love Tobias, for example. My son.'

A torrent of words welled inside him. *Tobias isn't your son. You stole him several years back from his family. What's more, you don't love him. You're fooling yourself. You took that child because of your sense of grandeur. Because of your need for legacy. Tobias was that insurance. The continuation of you. Tobias is nothing more than your selfish need. And, thankfully, after your incarceration, he was returned to his real mother to be properly nurtured.*

'That's nice,' Jake said, keeping his gaze on the speedometer as it settled down.

'I look forward to seeing him again.'

Jake's blood froze.

She must have noticed his expression because she laughed. 'Don't worry. I'm not asking you to get involved in that. I know you don't approve. But I do need your help with something else.'

'Woah.' Jake stared at her. 'No. I called you, remember? I asked you for help.'

'And I agreed.'

'Yes, so please don't complicate this.'

'I'm not.' She smiled. 'But surely you didn't expect my help gratis?'

He shook his head. 'Yes, I –'

'Why on earth would I do it for free? And please don't say compassion, or out of the goodness of your heart, or the irony of such a comment will send me hurtling across the central reservation.'

She was right, of course. How ridiculous of him to think Lacey came without strings. And how ridiculous of him to wind her up, too.

'So, would you like my terms?'

Jake took a deep breath. He exhaled slowly with the word, 'Okay,' trying to keep his anger in check.

'Oh, don't give me those puppy-dog eyes, Jakey. I mean *Jake*. My terms involve a particularly vicious one. A truly malevolent beast. Right up your street. Both of our streets.' She chewed her bottom lip as her gaze seemed to wander into some faraway place.

'Eyes on the fucking road!'

She shook off her reverie. 'Good idea. So, you want to hear about this monster?'

'Yes, but first, I want you to know we're heading to Salisbury just before Southampton.'

Lacey nodded. 'Now that has to take the award for worst suggestion ever.'

'I'm not suggesting it.'

'Wow,' Lacey said, indicating into the slow lane to take the next junction. 'I see you've learned nothing from your countless near-death experiences. Your suicidal impetuous streak still reigns strong.'

'I have to see my son.'

She bobbed her head from side to side as she processed this. 'Even if it kills you?'

'Yes.'

'And him, too?'

He flinched. 'I won't speak to him. I won't even get close. I just want to see him.'

'I see. And here was me, thinking we would just get on with tackling the problem at hand. You know; cup of tea, sofa, spit ball some ideas that may give us a fighting chance?'

'I already gave you the plan on the phone.'

'Yes, about that plan. Well. I admire you for it. I mean, you did come up with it out in the boondocks while pissed on homebrew. With that in mind, it's an absolute cracker, but you're back in the real world now. Article SE have got stronger since you left. They already had their paws on all crime in the Southeast, but they're *now* branching out in the North. It gives a new definition to levelling up. You can't solve this with brawn. You're not dealing with a local drug dealer.'

'You did get me the gun?'

'Of course. It's in the glove compartment. But back to my point; you aren't dealing with someone who grows his own weed and has created a problem in the local secondary school. You're dealing with Article SE. Think back to your *pre-fuck-off* days.'

'The plan is set. Although we can discuss it later, again, at your house in Southampton.'

'Best to. After all, the only thing Article SE will be interested in is your head on a platter. You killed their assassin, Borja Turgenev. You owed them a life of servitude. Instead, you fled the country, with your middle finger raised in their direction.'

'I know. Don't you think I know? But first, Salisbury, home, briefly. I need to see him.'

Lacey sighed. 'Okay. Although, your end of the bargain promises to be remarkably easier than mine. I just need help finding a doctor.'

It's about time, Jake thought, suppressing a grin.

'Don't even fucking think it.'

DR STEWART HOLDEN HAS A CARD TO PLAY

*D*r Stewart Holden's gaze swept between monitors in his control room.

Full-colour images. High definition. State-of-the-art equipment. Unlike the government-funded shit he'd been obliged to use at Princeholm.

To be fair, those flickering screens that revealed what was happening in the convalescence rooms at Princeholm had been reliable. He smirked. Unless, of course, he disconnected the feeds. Like he'd done with Lacey's, for example. Every single night. And the one in her corridor, also. 'At Stan o'clock ... party time,' he said, suddenly nostalgic over his evenings of research. There'd been other rooms, other *subjects*, but none had quite offered that same thrill, that same *curiosity*, as Lacey Ray.

He'd been careful with the camera footage, night after night, replacing the chunks of time when they'd been deactivated with older footage of the empty corridor and Lacey soundly asleep. Unless an IT specialist took a detailed look at the archived footage, it'd go unnoticed. *And why would they?*

The law had a narrative for the events already: Lacey had struck up a relationship with new nurse Amelia Banks, who'd assisted with both the syringe and the knife. Then Lacey had coerced Stan into making that booty call. He, of course, had met a foul end at the hands of the two. The cameras had filmed everything, including the moment when Amelia had been wheeled to freedom. Holden had been nowhere near; he was in the clear. However, returning to work would be suicide. His location would give Lacey an edge, so he'd been signed off on sick leave—an easy sell when your workplace had been the site of a homicide. He'd then gone into hiding with one major advantage. He knew what the law did not. He knew where the two killers were holed up.

Sycamore Street.

Of course, Lacey knew this well enough. She'd had him taken there for execution, after all.

That grunt Lacey had used to deliver Holden gift wrapped had insulted his intelligence. It'd been a poor move on her part. All it'd taken had been an offer of money. 'Don't believe me? Google *Felix Holden*, my older brother. Ah, there you go ... You get it now, don't you? Big-shot property developer? Stop playing silly buggers, young man, and name your price.'

The man had plucked a number from the air. Holden had agreed to double it. Then the bonds had come off.

Greedy men always ended up in holes—or, in this case, with holes *in* them.

He'd expected Lacey to flee Sycamore Street after his escape. But his stubborn girl hadn't moved. It was her way of teasing him. A 'come and get me.' She knew he wouldn't want her in the hands of the police, identifying his role in everything, and besides, he still wished to study her. Going up against her on her territory would be suicide though—especially while she had Amelia as an ally—so Holden had been forced to devise another plan.

A plan that involved here, his stone dominion.

His *other* place of research, paid for by his wealthy brother, Felix.

Who, ironically, was more corrupt and had more blood on his hands than he ever would.

His gaze moved to the monitor on the far left.

Keith Burston sat in the corner of the bare, stone room, looking at the camera in the corner. He always seemed to know when someone was watching him.

Seriously, Keith, how do you do that?

Lacey used to tell him she could hear the air whistle past his bent septum when he was standing outside her convalescence room, but right now, he was nowhere near Keith's cell.

Keith Burston had proven an interesting subject. A while back, ITV Studios had tried to make a docudrama of Keith. *The Corpse Rustler*. It was abandoned mid-production due to heavy protests about using such tragic events for entertainment.

Keith had strangled his victims and left them beneath his floorboards. Only when they were suitably decayed did he revisit them to satisfy his needs. Holden sat back in his swivel chair and considered. Since his arrival here, several months ago, Keith had been a tough nut to crack. *A very tough nut.* Holden stroked his leather-bound book of notes on the table.

I know how you think, how you operate, what you crave and desire—what you mourn and miss—yet still you resist.

'What have I overlooked?' he asked.

He thought for a time, but then, at a loss, decided all he could do was persevere until the answer was revealed. And, on that day, Keith could be broken. Because *everyone* could be broken.

It was inconceivable to believe anything else, for this made up the bulk of his life's work.

Men like Keith, women like Lacey, revelled in their immortality, their sense that they'd never be stopped. That the personal shutdown switch was inoperable or simply unavailable. Egocentrism on this level didn't lend itself to ever ending or to suicide. Those, like them, who played so close to the edge with a desire to one day be caught, only did so out of a heady desire to showcase their achievements—their sense of grandeur.

Holden, too, was like them. And he wanted so desperately to prove that everybody—Keith, Lacey and himself—had a breaking point.

Stewart and Felix's father, Kieran Holden, had also been a man of unusual tastes and interests. Kieran had been fortunate to live in an era when it was easier to explore and satisfy yourself without the threat of repercussions, especially when you possessed such wealth. From an early age, Kieran had seen the same passion for knowledge in his son Stewart. That same curiosity to develop. But times had been rapidly changing. They'd been entering an era where money was no longer a barrier to exposure. If anything, possessing wealth *welcomed* exposure. This was an era in which the lower classes were so desperate to expose the wealthy for what they really were. Add to that, advancement in criminal investigation, and things became a hell of a lot more difficult.

So Kieran made a deal with Felix. He promised him the land, the wealth, and every conceivable *opportunity* to fulfil his dreams on one condition. That he looked out for his younger brother, Stewart. That he gave him everything his heart desired. No matter how perverse or undesirable the request, he would satisfy it.

But the most important thing was that Felix kept the

wolves from Stewart's door, because they would most certainly come.

Now, Felix was a man of honour, and Kieran had known that, so Stewart had never needed to fear having his pipeline shut off. He recalled the look of joy in Felix's eyes when he'd decided to pursue a career in psychiatry, the relief in his demeanour when he'd taken that job at Princeholm Hospital; however, he also recalled Felix's expression of horror when he'd asked him to purchase the forgotten twenty-cell Victorian jailhouse in rural Wiltshire. The crumbling stone building had already been marked for demolition, and the landowner, a ninety-something childless close friend of the late Kieran Holden, had agreed to sell it if he could live out his final days there.

His request for Keith Burston, however, had been met with a laugh and a flat-out refusal.

Holden had been forced to remind his arrogant older brother of his obligations. *'No matter how perverse, remember?'*

'But how do you expect me to do that?' Felix had asked.

A way always existed when you were rich and had connections throughout every echelon of society, as well as being part of the criminal outfit the police dubbed *Article SE*.

Felix had paid a lot of money to have Keith's death faked in custody, so he could be brought here to occupy the first of Holden's cells.

'Why? Why this?' Felix had asked, his face creased in confusion.

'To learn.'

'About what?'

'About him. About me*, brother.'*

Holden's next request had also required a reminder. *'No matter how undesirable, remember?'*

Dead bodies weren't in short supply from a criminal enterprise like Article SE. Disappearing traitors were common-place. Yet, Holden had needed something more specialist.

He'd wanted them partially decomposed.

Digging up year-old hit victims hadn't been part of the glamorous life Felix had envisaged for himself when signing his life away to a criminal organisation, but he kept his end of the bargain to his father.

Corpses were delivered, and Keith was forced nightly to lie beside them. Forced to fill his nostrils with the cloying odour of death. Forced to gaze on rotten strips of flesh hanging from old, yellowed bones.

All the while chained to the wall.

Not allowed to touch them.

No.

Never allowed to touch.

Then during the day, the bodies were removed, and Keith would be left alone with a noose hanging from the centre of the room. A single chair sitting beneath it.

And if this sociopath had a shutdown switch, which Holden firmly believed that he did, he could slip the noose around his neck and flick it.

Go on, Keith, Holden thought, *prove me right.*

Of the twenty cells inside the crumbling stone structure, only two were in use.

Holden aspired to fill the others, and since his work at Princeholm was currently on hold; he'd have time to commit himself to that task.

His days of appeasing his wife and children were also behind him. For now. He'd packed his stuff and told them he needed time to get his head back together. The thought of one day returning made him feel rather queasy, but he expected it would one day be necessary.

Then he reflected on Lacey again and smiled.

He was certain he had her breaking point in his sights.

He moved his gaze to the second screen.

A ten-year-old boy stood in the corner of his cell. Unlike Keith, he wasn't looking at the camera, fantasising about Holden's dead and rotting corpse; instead, he stared off into space.

In the months he'd been here, the boy hadn't spoken. He'd simply stood when awake and sat while he slept. All in that same spot. That corner of the cell.

Betraying nothing over what made him tick.

Holden wasn't frustrated. He was simply intrigued. The boy was a puzzle waiting to be solved. And eventually that final piece would slip into place, and Holden could begin his research proper. Prove that unbreakable individuals were, in actual truth, breakable. Torment driving them to the same end as any other human being—no matter how atypical.

He'd been an easy catch, this young boy.

He'd killed his mother, a widow of a powerful man, who'd had his own strong connection to this world called Article SE.

The criminal bastards had been more than happy to make this child and the dead mother disappear. They didn't want the world to know that the dead CEO of Young Properties' son had committed matricide. It was particularly unsavoury and may reopen suspicions regarding Simon Young's more illicit operations. Felix, for obvious reasons, had plumped for the job. His seniors had no idea of Felix's true intentions. To deliver the boy straight into the arms of Dr Stewart Holden.

Three months ago, Holden had understood this was quite a turnup.

This was Tobias Young, after all. Referred to as Tobias Ray by Lacey, due to her delusional desires to call him her son.

The desire to reveal his catch to Lacey had been overwhelming, but the impact of the discovery was unpredictable. And his research was progressing just fine.

Still, it'd been a card available to play if needed.

Like now, for instance.

Now was a great time to play a card like this.

LOOKING DOWN THE BARREL
OF A GUN

*J*ake cracked open the car door, and Lacey gripped his arm. 'Think about what you're doing. Think carefully.'

He stared at the primary school playground.

From this distance, it was a large congregation of young children. Sealed behind wrought iron fences, locked gates, and a smattering of teachers, his eight-year-old son would be at play. Protected, to a certain extent, from the outside world.

'Do you reckon I think about much else apart from Frank?' Jake said.

'Well, you need to. You're staring down the barrel of a gun.' Lacey tightened her grip on his arm. 'So coming here should be the last thing on your mind—'

'Could you let go?'

'Listen. When I'm staring down that barrel, I think about nothing. Nothing at all. It's the only way.'

'Enlightening.'

'It's supposed to be. You should use it. Stop thinking. Stop being distracted.'

'I'm not wired that way.'

He looked over at the congregation of children again. He wondered if his son was among them. The boy he'd not seen for so long. He turned and eased his foot onto the pavement.

'Think about it.' Lacey refused to lessen her grip. 'When death comes calling, blankness, emptiness. You just *are*. You just *be*. Then you survive.'

'Thanks for the TED talk, but I've made it this far on my own.'

'Have you? You're covered in scars. Inside and out. Who knows where the next cut might be?'

Jake pulled away from her arm. 'It'd probably be a fucking blessing.'

'I don't fear death, and I consider that a healthy approach. Wanting death, though? That, I don't understand. You step out of this car, you risk everything. Yourself, your son. And most importantly, me.'

'It won't be a problem.' He yanked his arm from Lacey, thrust up the hood on his jacket, exited the car, and gently closed the door behind him.

He approached the wrought iron fence with his head lowered slightly so his face stayed within the shadow of the hood; there'd be a significant number of cameras around here.

The temptation to clutch the bars on the fence and to scan the crowd for Frank tugged at him like nothing he'd ever experienced.

You risk everything.

Article SE had enough of a presence in the police force. If someone sighted and reported Jake, the bastards would rise, quickly, from the shadows, and he was yet to make his play.

Who knows where the next cut might be?

He'd only been here for seconds but seconds too long, so Jake turned before he reached the fence, thrust his hands in his pockets, and skulked by.

One opportunity. That was all he'd allow himself. *One oppor-tunity to see Frank.*

He threw brief and furtive glances into the playground as he passed. Too many children of all ages bounced between each other, burning off the agitation that came with sitting in classrooms for too long.

Too much chaos. His heart sank.

He glimpsed a group of smaller boys playing football up ahead closer to the fence. He thought of the photograph in his possession of a younger Frank in a Southampton FC kit. The picture was ingrained in his mind. He'd stared at it nearly every night since he'd fled the UK. And nearly every morning, he'd woken with it pinned to his chest.

Now Frank was eight.

So much lost time.

He drew parallel with the group of boys playing football.

Frank? Are you there?

A tall, suited male teacher was pretending to referee the game, but really, he was just trying to keep the children under control and prevent them from rolling around in the dirt.

Jake used quick glances at the children mindlessly chasing the ball with no strategy or clue. His whole being ached as he realised that even if Frank was there, he may not even recog-nise him.

So much lost time.

He was close to the end of the fence now. The knowledge that his son could be somewhere here, thriving, living his life, would have to be enough for—

His eyes widened.

Frank.

Yes. It had to be. Frank. The boy bursting away from the others with the ball at his feet. Taller than the other children, as Jake had always been as a child.

Frank's face hadn't changed all that much. But he was bigger now. So much bigger than how Jake remembered him.

He hoped his grandmother had bought him another Southampton kit.

If not, then that would be the first thing he would—

His son scored a goal, wheeled away cheering, and Jake smiled. He was cast back into his own childhood, where his own father used to watch him play for a local team every Sunday.

Who watched Frank now?

I'll put this right, Frank. I'll put this right, and you can play as much football as—

His insides turned cold.

The male teacher was staring at him.

Jake, in his reverie, had mindlessly approached the fence and gripped it. *You bloody idiot.*

He turned away, thrust his hands in his pocket, and continued his journey.

His mind whirred. It was probably a warning glance. A 'back away, fella; I don't recognise you' look. After all, many parents probably walked by and threw smiles and waves at their children. But Jake's hood was up, and he'd be unknown to the teacher. Caution, a quick shooing away, that's all it was.

Focus instead on that moment.

The moment you saw your son score that goal.

Did you see his run?

What a run!

Dribbling like the best of them!

He *knew* then that he would buy his son a new kit, that he'd take his son to St Mary's Stadium again, that he'd see his son play for a local team.

He just knew.

But then, he had to know it, didn't he?

The alternative didn't bear thinking about.

He saw Lacey had moved the car, so she was against the curb just ahead of him.

He climbed in the vehicle and closed the door.

'Did you see him?' Lacey asked.

He nodded.

'And did anyone see you?'

'No,' he lied.

She shook her head. 'I hope you don't regret this moment.'

He brushed back his hood and glared at her. 'Regret? It was one of the best moments of my life. I'd happily look down the barrel of a gun every day for a rush like that.'

She regarded him for a moment, looking confused. She reached for his face and drew her fingertips beneath his eyes. Then, after looking at her fingertips for a moment as they glistened under the light, her confused expression melted away. 'I don't think I've ever seen you cry before.'

$\sim$

ON THE WAY TO SOUTHAMPTON, Lacey explained her doctor problem to Jake, and he was sickened to the core.

Jake had dealt with his fair share of people who were lacking in humanity, but he'd never become desensitised. He imagined that the day he did would be the day he lost his own humanity.

After she'd finished her tale, he not only felt sympathy for her but rage and anger towards the beast who'd orchestrated such heinous things.

Still, he couldn't lie. The fact that this monster, Dr Stewart Holden, was out there, watching and preying, potentially readying himself to strike, was an absolute bloody nightmare for his own situation. And, if he'd known, he certainly wouldn't have called on Lacey.

He heard Scott's voice in his head. *'And this is why I said it was a gross misjudgement.'*

He sighed.

'Go on,' Lacey said. 'Speak your mind.'

'This complicates things.'

'Things are always complicated.'

'But a message on a corpse saying, *Let's play*? That's a whole new level of complicated.'

She guffawed. 'Fucking head doctors. They always have such a taste for the dramatic. Show ponies.'

Jake made a point of looking at Lacey, grinning knowingly.

She smiled at him. 'At least I'm not cruel to people who don't deserve it.'

'I dunno. You weren't kind to Sheila that time.'

'An act.' She waved him away. 'Barely touched her. It was just to get at you. I'd never have harmed her.'

'So that's okay, then, *because* your cruelty was aimed at me? You think I was deserving?'

She rolled her eyes. 'Don't sweat it. I realised before any real harm was done.'

'Realised what?'

'Realised we're more alike than you realise, that you couldn't help some of the mistakes you made.' She looked at him again. 'In your infancy.'

'Infancy? What're you talking about?'

'Some of those stories you told me before speak volumes.'

On the long journey up from London, Lacey had probed and probed until Jake had relented and told her some of his tales about his time in New England.

'You're talking about situations out of my control,' Jake said.

Lacey took her focus off the road to glance at Jake. 'It sounds like you went wholeheartedly into some of those situations.'

He glared at her. 'Look at the road, please. I killed because I had to.'

Lacey shook her head, tutting. 'Still not accepting the truth.'

He gritted his teeth and clenched his fists.

She was intolerable.

He looked out the window at the world rushing by.

She was right, though.

He'd had chances to spare lives before, chances he'd not taken. Death usually seemed the best option.

Jotham MacLeoid in Blue Falls, for example.

Would Jotham have ever stopped killing innocent people?

Not a fucking chance.

He took a few deep breaths and relaxed his jaw and unclenched his hands.

'Anyway,' Lacey said, 'there's something else regarding my game with Dr Holden.'

Jake sighed. 'Please don't call it a game. I don't want to enter into that ridiculous mindset. You both want to kill each other. Let's just keep it black and white.'

'Actually, I don't think he wants to kill me. That's part of the reason we carried on staying in the house he escaped from.'

Jake's blood ran cold. 'Come again?'

'Sycamore Street. Where he left his message to play—'

'Carved into a fucking dead man's chest?'

'Yes, that's the one. As I said, it's nothing to worry about.' She activated the windscreen wipers when a sudden summer shower materialised.

Jake felt his stomach turn over. *Are you completely insane?*

He didn't ask it, because wasn't the answer obvious? Plus, it would just inflame her. 'I'm not comfortable with this.'

'Well, you need to get comfortable with this, or I'm not helping you. This is *exactly* why you need to think of it as a game. He doesn't want me dead. That's not how he operates. He thrives off suffering and pushing his victims to a breaking point. He hasn't yet found mine, and he wants to find it badly. So very badly. He'll not attempt to move on me in the house on Sycamore Street because he may be forced into an outcome that would disappoint him immensely—one of our deaths.'

'He could just have the authorities pick you up and return you to your convalescence room.'

'But why? They'll return me to a different facility, not to one where I killed someone. Sure, he might organise a transfer for himself, but he's currently signed off with stress and in hiding, so he's unlikely to have the pick of placements when he returns.' She smiled. 'Throw into that the fact that I kept the body of the man he killed and inscribed with his message.'

'What? The body's still at the house!'

'Yes. Concealed away, out of sight, several months back. Wrapped in plastic and hidden beneath the floorboards under the carpet in the lounge, which already stinks to high heaven of cat piss, so you won't know he's there. Him ... or any of the others.'

'Others?'

Jake realised he was clenching his fists again. *It just gets fucking worse!*

'Yes. Which leads us to the next important discussion point. Carrie.'

'Is this your true love?'

'You need to be cautious around her.'

'So I don't end up beneath the floorboards?'

'No, you'll be safe at our home, I promise. You're my guest, and she knows how strongly I feel about you.'

'Let's hope she's not the jealous type.'

Lacey didn't reply.

Jake glared at her. 'Is she?'

'To be honest, I can't answer that. I told you before that she was changeable. Adaptable. I never really expected her to take the turns she's taken, to flourish so quickly and dramatically. And I admire those things in her, but it doesn't come without its costs. She's volatile and more unpredictable than before. She certainly possesses less of a code than I did.'

'I think I'll just go to a hotel.'

'That'd be ridiculous. Southampton is the main hub of Article SE. One sighting at this stage and we're all dead.'

Still, keeping you at arm's length is hard enough. And now another one, who's worse than you! I think I'd prefer to take my chances with another Article SE hitman!

'Besides, I've given you my word that you're safe, and that should be enough for you,' Lacey said.

Jake responded with a sigh.

'I'm just asking you to be discreet. She loves me, and I really don't see this being an issue.'

And there it was again. That word. Love. And it filled Jake with dread, because what was love to people like this? Did it exist? Was it not just a form of pathological obsession? But he didn't want to re-tread old ground and antagonise her.

Instead, he reached for the radio. 'I have a headache and need to think.'

'And music helps with that?'

'Yes.'

Except, it wasn't music; it was the news reporting on a terrorist incident in Salisbury. At the High Street gate. Jake had heard about it prior to leaving the states. It'd made international news due to the heinous nature of the attack that had left fifteen people dead, including three police officers, two paramedics, and a child. Details had been vague at the time, and Jake hadn't revisited the story since landing, so he listened intently. The newscaster was confirming that one of the victims was the recently kidnapped child, Matthew Brace.

Six years old.

'This *fucking* world.' He looked at Lacey. Her expression hadn't changed, nor did she offer any views on the matter.

He listened to the names of the dead paramedics and the residents who'd run towards the bomb sight when they'd seen the gun-wielding terrorist. Then they moved onto the three dead officers, those who'd have been Jake's colleagues had he not flushed his life and career down the toilet.

DC Sonia Jones. Widowed mother of three. History of social work. Destined for greatness.

DC Rob Wood. Young and ambitious with a noticeable eye for detail.

When Jake heard the name of the third and final deceased officer, he demanded that Lacey pull over onto the hard shoulder.

He threw himself from the vehicle, staggered forward, fell to his knees, and vomited.

THE DEATH OF DCI MICHAEL YORKE

Two days before the terrorist incident

*a*t the front of incident room 2, DCI Michael Yorke panned his gaze from one serious face to the next.

This was no small task force. Twenty-five strong. Mixed gender and drawn from different departments. Yorke had demanded a team full of experience.

His request hadn't been ignored. There'd been no need to convince any of the penpushers handling the budget to cough up funds.

When a six-year-old child went missing, you got what you wanted. Full stop.

The parents and the press would expect nothing less.

And neither did Yorke.

Still, as he surveyed their faces, he sensed despondency.

This was a team full of people who were used to cracking the hardest cases imaginable. Yet, in the space of three days, they'd not even scratched the surface.

Three days and ...

Jesus.

Three sodding days!

Some members of his team were even suggesting the boy must be dead.

He wasn't having resignation creep into this usually hardened group.

He narrowed his eyes and silenced them all with a sweeping stare. They'd never question his authority because everyone knew he'd solved two kidnappings already. He'd brought home two boys, even adopted one of them—Ewan Brookes.

Then, he reviewed the details of the case with them. Every piece. Every fragment, even though it was already tattooed into their memories. Because that was how you restored the adrenaline. You returned to the beginning.

The parents, Mia and Greg Brace, were minted. Three days prior, they'd had very little to worry about other than the needs of their beloved six-year-old, and even they were mainly catered for by a Lithuanian au pair. Greg was the major shareholder of a pharmaceutical company called Noracell, while Mia had inherited a serious amount of land. Noracell leased a chunk of this land and had erected a factory, filling Nia's pockets with the rent money. The whole situation was very win-win for Mia and Greg Brace. Cash poured in through a lot of taps.

On Saturday, Greg, who hadn't been born into money but was enjoying it nonetheless, had donned his flat cap and tweed jacket, and with his six-year-old and golden retriever Winnie had gone for an afternoon stroll in the woods at the edge of their land, which was a considerable distance from the Noracell factory.

Because he was with his child, he'd not taken a gun to

hunt with, although, in retrospect, he probably wished he had, because two men in balaclavas had confronted him in the wood. Winnie had tried to scare off the intruders with loud barking, but the bastards had been armed with sawn-off shotguns, and when close enough, they'd threatened to shoot the dog unless Greg restrained her.

Greg had held Winnie back with one hand and manoeuvred his son behind him with the other. He promised the gunmen riches beyond their wildest dreams. They weren't interested. One stepped forward, forcing Greg aside with a wave of his shotgun, then swooped up the child.

Greg had begged, tearfully, for his son back as the other man trained his shotgun on him. In his statement, he'd claimed that fighting would've been suicide, and could've easily led to his son's death. As the two men sprinted away through the woods, Matthew, in the arms of the biggest one, pleaded with his eyes for his father to fight.

Greg had considered releasing Winnie to chase them down, but he'd been fearful that she'd be dead before she could draw blood, and then they'd kill his son out of spite too.

Many of Yorke's taskforce had suspected Greg at one time or another during the previous few days. For some, his narrative just didn't add up, and they believed that a father would surely want to fight harder to stop the kidnapping. But fear affected everyone in remarkably different ways, so Yorke had instructed everyone to keep their options wide open.

Nia Brace wasn't Greg's biggest fan, either. In fact, Yorke had watched Mia slap Greg when she'd heard his tale of woe. *'You always cared more about that dog than your own son!'*

Yorke, meanwhile, had taken more than one good look into the eyes of the broken father and believed his devastation to be real.

The Lithuanian au pair, twenty-three-year-old Rozalija Andris, had been taken to pieces by some of Yorke's most aggressive interviewers. This was his call, which made him feel even more sympathetic when she broke down during the interviews. But he knew his calls were right. A missing child trumped all. Still, after Yorke had become suitably convinced of her innocence, he called off his heaviest interrogators and listened sadly to her desperate pleas to return to Lithuania, to live out her days simply caring for her elderly parents. It seems the world, and the adventures it could hold, weren't all they were cracked up to be. She was desperate for a return to her quiet life. Of course, she'd have to wait until the investigation was concluded before she flew home.

Rozalija was given hotel accommodation while the investigation was underway, and Yorke had visited her the previous evening to check in on her. She'd been beside herself, distraught to the point that Yorke had been genuinely concerned about her wellbeing. He'd managed to settle her and had offered her his work phone number so she could get in touch with him if necessary. Unfortunately, due to a security leak, all work numbers had been changed the previous week. Yorke's work phone battery was dead, and he couldn't, for the life of him, remember the new number. So, in a moment of rashness, he'd given her his personal number instead. Unprofessional but needs must. He'd explained it to Patricia that evening just in case he took a phone call from a strange woman late at night. He also made a note on his planner to have his personal number changed once Rozalija had returned to Lithuania.

Yorke concluded his recap by drawing attention to the gunmen. After kidnapping Matthew from the woods, they'd vanished into thin air.

Except *nobody* vanished into thin air these days.

Yet, apart from Greg, there wasn't a single witness to these men that came into the woods. Yes, the property was out in the sticks, but still, someone *always* saw something. Someone walking their dog down a dirt road, perhaps? Or a camera outside a local shop?

And to date, not a single ransom note. Three days! Had that even happened in the history of kidnappings?

All other lines of inquiry had so far yielded nothing.

Yorke felt the investigation spiralling. Another day and he suspected everyone would be calling to have that patch of woodland excavated. Although, he just couldn't believe that a six-year-old boy with Greg's DNA all over him would be unearthed. Still, it wouldn't be long before he'd be *forced* to bring his thinking more in line with the others.

So, with that in mind, he assigned tasks, watched his disgruntled team file out, and decided to take one last run at Greg and Mia Brace.

~

WHEN MIA OPENED the door to her home, Winnie was first to greet him.

Yorke, having grown fond of the golden retriever during his visits over the past three days, knelt to stroke her. 'Good girl.' The long tongue sliding up the side of his cheek didn't bother him. Rosie, his cockapoo, could lick with the best of them, and his days of being squeamish over dog saliva were long gone.

When he stood to greet Mia, he saw that the three days had seriously taken their toll. Pale skin, darkness around the eyes, and a dishevelled look. He sympathised immensely with her. He could only imagine what it felt like to lose a child. His daughter Beatrice was safe at home with Pat, his wife, and long may that continue.

Yorke had phoned ahead to Mia to explain he'd no news regarding Matthew and that he was only stopping by to clarify a few things in their statements. The last thing he'd wanted to do was turn up on her doorstep and give her a tremendous rush of hope as she sprinted down the stairs and fumbled at the locks. That would be cruel.

'He's pissed. Again.' Mia stepped backwards to allow Yorke access. 'You won't get any sense out of him. He wasn't even awake when I last looked in.'

Yorke offered her a smile. 'I'll try to be as brief as I can; I know it's late.'

She lowered her head slightly. 'You said that there was nothing new.' She toyed with the knot on her dressing gown belt. 'Is that right?'

'I'm sorry.'

She nodded and fiddled with her belt some more. 'Do you think Matthew's dead?'

She hadn't asked this before, but since nearly everyone else around him seemed to be rapidly losing hope, he wasn't completely surprised. 'I can't answer that.' *But it's looking more and more likely.*

She looked up. Closer to her now, Yorke noticed the darkness around her eyes was more pronounced than he'd first thought. She clearly hadn't slept in days.

'We need to prepare for all eventualities, but my team aren't giving up. Shall we go and sit in the lounge?'

Mia was a keen horse rider. Pictures of her show jumping were spread around the quaint lounge, alongside the pictures of Matthew in various stages of his short life—pictures that tugged painfully on Yorke's attention. Yorke refused a drink and asked Mia if she could possibly get Greg. She offered to try.

Less than a minute later, she returned with a disappointed look on her face. 'He's out for the count in his office. There're two empty wine bottles beside him. Even if I did wake him, he wouldn't make much sense to you. He's a *fucking* idiot.'

Yorke inwardly sighed. He hadn't heard her swear before. The cracks were really starting to appear in Mia.

Disappointed that he couldn't speak to Greg, to once again put the narrative that had divided his team under a microscope, he started to stand. 'It might just be best if I come back first thing—'

'This is all *my* fault.'

'Sorry?' Yorke was half-standing.

Mia sat down. 'My fault. I ...' She buried her head in her hands.

Yorke sat beside her, studying her.

'I should have just listened to him. He's an idiot, but it looks like he was right, after all.'

Sensing something potentially game changing, Yorke leaned in but kept his voice gentle despite his rising adrenaline. 'Listened to what?'

She didn't respond.

Yorke pressed, sharpening his voice a tad. 'Please. What did Greg say?'

Her hands dropped away, and she glared at Yorke with wide, furious eyes. 'That I was making a mistake by calling you!'

Calling me? She'd never called him directly, unless Greg had meant, 'The police?'

She nodded. 'And now look what has happened!'

She put her face back into her hands.

'Mia?' Yorke said.

She sobbed gently. He had to stop her retreating into herself. This glimpse she'd given him into Greg's behaviour was essential. So far, Greg's hesitancy in contacting the police had gone unmentioned. 'What happened?'

'Nothing,' she murmured. 'Nothing at all. That's the point. Where's the ransom demand? He said I'd ruin everything by calling the police.'

Yorke clenched his fists. *Greg, why tell your wife not to call us? Who in their right mind says that after watching their son disappear with armed nutcases?*

'I didn't listen,' Mia continued. 'I thought he was insane.'

I'd agree.

'So I called.'

Good move.

'He made me promise not to tell anyone about his reluctance to get the police involved.' She looked ceilingward. 'Screw you, Greg! Festering away up there, pissed, while I pick up the pieces.'

'Mia?'

She refocused on him.

'You did the right thing by calling us.'

'Did I? Then, where's Matthew?'

Yorke flinched, but then steeled himself again. 'Do you know how Greg reached the conclusion that contacting us was a bad move? Did he mention the kidnappers saying anything to him?' *He certainly never mentioned anything like that in his statement.*

'He was *adamant* that kidnappers never ever appreciate you contacting the police and that it was often a sure-fire way to destroy your chances of getting the person back alive.' She pressed her fist to her mouth, and a tear streaked her face. 'Sounded reasonable. I mean, you see it in the movies all the time, don't you? Still, my son had just disappeared.

How could I sit tight? Come hell or high water. I phoned you.'

'And if the kidnappers never actually made this demand, then you weren't disobeying any rules.'

'So why is there no *fucking* ransom demand,' Mia said.

True. The biggest anomaly in this whole bloody case, unless ... Yorke felt something click. *What if they'd delivered the ransom demand there and then? To Greg alone? And if it had been delivered, you could bet it wasn't money, because why'd you keep that secret? They were loaded! What did they ask you for, Greg?*

'I can understand the frustration, I really can, but you've made the right decisions all along, I promise, and I think we're close.' *Was this a lie or born from a sudden surge of confidence that Greg might hold the key?* 'So I need you to keep trusting us, *me especially,* just a little longer. Can you do that?'

She glared at him, then her expression quickly softened. 'Do I have a choice? I've lost everything. What do you want?'

'My next question might come out of the blue, but I need you to take it seriously, and I need you to think hard before answering it.'

'Of course.'

'I know he's your husband, but this isn't about protecting Greg right now. This is about finding Matthew.'

She paled. 'I ... don't follow. Greg can't possibly ... I mean ... no. It's not possible.'

Yorke nodded, sympathetically. 'Just think back through the last few days since Matthew disappeared. I know that'll be hard, but I'd like you to try. Focus specifically on Greg. Apart from the drinking, what else has he been up to? Anything that struck you as odd? Out of the ordinary?'

She slowly shook her head and appeared on the verge of vomiting. 'No. He can be a pig ... but not his own son ... no ... not that.'

'I'm sorry, but could you try?'

She nodded now. 'It's a blur. The whole thing's just a blur.'

Think, please, just think as hard as you can.

'He's spent a lot of time at the factory, but that's usual. He *always* spends a lot of time at the factory.'

But isn't that odd in itself? 'The day *after* Matthew was taken?'

Mia regarded Yorke, as if she, too, was realising something. 'The *same* day.'

Yorke kept his demeanour in check. He wore his best poker face, kept the tone of his voice matter-of-fact. 'Did he tell you why?'

'Yes. He said he wanted to thank the staff for their support. He said many of them had been contacting him to wish us well.'

Yorke quickly reviewed what he knew about the Noracell factory.

A newcomer in the pharmaceutical world but by no means a smaller hitter. It'd already unleashed several new vaccinations on Europe and had enjoyed soaring share prices this summer. However, like most pharmaceutical companies, Noracell valued its privacy—or, to use more coarse a term, its *secrets*. Noracell was a regular Fort Knox. Two days earlier, Yorke had briefly visited. On this short tour, he'd counted more security guards than scientists, although he hadn't delved too far into the building. This, of course, made a man like Yorke suspicious, but Greg had assured him that this was regular practice for the type of company that had a lot to lose by leaving itself 'wide open.' Still, the sheer weight of security had bothered Yorke. No one's health would fare well if they broke into this building—rather ironic, considering the whole premise of the place was to make discoveries that improved wellbeing.

Still, up until Mia's comments, Yorke hadn't considered it necessary to seek out a warrant. He knew it'd be a 'slower than usual' process when it came to industries like this one. After all, those with vested interests higher up the food chain would undoubtedly have something to say on a pointless search of such a profitable company.

But right now, he was giving it serious consideration. And he reckoned he could bypass the usual bureaucracy and red tape which went with industries like this. After all, if Yorke shouted loud enough about a missing six-year-old, would anyone really want to attach themselves to a refusal?

'I know we've spoken to you both at length about Noracell,' Yorke said. 'And I get that your husband likes to keep a lot of what you do confidential; however, I'm going to ask you a serious question, Mia. Do you think there could be any connection between Noracell and the kidnapping of Matthew?'

She thought for a moment. 'No. Only in what I said already, that it's public knowledge that Greg is extremely wealthy, and I suspect the kidnapper knew the financial rewards would be significant.'

'So, apart from going in to express his gratitude, can you think of any other reasons Greg has spent so much time in Noracell over the past few days?'

'Keep himself busy. It's always been his way with trauma. Unless ... it's to get away from me? Yes ... that could also be a reason. He can't stand watching me cry, never could. I think in his own way, he's rather sensitive and understanding, but he does become rather awkward and wooden around displays of emotion. I think he's potentially autistic or something, but ... sorry, I'm off on a tangent.'

'No, this is all helpful. Do you know anyone you can speak

to who works in the factory, who may have an inkling as to what he's been keeping himself so busy with?'

'Yes, but ...' She stiffened. 'I think you're barking up the wrong tree. As I said before, my husband has his faults and can be an obnoxious prick, but he loves Matthew.'

'I'm not disagreeing with you.' Yorke offered her a smile. 'But I'm worried that your husband may have been put in a situation that has compromised him in some way. He may still be acting in your son's best interests. I asked you to trust me. I'm not trying to cause any problems. We're all after the same thing. Do you know anyone?'

'Yes. But probing Greg's activities at the factory will be considered sacrilege! You're asking me for inside information.'

'Does that mean you won't?'

'No,' Mia said with a flicker of light suddenly coming into her eyes. 'Fuck him. He's not exactly been supportive.' She stood. 'I know the chief of security, Tom Fields. In fact, I knew him before Greg. Strike that. You want open and honest? Let's do that. I dated Tom in another life. Greg has no idea. Wouldn't do good for a man with Greg's ego to know that one of his underlings knows his wife carnally, would it? Doesn't matter how successful an egotistical man gets, he never loses that shallowness, never shakes off his coil of immaturity. Tom will give me whatever I ask for because he's fond of me.'

'Thank you.'

Just before Mia left the room, she turned back to Yorke. 'I'm fond of Tom too, but that's a story for another day.'

Seems there are a lot of stories for another day around here, Yorke thought as she exited the room.

And that was the problem. Secrets within the gentry were no surprise. But when they hindered kidnapping investigations, they went from being eye-rolling scandals to blood-boiling revelations.

As he waited, he struggled to keep his fury at bay. Not only did he have to work at keeping his breathing under control, but he was forced to make a silent vow to himself.

Unless she brings me something relevant from her ex-lover and potential future squeeze, I'll round up my entire team and sweep through here tomorrow like a bloody tornado.

～

Mia did deliver something very relevant. However, it didn't prevent the tornado. If anything, it was the catalyst for a career-high mammoth twister.

As he'd hoped, it wasn't as hard for Yorke to get a warrant to search the Noracell factory as he'd first suspected. Not that he intended to go inside it. Caution was order of the day after Mia's revelation.

So, as armed response took up various positions around the Noracell factory, Yorke hung back behind the first line of trees in the wooded area with his binoculars and with hope that the brief conversation with Mia the evening before would bring this whole sorry affair to a close.

～

'This is wrong. Completely wrong,' Mia had said at the lounge door. 'Tom certainly doesn't know what to make of it, and I don't either.'

Yorke stood. The surge of adrenaline was too strong.

'Greg has given everyone the day off tomorrow. *Even* the security.' She paused to shake her head. 'That never happens. *Has* never happened. Security works twenty-four hours on rotation. But from tomorrow at five a.m., they're to leave the premises for twelve hours.'

'Why?'

'The place apparently needs fumigation of some kind. Something compromising research. For health and safety purposes, they need to clear out. Except, why not just keep security nearby? It didn't make sense to Tom, but Greg was in no mood to argue when he delivered the instruction. Most of the other employees are over the moon at the day off, so they aren't about to question it! This is unprecedented. What's Greg playing at? Let's hope word doesn't get out that the building isn't secure.'

Word would *most certainly* be out.

This was the ransom demand.

Vacate your factory.

At four a.m., Yorke sent officers to wait near the Brace residence in case Greg decided to leave early and potentially head to the factory to meet whoever may be coming. If necessary, he would have to be taken into custody.

Yorke had called on both the counterterrorism specialist firearms officers and specialist firearms command. A fair number of officers were in the field under the orders of Commander Pedal. Such were their skills, Yorke couldn't see a single one with his binoculars. He knew some were concealed behind a row of parked cars at the far end of the carpark, while another batch lay in wait near the entrance behind the large ornate fountain.

The minutes ticked by, slow and agonizing, as Yorke, DI Harnett, DC Rob Wood and DC Sonia Jones waited for any signs of activity from the wooded area, out of harm's way. He saw anxious glances on his colleagues' faces. He knew what they were thinking: *What's the boss playing at? Was armed response on this scale a kneejerk reaction?*

No, Yorke assured himself. *Something's coming.*

But, by ten a.m., doubt picked at Yorke. 'Shit,' he said,

lowering his binoculars. 'I'm going to contact Hawkes at the Brace residence. Find out if Greg has managed to get a warning—'

'Sir ... quick, look!' Sonia said.

He hoisted the binoculars to his eyes as his radio crackled into life. 'Confirmed sighting. Black van. Main entrance road.'

Yorke watched the black transit slither down the main entrance road as an officer read out the licence plate over the radio.

Yorke bounced his binoculars between the strategically placed row of vehicles in the carpark and the fountain. He caught the tiniest flickers of shadows and clothing but not enough to give the game away. Not unless you were scrutinising those areas like he was.

The van pulled into the carpark and positioned itself near the entrance, close to the fountain and close to the row of cars.

The visitors were now flanked. Game on.

Yorke held his breath, expecting the doors on the transit to suddenly fly open.

They didn't.

Come on ... come on ...

He exhaled. *Do they know we're onto them?*

Yorke tried to suppress his angst, but time seemed to move slower still. His finger twitched on the radio. He wasn't in charge of armed response—that would be Commander Pedal —but he considered suggesting politely that they storm the vehicle. Pedal would be wearing an earpiece. There'd be no sound to betray his team's presence.

Yorke sweated.

If the kidnappers caught wind, it could turn into a chase. But, if response moved in now, suffocating them from each side, demanding they exit the vehicle, it could be salvaged.

He pressed the button on the radio—

No need. The side door slid open. *Here we go.*

He released the button.

Two individuals wearing balaclavas slipped out. The tallest of the two reached in for a large heavy-metal case. Then the other reached in for his.

The radio came to life. It was one of Pedal's men watching from a safe distance like them, feeding information into the earpieces of those on the ground regarding the men's descriptions and their activity. 'Suspected explosive cases.'

Yorke's blood froze.

They're here to blow up Noracell.

The two terrorists marched towards the factory's entrance, while the driver and the passenger came free from the front and went for their explosive cases too.

Yorke suspected that Pedal would have preferred to grab all four at the entrance, but the first two had quite a head start on the others and were almost there. It'd get messier if any of them entered.

Commander Pedal's voice burst from the radio. 'Unit A. Entrance. Unit B. Van. *Now.*'

Five men, concealed behind the vehicles at the side of the carpark, emerged. They fanned out quickly, full-body armour, Glock 17s raised, and marched on the van.

Another five emerged from behind the fountain, also ready for combat.

Ten in total. Outnumbering the four men considerably.

Odds were in armed response's favour. The odds of the terrorists surviving? Well, that was a different matter.

And Yorke needed them alive.

They *still* had Matthew.

Yorke chewed his bottom lip.

Armed response's loud calls for surrender travelled up to Yorke and his team.

Through binoculars, Yorke watched the two terrorists who'd already made it partway to the factory entrance lower their explosive cases and put their hands in the air.

Tasting blood, Yorke parted his teeth and released his bottom lip.

Yorke heard shouting and swung his binoculars to the other two terrorists who were being flanked by the officers coming from behind the line of vehicles.

Come on. Follow the example of the other bastards ... hands in the air.

The two officers were retrieving something from the van. When the sharp reflection of sunlight on the guns stunned Yorke's vision through his binoculars, he pounced to his feet. '*No!*'

Rapid-fire gunshots.

Yorke charged forward. Pointless. It'd be long finished before he got within spitting distance. And spit was all he'd have. He didn't have a gun.

Realising this, he paused and looked with his binoculars again. The other two terrorists who'd 'seemingly' surrendered had pulled their semi-automatics during the chaos and unloaded on those who'd flanked them.

The air was rent with gunfire.

Shit ... shit ... '*Shit!*'

And then, as suddenly as it'd started, it was over.

All four terrorists were down.

Yorke scanned the crowd of officers.

His heart fell when he saw one of them on the ground.

Binoculars banging off his chest, Yorke ran.

~

A BULLET HAD SLIPPED past the officer's armour and grazed his leg. There'd been a lot of blood, but much to the relief of everyone, she'd made it.

The only positive.

Unless you counted the preservation of Noracell as a positive too, but the jury was out on that one.

All four terrorists were corpses.

Yorke sat in his office, head in hands.

He'd just finished interviewing Greg Brace, fighting to keep his voice at a reasonable volume and the furious tone from his voice. Hard when the bastard completely refused to talk.

'No comment.' A quick whispery exchange with his lawyer and another, 'No comment.'

At one point, Yorke succumbed. He jumped up and pounded the table with his finger. 'What about Matthew? Your son. *Your son!*'

For a moment, it seemed as if the weasel's wall would come down, but the vermin simply lowered his head and shook it, before having the audacity to look back up to say, 'No comment.' Yorke had forced himself to leave the room at that point for fear of making a move which would end his career.

Yorke rubbed at his temples, thinking.

Greg had provided the terrorists, all men and all still yet to be identified, with key cards to get them into Noracell. The fumigation stunt was just a way to get everyone off site. Greg had *known* his factory was about to be razed to the ground, as payment for his son's life. This was all obvious.

The explosive ordnance disposal team had been on hand to secure the bombs and had neutralised them before transport. Yorke had already been informed that these explosives weren't the work of amateurs.

Counterterrorism were also firmly involved and part of the

large-scale team who were now scouring the factory. Yorke had been waiting hours for an update on this and was going out of his mind. Seeing it was five o'clock, Yorke called it a day and headed home. He'd get an update later for sure, and sitting here, twiddling his thumbs, while he could be sharing a takeaway and drinking a pint of Summer Lightning, or two, with Patricia was a poor use of his time.

He stood and reached around the back of his chair for his suit jacket.

He started to put on his jacket when a knock sounded at his office door.

'Come in.'

The door opened.

Yorke looked up, nodded, sighed, then replaced his jacket on the back of his chair.

At least he might actually start getting some bloody answers.

∼

'YOU REMEMBER what happened last time you were in my office?' Yorke asked.

Chief Constable Riley Robinson didn't respond. He just sat in a chair opposite Yorke.

Yorke pointed at the scar on his right cheek. 'Does this remind you?'

Robinson smiled. 'I've had a fair number of 'fuck you' receptions, but that one really will take some beating. How've you been, Mike?'

Yorke smiled. 'I've been better, sir. But then, I guess you already know that. In fact, I suspect you're here to enlighten me as to what the hell is going on around here. Although just by walking in, it becomes obvious.'

Robinson ran SEROCU–the southeast regional organised crime unit. Yorke suspected that not only was he about to find out that the kidnapping of Matthew Brace and the attempt on the Noracell factory was connected to organised crime but that it'd also be linked to Article SE. Nothing brought the main man of SEROCU flying through your door quite like Article SE.

Robinson sat back in his chair and ran his hand through thinning white hair before nodding. 'First, thank you, pal.'

'For what?'

'Well, if not for your intuition, half of Wiltshire's police force would still be bumbling around in a false kidnapping case, and SEROCU would have lost the motherlode, and I mean *the motherlode*, of evidence to a mushroom cloud over the plains of Wiltshire.'

'What's in that factory?'

'Well, the ground floor does a cracking job of pharmaceutical research, no question. They put out a vaccine this year; did you know that?'

Yorke nodded. 'Sent their stocks rocketing. You're about to tell me the pharmaceuticals are a front, aren't you?'

'Indeed. But what a bloody lucrative front, eh? Turns out the first floor is a weapons factory.'

'Shit.' Yorke leaned forward on his desk.

'Shit, indeed. The bombs and firepower are one thing—I can just about keep myself composed on that one—but the bioweapons they're developing on the first floor, well, they really do have me flustered.'

Yorke shook his head. He really hadn't seen anything like this coming. He thought back to the kidnapping and the events over the previous three days. In no way had it ever felt in connected to Article SE. 'We should have let the bloody factory burn!'

'No, the evidence is good. We'll be able to snap off a few of Article SE's branches with it. Still. We need more. A *lot* more.' Robinson leaned forward. 'I want to bring you into the loop now.'

Yorke made a show of looking at his watch. 'Better late than never.'

'Better you get nailed-on intel rather than half-arsed assumptions.'

Yorke nodded. 'Go on.'

'Greg Brace—did you twig anything peculiar about his background?'

'Not that I can recall. Shall I dig out my notes?'

'Don't bother. It's all bullshit anyway. He's completely manufactured. Greg Brace was the identity given to a five-year-old Dominik Sokolov, a Russian immigrant. He was the son of a fleeing GRU agent called Igor Sokolov.'

Yorke's blood ran cold. After what the Russian hitman Borya Turgenev had tried to do to him and his family, hearing about *that* country's involvement was not something to relish. 'Why wasn't there a flag on him?'

'When it comes to these fleeing GRU agents, you folks don't even get a wink or a polite "fuck off." But what did surprise me was that we at SEROCU didn't get squat, either, when you threw Greg's name into the database. Fucking unusual, pal, and a fucking disgrace. There's some rank history in our force. *Rank*. But secrets hide, and so, by their very nature, they can be found. And we found them. Dominik's—aka Greg's—ex-GRU agent father, Igor Sokolov, who was provided with the name Patrick Brace on British soil, brought him to this country when he was five years old. Patrick, God rest his soul, has been dead ten years. Apparently, the intel he provided was some of, if not *the* best we received during the Cold War. But you don't get a statue for that! What you do get is the honour of having your identity locked away in a dark and dusty government vault. However, governments are incompetent, and SEROCU is anything but. Once you'd put Greg on our radar today, it took us less than an hour to empty that vault. And I didn't even have to use my best officer.'

Yorke nodded. 'Okay, just slow down a second. So, if Patrick is dead, then why has Greg been targeted? He was five at the time; he hardly had any part in his father's defection, probably can't even remember it.'

'No, precisely, the Russians aren't seeking revenge against Greg. You're exactly right; why would they? And now, in a peculiar turn of events, we discover that Greg is *actually* on the payroll of Article SE.'

Yorke rose his eyebrows. '*What*?'

'Yes. Only took us five minutes to detect his bloody face on our multitude of surveillance photos on suspected Article SE meetings and activities.'

Yorke struggled to put it together in his head. 'This doesn't make sense, working for Article SE? Article SE *have* Russian affiliation and investment. Why would the son of a fleeing GRU agent work for them? Hide in plain sight?' Yorke shook his head; this was madness. He felt like he'd just walked straight into a British spy novel. Ask him about serial killers, corrupt businessmen, or drug dealers and he was like a Google search engine. But Russians, shadowy organisations like Article SE, and weapons factories? Well, let's just say he was yet to receive a training session on that one. 'Talk about a kick in your father's teeth. Working for the people he'd risked his life to escape!'

'I'll be honest,' Robinson said. 'I don't know the reason. Maybe Article SE simply threatened him? Expose the truth of who he was to their Russian affiliates? Or was it just the usual? Money?'

Yorke sighed. 'Well, feel free to take a run at him and see if you can get passed the "no comment."'

'Already have done. And no, we didn't. But we're authorised to turn up the heat hotter than you guys can, but I'll hold off on that just now.'

Yorke guffawed. *'Already have done!* Why do I feel like you've marched in and taken over?'

'We're on the same side, pal.'

'Hmm ... anyway, let's hear what else you have.'

'Okay, well, it stands to reason that Article SE or the Russians won't bomb their own factory. I've been around Noracell today. The profits they're making from that weaponry will be staggering. And some of that bioweaponry? I imagine you can pull a number out of the air if you develop something that could bring the world to its knees.'

Yorke sighed; it didn't bear thinking about. 'So if neither Article SE nor the Russian investors have kidnapped Matthew Brace, who the bloody hell has? Who else would have the balls to take on Article SE apart from you? Are MI5 involved? Was it them?'

'Well, it wasn't us. Give me some credit! A six-year-old boy? And, as for MI5? Kidnapping a kid to orchestrate the levelling of a weapon's factory—not very British, is it?'

'Well, whoever it is must be either stark raving mad or willing to die for whatever their sodding cause is.'

'And that is the nail on the head. The sodding cause.' He lifted his briefcase onto the table, cracked it open, and removed a photograph. 'Taken five years ago.' He slid it over the table. It showed three men and two women approaching separate vehicles outside a derelict building. 'Back when we had eyes on them.'

'Who're they?'

'You remember the attempt on the Russian embassy in London five years back?'

Yorke nodded. 'Yes. A near miss.'

'Not really. That's what the media led everyone to believe. We were all over it.' He smirked and prodded the photograph. 'We had these in our crosshairs long before that one got out of hand. This is your sodding cause.'

Yorke took the photograph and studied it.

'All of them British born,' Robinson said. 'And all with one thing in common.'

The five figures in the picture were suited and booted. They looked like they were leaving a business meeting in Silicon Valley rather than a clandestine meeting in a derelict building.

'Just like Greg, these individuals are descended from ex-GRU agents. Except these happy few'—he nodded at the picture in Yorke's hands—'have no desire to pander to Article 5E.'

'I'm guessing their parents weren't as lucky as Greg's father?'

'No,' Robinson said. 'I couldn't tell you how many ex-GRU agents have been assassinated in the UK over the years—there's little transparency in that regard—but I can assure you that it's more than a few. Car bombs, nerve agents, house fires—they've kept it varied. Every one of these individuals have experienced loss because of it.'

'But you got them five years ago when they tried to hit the Russian embassy?' Yorke said.

'Alas, no. The plot was foiled, but at a cost. These folks vanished before we could detain them. Press made it sound like we'd hit it out the park when we had rounded up the bombers, but they were just a couple of bagmen.' He tapped the picture again. 'The orchestrators had disappeared. Not about to set the newshounds straight, were we?'

'I guess not, but you haven't managed to find them in five years!'

'No. Not a trace. And we estimate there's more in this terrorist cell now. Maybe ten or so.'

'Less after this morning.'

'True.'

'Are you sure it's this particular cell?'

'I *know* it's this cell. Someone is striking out against Article SE. This factory is, sorry, *was* of massive importance to Article SE. Ironically, this cell has succeeded, because the factory, one of the syndicate's success stories, is in our hands now, but that wasn't what these folks wanted. They *wanted* fireworks. Why else go to this extent? Kidnap Matthew and make Greg betray Article SE? They wanted to send a message in fire that they're back again, and this time, they mean business.'

'Shit. If you're right ...'

'I am.'

'Then this isn't over.'

'Is it ever? But right now, we can be certain that Article SE will want blood for this. So if we let this play out naturally, this cell will most certainly fall. I mean, how many remain? Half a dozen? Seven at the most?'

'But you don't want to let it play out. Do you?'

'It'd be pointless. Imagine what they know and have on Article SE; the factory could just be the start! This could be the way to finally get the bastards good and proper.' He leaned forward. 'So we need to find this cell before they do.'

'Guess you better increase that heat on Greg,' Yorke said.

Robinson guffawed. 'Pointless! The lawyer in there with him will be from Article SE. He breathes anything about his connection to Article SE and he's a dead man walking.'

'He probably already is.'

Robinson nodded. 'Yes. But Article SE don't want *any* fireworks. They know we have a bucket load of potential evidence to use against them from this factory. Last thing they'll want is to establish a clear link. They won't want to come out of the shadows to hit Greg. Greg will be offered a cleaner way out. Protect Article SE, take the jail sentence, and live out your days in jail, comfortably. Article SE have ways and means to provide comfort in jail.'

'But what about his son? Matthew? Does that factor into Greg's plans moving forward? Is he that spineless?'

'I suspect he must love his lad or he'd never have agreed to the bombing of Noracell. No, I suspect he's on a promise from Article SE that they'll do whatever they can to find his boy. If he talks to us, then they will have to move on him, and no one will look for his son anyway. Thus, he has another incentive to keep schtum.'

'I'd look for Matthew whatever. In fact, I still will!'

'I don't doubt it. That's kind of what I'm counting on.'

Yorke creased his brow.

'Because it's all we have,' continued Robinson. 'We must find this cell before it's wiped out. This is the first time in ten years, Mike, I felt like we've had the bastards against the ropes. We cannot fuck this one up. We just can't.'

'I get it, but I'm more concerned about the boy right now.'

'I know ... so let's help each other. Talk me through everything on the kidnapping, then from tomorrow morning, I'll be in your briefings. Is that okay? I'll be a polite presence; this is your world.'

'You'll be a lingering bloody shadow.' Yorke smiled. 'But it might wake up a few of the miserable bastards in my incident room.'

'Happy to help.' Robinson grinned back and winked. 'Now,

obviously I know the ins and outs of today, but take me through the entire investigation from when it started three days ago.'

~

THE DAY HAD BEEN long and fierce.

Desperate to sleep, Yorke went to bed early, but his mind had other plans for him. It raced long into the night, loaded with dead terrorists, chemical weaponry, and a missing six-year-old boy. At one point, Patricia noticed his restlessness. She came over to hug him and to ask if he was okay. He'd never deviated from his default response to that question and wasn't about to start now. 'I'm fine.'

And she, in turn, was not about to deviate from her default response to that answer. 'Bollocks.'

He laughed and turned onto his side, kissed her, then closed his eyes. 'You know how it is, when the days are long and the caffeine intake gets out of control.'

She opened her mouth to usher the same response as before, but he pinned his finger to her lips before she could issue it.

He kissed her on the forehead, closed his eyes for a while to feign sleep, until he heard her breathing become shallower. He rolled onto his back and looked up at the ceiling. He kept his gaze on it as his thoughts swam through a swamp of events, hypothesises, and briefings, before it crashed into the brick wall of Article SE.

In some form, Article SE had always been there, but the way it had evolved in Yorke's career was terrifying. This organised crime syndicate was an umbrella over every conceivable profitable crime in the Southeast, not just the obvious human trafficking and drugs but also sweatshops, illegal organ removals, and the breeding of children for sale. Each of these 'branches' of crime still existed as its own entity, and so could be raided and shut down, but the ultimate control came from the shadows, where the puppeteers involved ensured they were so far removed that they were impossible to identify.

Although those at the head of Article SE dangled its umbilical cord to feed and nourish these industries, while absorbing the profits through its seemingly endless number of roots, following the umbilical cord or roots simply got nowhere. There were too many layers from top to bottom, and when necessary, at a moment's notice, they could break a layer.

And survive.

Article SE was a malignant mass, swelling and growing at an alarming rate. It had already branched out into the Southwest and was now working its way northward, too.

Its power was terrifying.

Its eyes were everywhere, monitoring everything.

The government, the police and the health service had been infiltrated. Shit, even SEROCU itself could have been compromised. Robinson would be no fool. He'd measure and control everything he said to his staff and look for leaks on a daily, potentially, hourly basis.

Eyes.

Everywhere.

Suddenly feeling like a train had hit him, Yorke sat upright.

Novacell had been important ... essential ... ground-breaking. Had Article SE really left their flagship gamechanger to the eyes of one man? Greg Brace. A Russian immigrant?

Not on your nelly!

He redressed in his suit.

But if that was the case, wouldn't they have known about the bombing? Cut it off at the source?

Yes ...

Unless the eyes themselves had been taken away ...

Yorke charged down the stairs.

... And moved to another location, a hotel, for example, where they could no longer see what they were paid to see.

He darted from his house, beeped his car alarm, and dived in behind the steering wheel.

There was no doubt in his mind that these eyes belonged to the twenty-three-year-old Lithuanian au pair Rozalija Andris.

~

FASTENING the top button of his shirt to keep the cold from the nape of his neck, Yorke studied Rozalija's pale face.

He looked into her wide eyes. He thought of the desperation he'd seen in them all those nights back. Now he saw only emptiness. She was gone. Along with all her hopes and dreams of salvation.

His eyes moved to her neck, and the bruises.

Strangled.

He turned away from the body, his fists clenched.

Article SE would have approached her after she had scored the au pair job. Offered her more money than she'd ever seen in her life. He imagined there'd been many happy faces in the Andris family when that money had started arriving in Lithuania.

But taking their money was like drinking from a poison chalice, and the Andris family would later wish they'd questioned Rozalija over that sudden influx of cash rather than turn a blind eye to it.

He went to the hotel balcony, gulping deep breaths.

Below, the cavalry entered the carpark; he'd contacted them on his journey over. He'd never expected to find a dead body. He was stunned. His backup would be too.

He hoisted out his phone and dialled Robinson. After he updated him, Yorke asked, 'Did Article SE do this?'

'I don't think so. What would be the point?' Robinson said. 'Like I said before, regarding Greg, it's not in their interests to draw attention to this situation - make a song and dance out of it. They can easily buy silence. Money is no object.'

'But how is this in the cell's interest? Killing a young woman?'

'Were you not listening in the office earlier?'

Fireworks. 'I thought they were after revenge, justice, when really, they're just another set of bloody monsters.'

'They're fucking terrorists, pal. They're the same the world over.'

Yorke sighed.

'We dropped the curtains on their show at Novacell, so now they're having to look elsewhere,' Robinson said.

Rozalija Andris.

Yorke couldn't shake the image of her pale face from his mind.

'Mike?'

'I'm here, sir.'

'I think their message is clear. We're one step ahead of you, and not only do we want your attention, but we want the attention of the world.'

Yorke felt another realisation fall onto his shoulders. Crushing him. Threatening to send him over the balcony. 'Matthew ... shit! What'll they do to him?'

Silence.

'Do you think? No...' He couldn't get his words out. There was no need to. He knew the answer.

'That's why you've got to be quick, pal. Time is running out.'

'You've not found this cell in five fucking years! And you expect me to find it before ... before ...'

'The next firework?' Robinson sighed. 'Yes. I know I'm asking the impossible, but what other choice do we have?'

～

NO OTHER CHOICE.

Robinson was right.

Which is why, after he had locked down the scene and forensics had begun processing, Yorke returned home and lay in bed, desperate for some rest before the morning briefing.

He stared ceilingward, hoping for another revelation.

None came.

Neither did sleep.

～

BRIEFING, as it'd been on the previous four days, was a complete washout.

Rozalija's crime scene was clean. The hit had been professional. They were waiting on some fast-tracked tests, but as was the norm in this incident room, nobody was in a confident mood.

As a result, Yorke lost his temper. Yorke *never* lost his temper with his team. He always went out of his way to value and respect them, but when DI Grant Harnett said, in a melancholic tone, 'One dead end after another, these bastards are bloody slippery,' Yorke had retorted with, 'No shit, Grant!

They've kidnapped a kid, and if not for a few lucky questions night before last, they'd have blown up a bloody weapons factory! But guess what? Our job is to keep on sodding-well going.'

Harnett looked down.

In fact, most people in the room looked down.

Yorke felt an overwhelming sense of guilt and brushed a chair out of his way. Unfortunately, the chair toppled, which hadn't really been his intention. However, it intensified the sudden cold atmosphere.

On the way out of the silent incident room, he leaned over Robinson. 'You want to tell them what's coming, sir? The fireworks?'

Robinson didn't look at him or speak.

A good thing. Yorke had suddenly descended into a very dark place. Any comment from the SEROCU leader may just trigger a response that would probably cost Yorke his career.

∾

YORKE PACED HIS OFFICE, wired on exhaustion and bouncing through every second of the last four days, wanting desperately to identify an adhesive that brought the fragments together into a whole.

He'd been summoned by Superintendent Joan Madden to her office because of the outburst but was ignoring the request.

He stopped after he felt a very familiar tug of intuition— the same tug, in fact, that had taken him back to Mia and Greg for the revelation regarding the factory, and then, during the middle of the night, to Rozalija, albeit too late.

A fierce knock sounded on his door, and he turned, annoyed, that someone had interrupted his epiphany.

Sonia stood there, holding a cup and smiling. 'Coffee? Decaff, though.' She raised an eyebrow. 'For obvious reasons.'

Yorke felt the frustration drain from him. He smiled at her act of kindness. 'So, you're offering me a cup of hot water?'

'Think yourself lucky, sir. Some of the others wanted to bring you a cup of arsenic.'

Yorke laughed. 'Grant, in particular?'

'No, he was looking for the key for the gun cabinet.'

'If such things existed, it'd be well deserved.' Yorke took the cup from her hands. 'I may even stand close to give him an easier target.'

'Don't be so hard on yourself. Not like you lose it often. In fact ...' She tapped her bottom lip with her finger, playacting that she was giving it some thought. 'Have you ever lost it? At least everyone now knows you're human, like the rest of us.' She smiled and looked over her shoulder to check that the door was closed. 'Now, Superintendent Joan Madden on the other hand ...'

'Yes,' Yorke said, perching on the edge of the desk. 'When she's calm, you know something's amiss.'

'So go easy on yourself; you're exhausted.'

'Yes but being a dick won't get us any closer to Matthew.'

'We'll get there. Your track record speaks for itself.'

'My track record means nothing. You know, if Matthew dies, that's on me. If that factory had been allowed to blow, he could be home with his family by now.'

'And you believe that, sir, honestly?'

Yorke shrugged. 'Ask me when this is all over and I've had a good night's sleep, and I may give you the answer you want to hear, but right now, this whole bloody thing feels firmly at my door.'

'These people are ruthless. Look at poor Rozalija! If

Matthew doesn't come back, this isn't on you. This is on the behaviour of malicious people.'

Yorke smiled at her. 'You're doing great, you know. None of what I said out there applies to you.'

She blushed. 'Thanks, sir.'

'No need to thank me. You were made for this. You remind me of someone I used to work with. Sharp as a tack.'

His mind wandered to DCI Emma Gardner, currently operating in Yorkshire—or 'The Wilds of Yorkshire,' as she put it.

'Where do we go next, sir?'

'Good question. They're putting on a performance, aren't they? This cell. We changed the terms of it, but it remains a performance, nonetheless. They want Matthew for their final hurrah, to make Article SE really understand what they're up against.' Yorke's mind leaped back to that intuitive pull, and it dawned on him, like a bulb exploding in his head.

Could he put himself one step ahead? For once?

'We need to get to Mia. Greg is out of the picture. That leaves her. Just her. If they want to carry on playing, that's all they've left.'

'So, she's in danger?' Sonia said, turning for the door.

'No. It's not that simple. Mia dying before they return the child, what does that serve? Nothing. To inflict maximum damage, they need to revive the ransom demand.'

$\sim$

YORKE HAD BEEN RIGHT *AGAIN*. Unfortunately, he was also late *again*.

By the time they got to Mia, the cell had delivered the ransom demand to her, and Yorke's hope of putting a trace on the line had passed its sell-by date.

Mia was to place money into the bin of a local park, early the next morning.

She was determined to do so.

The requested amount was ridiculously small, considering Mia Brace's wealth. And, considering all that'd come to pass, it was very unlikely that this cell didn't know their audience. So Yorke faced up to the stomach-churning, skin-crawling reality. *This is more bullshit.*

More fireworks.

Seeing lives being toyed with so frivolously was tearing Yorke apart inside, but he had to keep himself firmly under control now; there couldn't be any repeat of the behaviour in the incident room earlier.

The whole afternoon was designated to planning the ransom drop. They left no stone unturned. Yorke had warned Mia beforehand that if it went wrong and they ran with Matthew, there would be no backup, and she could potentially lose him forever. She'd agreed to the police having limited involvement. A 'light touch,' she'd insisted.

Yorke and his team reviewed their plans a second time.

This was anything but a light touch, but Mia didn't need to know that.

Surveillance on the park would come from the air and the ground. Armed response from yesterday's factory shootout would be in attendance. Hidden, but presence would be heavy. If the kidnappers came, they'd swoop, even if Matthew wasn't there. Because he wouldn't be there. Yorke was certain of it. And if by some miracle he was, he'd be dead, so letting them go would be unthinkable. If Yorke could get his hands on just one of these bastards, he wouldn't hold back on tearing the truth from them come what may.

Then everyone went home to rest for the big day.

And Yorke stayed behind to talk to Robinson.

'It won't play out the way we think tomorrow,' Yorke said.

Robinson nodded.

'It's probably a trap.'

'We've done everything we can, pal,' Robinson said. 'We've left surveillance on the area the entire night. Anybody who moves into that drop zone tonight will be scrutinised and logged. Nobody is setting traps. It's the same tomorrow when the drop happens. Eyes will be on anyone who enters that park. The hint of a weapon, a bomb—well, it'll be all over before anyone crosses the threshold.'

'All sounds too easy though, doesn't it?'

'Yes, it does,' Robinson said.

'Gut feeling?'

'We're not getting Matthew back tomorrow.'

'I was afraid it was the same as mine.'

'But we don't have any choice. We must go.'

'And dance to their bloody tune?'

'Can you hear another one? If so, fella, please let me know.'

∾

YORKE'S WHIRRING brain didn't want him to sleep. His exhausted body had other ideas, mind you. And, for a time, he spiralled halfway between sleep and wakefulness in that montage of mayhem that had plagued his week.

When he was pulled from the darkness by the beep on his phone, he felt a strong surge of irritation. But, he knew, he had to force it back, because, if he rose to it, he'd have no chance of getting more sleep before the six o'clock rise.

An unknown number had sent the message. Before he played it, he felt Patricia's hands around him. He leaned over, kissed her, and apologised. He left the room, closed the door behind him, and played the video.

A closeup of ashen-faced Matthew Brace, coughing and moaning for his mother. A zoom-out to reveal his location. The closed High Street gate. North side. Recognisable by the Stuart royal coat of arms.

Everyone was getting a good night's sleep for a drop that would never happen.

But Matthew was alive!

Christ, he was alive!

THERE'S ROOM AT THE INN

*D*r Stewart Holden's gaze bounced between the two screens.

Keith 'Corpse Rustler' Burston stared at the camera mounted in the corner of the room.

Tobias Young—or Tobias Ray, as Lacey would insist—stared at nothing.

Holden dampened his top lip with his tongue.

I simply can't wait, Lacey, to play this card.

He panned to the next cell. *Empty.* Then the next, also empty.

Eighteen empty cells in total.

Not for long.

He thought of Lacey, Amelia, and his brother's impending delivery.

Soon it would only be fifteen empty cells.

Growing.

He looked at the picture on his phone again that Sam Lynn had just sent him.

Sam was a freelance private investigator, who Holden had carefully vetted. After becoming convinced that money was

Sam's idol and that morality didn't figure, Holden had set him to work on following Lacey. His updates from her world were regular, and Holden ventured outside his prison hourly to catch a few bars on his phone and update his messages.

This picture was interesting—a ridiculously large, well-built man with a shaved head climbing from Lacey Ray's car outside the house on Sycamore Street.

Bravo, Sam, good shot! I can even see the scars on the big man's face. How do you do it? You're like the invisible man.

Holden reclined in his chair and closed his eyes.

Who're you then, big man? Are you just an unfortunate who Lacey picked up? If so, it's highly likely that your time on this earth has since ended, or in the process of doing so.

A knock came at his control room door.

Felix.

He'd seen him minutes ago through the camera at the prison entrance with his delivery, punching in the keycode. Holden stood and stretched. Things were about to get more interesting.

He stood, threw a smirk at the still-staring Keith on the monitor, and went to unlock and open the door.

Felix Holden stood there in the gloomy stone corridor. His suit was expensive and pristine. His shoes shone.

'You didn't have to wear your Sunday best, brother. Look around.'

'Believe it or not, you're not my only stop today. Although, I hope to make this the briefest of them all.'

Holden snorted. 'I still don't get it though. Why have as much money as you have if you can't just wear what you want?'

'I'm wearing what I want.' Felix wiped the back of his hand over his forehead. 'There's no air in this fucking place.'

'It's a Victorian prison, brother. Thick walls, narrow

windows. No one was brought here to enjoy the flow of fresh air. It was a place of punishment. *Real* punishment, not like the ones—'

'Give the history lesson to someone else, please. It's a bright summer's day outside, and I want to go and enjoy it. Where do you want Vinnie?'

'Depends. I need to look at him first.'

'*No.* You told me this was what you wanted.' Irritation burned bright in his brother's eyes.

Oh, Felix Holden! That promise to our father is a part of your soul. To support and protect your brother through thick and thin.

Holden's top lip curled up. Of course, when he'd made that promise, he'd probably not expected so many *thick* times.

Felix continued to express his annoyance. 'For fuck's sake, Stewart, it's not like there isn't room at the inn.'

'Well, if he doesn't fit the bill,' Holden said, thinking of his refrigeration unit, 'I'll make use of the body.'

He nodded down the corridor to where Holden's gift was. 'Jerry has him.'

Holden stepped into the corridor and looked right.

Jerry, also suited and booted, held a catch pole. The wire loop at the end of the long fiberglass shaft was tightened around another smartly dressed man's neck.

Vinnie Russell, who was one of Felix's heavies, had gotten one hell of a surprise when he'd turned up to work this morning.

Kneeling, Vinnie had his hands secured behind his back. His gaze darted angrily between all three of them. He was sweating, despite the cold, while the tape on his mouth puffed in and out as he struggled to get enough air through his nose.

'Treating my guest well, I see?' Holden smiled at Felix.

'Like fucking royalty to how you're going to treat him,' Felix said.

Holden approached Vinnie.

'I wouldn't get too close,' Jerry said. 'I've seen this fucker go. He's an animal.'

'Best keep hold of that pole, then,' Holden said and knelt so that he was directly in front of Vinnie. 'If I remove the tape, will you be good, little bunny?'

Vinnie stared hard at Holden.

'If you try to bite me, I'll take out all your teeth before I show you to your room. If you look into my eyes, you'll see I'm not bluffing.' He allowed a few seconds for Vinnie to see the truth in his eyes. 'Clear?'

No response.

'*Clear*?' he repeated, sensing he may have to give Vinnie a quick taste of his punishment for dissent—the cattle prod.

Vinnie nodded.

'Good choice.' Holden tore off the tape.

Vinnie gasped and sucked in air.

'Shall we get you more comfortable?'

'Who ... the *fuck* ... are you?'

Holden smiled. 'We've plenty of time for me later, Vinnie. First, let's start with you. I've been made aware that you've *certain* tastes? Is that right?'

Vinnie's gaze darted from Holden to upward in Felix's direction. 'Boss?'

'Just answer the question,' Felix said.

'I don't understand! What's happening?'

Holden sensed Felix come alongside him. 'It's over, Vinnie. You've been loyal to me, but—'

'Then, why this? What the fucking hell is this?'

'If you let me finish ...'

Vinnie nodded.

'You've been loyal but ... well ... I had a few gripes.'

'Gripes? I did everything you—'

'*Everything?*'

Vinnie tilted his head to the side. 'Yes ... more or less.'

'*More or less?* I gave you a position of responsibility. I asked you to *tone* it down. You didn't. I don't mind someone enjoying their work, but no one—I mean, no one—should take that much pleasure from it.'

'I'm fucking good at it.'

'Only in that the people you were asked to kill did always end up dead.'

'So, I *delivered*, then!'

'You did. But the *manner*, the *methods*. It just gets people talking, you know. It doesn't marry up with the image we're trying to project these days.'

'Smart suits and all,' Holden quipped.

'So, you're leaving me here. With *him*.' Vinnie nodded in Holden's direction.

Felix sighed. 'Yes. In a way, I'm sorry about that. I wouldn't wish it on anyone. Even with your sick, fucking tendencies, I'd have given you a quieter exit. Jerry here could even have done it while you were stirring sugar in your coffee this morning. But be this as it may, this is where we find ourselves.'

Felix narrowed his eyes, then growled as he tried desperately to wrestle his hands free. Jerry tightened his grip on the catchpole so that Vinnie winced and yelped every time he moved his head too sharply.

Holden stood and watched him fight against his bondage, until the metal loop around his neck cut off too much oxygen for him to continue. He lowered his red sweating face, gulping at air.

Eventually Vinnie lifted his head and glared at Felix. 'You're not top of the fucking food chain, you arrogant prick.'

'No, but I'm high enough on it. And, more importantly, higher than you.'

'Do *they* know about your little freak show?'

'It's not important to them.'

'What about the image *they're* trying to protect? Not sure they'd like this carnival side line.'

Holden regarded his brother. He was trying to appear unrattled, but Holden could sense something behind his eyes. *He's right. They wouldn't like it, would they, brother? You may be a big-shot property developer, but feeding me wouldn't be good for your image, and it certainly wouldn't be good for theirs. I imagine you want to keep this well and truly quiet.* He eyed Vinnie. *But don't worry, brother, this one won't say anything, because he isn't going anywhere.* He knelt again. 'Vinnie?'

Vinnie refocused on Holden. '*What*?'

'Is it true that you like to skin people?'

'Untie me and I'll fucking *show* you.'

Holden smiled. 'All in good time. But I'd like that. For you to show me.'

'You wouldn't.'

'We'll see. I researched you a little. I hope that's okay?'

'Fuck you.'

'You were brought up on a farm. Is that where you learned to skin animals? Did your father teach you?'

'Fuck. You.'

Holden smiled again. 'Did you start with rabbits, work your way up?'

Vinnie spat in Holden's face.

Holden grinned as he wiped away the spit with the back of his hand. Then he stood. 'We're going to learn together, Vinnie. In time, you may appreciate me. I'll teach you a lot about yourself.'

Vinnie eyed Felix again. 'Don't leave me with this nut job. *Please.* You've my word, boss. I won't do it again.'

'It's done,' Felix said. 'And this is best for everyone.'

'I can be like a father to you, Vinnie. I bet your father didn't understand you, did he?' Holden asked. 'They never found his body. Did you burn his body after you skinned him, perhaps?'

Vinnie glared at Holden. 'Fuck you.'

Holden smiled at his brother. 'I'll take him!'

Vinnie moaned quietly.

'Where do you want him?' Jerry asked.

'Down the corridor. I left the door of his cell *wide* open.'

Jerry yanked gently on the catch pole, guiding Vinnie to his feet. Jerry kept the pole extended fully so Vinnie could get nowhere near him as he led him down the corridor. At first, Vinnie obeyed and continued moaning, but several metres down the corridor, the sad noises turned to shouts and screams, and he tried to make a move for Jerry.

Felix, still beside Holden, went for his gun beneath his suit top.

Holden put a hand on Felix's shoulder. 'No. Wait.'

With his foot, Jerry swept Vinnie's feet from beneath him. He went to his knees again.

'Have it your way,' Jerry said, pulling hard on the pole.

Vinnie gasped and cried out but couldn't reach his neck because his hands were restrained. He was forced to shuffle forward on his knees after Jerry or risk strangulation.

He half-scurried and was half-dragged into the open cell.

Jerry stepped back out the cell, slammed the door, and turned the key.

'Fuck you, Vinnie, you sick bastard.' Jerry turned and headed towards Felix and Holden. 'You can keep the fucking catch pole.'

'Listen,' Felix said, 'if he ever gets out of here, I'm fucked. Everyone, apart from me and Jerry here, thinks he's dead. And Jerry ... well, Jerry'—he clapped a hand on Jerry's shoulder—'is like a brother to me, so he's all good.'

'The brother you never had,' Holden said.

Felix grinned. 'Come on, Jerry. Let's go.'

'One more thing,' Holden said.

Felix lowered his head, clucked his tongue, and shook his head. 'Jesus ...'

Holden reached into his pocket for his phone and showed Felix the picture of the big man sent by Sam. 'I need you to find out who *that* is.'

Felix sighed.

'And that's it,' Holden said, sensing his apprehension. 'Then, for a time, I'll leave you be. You can go about looking smart, doing your thing. *Shining.*'

'That's what you always say, but your phone calls come thick and fast. Give me that fucking picture, then.'

There was no reception, so Holden used Airdrop.

As they walked away, Felix called over his shoulder, 'Not even a fucking *thank you.*'

'Thank you, brother,' Holden called out. 'I'm so glad Father taught us *both* the true meaning of family.'

Vinnie howled and bashed on the cell door.

THE ONE WITHOUT THE HEART

*A*fter parking on Sycamore Street, Lacey glanced at her passenger.

Jake had his head against the glass and his eyes closed. He wasn't asleep, just despondent over the news of his ex-colleague's death.

Oh, Jakey. Your sensitivity will be your undoing.

'We're here,' she said. 'And I need you back from wherever you've gone.'

Jake grunted.

She waited, scanning the street to check no one was watching them. 'Remember that your grief isn't part of this adventure,' Lacey hissed.

'Adventure? We aren't hunting diamonds in the Amazon! I needed a killer, one without a heart. That's where you come in. Don't try to make this glamorous.'

Lacey nodded. *Watch where you tread. Forget sensitivity, a complacent tongue around me may undo you first!* 'Open your eyes. We're on Sycamore Street. I told you before that Dr Stewart Holden *knows* about this place. Now, if you want to draw attention to yourself, by all means, go ahead.' She checked her watch. 'But if you're not inside in two minutes, the door will be bolted, and you can go on your merry way. Then I'd give you twenty-four hours before someone cuts out that bleeding heart of yours. What a pair we'd make then, eh? The ones without the hearts.' She gave him a wink.

He opened his eyes and looked at her. His cheeks were red from tears.

She shook her head. Jesus, people and their emotions! It must be like wading through mud. Much better to run, dance, and frolic in freedom.

'Yorke was no good for you, Jake. He was an idealist.' Lacey cracked open her door. 'He'd have swept you into a jail cell as soon as he saw you again and slept all the more soundly for it.' She swung her legs outside. 'He's better off dead and out the fucking way.'

Jake's hand clutched her arm. She looked at it, then into his angry face. She smirked. 'Sadness, frustration, despair— it's all there. A fucking catalogue of emotions. So tell me now, where do you think these emotions will get you? Do you think it will get you Frank back? Do you think it will get me Tobias back? I've watched you grow, Jake, and wherever you've been has certainly hardened you more than I even thought possible. But even with all that change, your emotion is still in charge. You need to deaden it. Do you hear me? *Fucking deaden it.*' She glared his hand. 'And take that off me before I deaden you.'

Keeping hold of her, he retrieved the gun she'd acquired for him from the glove compartment with his other hand. He pointed it at her. 'Unless I deaden you first?'

Her smirk didn't fall away. 'So natural. Even in your left hand'—she nodded at the hand on her arm—'when you're right-handed. You're a born killer.'

'Mike was better than me, and he was better than you.'

Lacey shrugged. 'Depends on your definition of *better*, I guess. For me, it's about staying alive. He didn't manage that so well.'

'Fuck you.'

'Shoot me.' She smiled. 'Kill me. By all means. Then I guess you'll have proven me wrong. Lacey Ray undone by a gun she purchased for a man she agreed to help. The stupidest bitch who ever walked the earth.' She bit her bottom lip and looked him in the eyes. *Capable, yes. Willing, no. Not yet, at any rate.* 'Go on. *Do it.*'

He lowered the gun and released her arm. 'No, I need you.'

More than you realised it seems.

'Okay. Now listen. I warned you about Carrie already. It'll be fine, but she doesn't do well around people, especially men. Just be mindful of how you step.'

'She can't be worse than you,' Jake said, cracking open his door.

∼

JAKE'S closest friend was gone. He needed to process it, and quickly, but he'd no idea of how to do that.

When Lacey slammed the front door behind them, he flinched and leaned against the banister, the nausea from when he'd heard the news earlier suddenly returning.

'Okay, the carpets are grim.' Lacey slapped his back. 'But don't go decorating them anymore.'

He shook his head. He was sick to death of her sarcasm.

Mike was gone. Gone!

How? You were the best. You always seemed to be one step ahead of everyone.

The nausea intensified as he thought of Patricia, Ewan, and Beatrice.

Good people.

Mike's people.

He needed to go to them at some point, once his son Frank was safe. Put his arms around them. *Damn the consequences.* Let them arrest him, investigate him. He owed Yorke at least this much. His arms around Yorke's broken family, his condolences, for what they were worth, his offer to support them as best he could from this day on.

If he even lived that long. Because Michael Yorke was the best there ever was, and if he'd fallen, then what fucking chance did the rest of them, him especially, really have?

The world pulsed around Jake. He took some deep breaths.

Stay in control.

A big fucking ask in one of the worst moments of his life.

Frank. Think about Frank. This is all about him. Remember? All about him. It must be.

With his breathing under control, he straightened and turned to see Lacey removing her shoes.

'Focused?' she asked, bending down to line up her shoes neatly beside some other ones.

'Focused enough to realise that those expensive shoes are out of place in this shithole.'

'Have to admit that it's genius though! Who'd suspect that Lacey, a woman with such fine tastes, would live in such a dump?' She pointed at his scruffy trainers. 'Make sure you take *those* off.'

He creased his brow. 'Why? The place is disgusting.'

'Let's not make it worse then.'

Jake removed his trainers and tried to place them next to Lacey's line of shoes.

Lacey put her hand on his arm. 'The other side, please.'

'Snob.'

'Everyone has a weakness. Now you know mine.'

'What? Shoes?'

Lacey shrugged. 'Hey, the world works in mysterious ways. When I worked as an escort, some of them used to have their hands all over me, but it meant little. Just money, you know? However, if I saw them touching my shoes with no respect, I'd cut off their fucking hands.'

'Wow,' Jake said, shaking his head. 'Just, wow.'

Lacey shrugged. 'Carrie must be out. If she wasn't, she'd have met us at the door.' She yawned. 'Now, that was a lot of driving. I'm going to lie down.' She started up the stairs.

'Hey, wait. We've got to crack on.'

Lacey checked her watch. 'Later. We've made good time. Rest will help.'

Jake sighed. Lacey was right. They had hours to spare before their target would be home from work, and rest was a good idea. However, after hearing that Lacey shared the house with another psycho, he wasn't too keen on closing his eyes.

'Oh,' she said from the top of the stairs, 'the lounge is the first door on the right. Hunker down in there.'

'Is that where that body is?'

'Beneath the floorboards ... *relax*. Also, stay out the kitchen. The door directly opposite you.'

'Why?'

'Carrie's working on something in there. She mightn't appreciate anyone seeing it until it's finished. You know how precious people can be about their artwork.'

'Can't I just stay upstairs?'

'No,' Lacey said, turning the corner. 'And remember, stay out of the kitchen.'

Jake heard her bedroom door close, then his gaze flew to the closed door opposite. He felt a cold stone of dread in his stomach.

The kitchen.

He turned into the lounge. He surveyed the yellowing carpet and the curved edges where they should have been attached to carpet grippers. It wouldn't have been too difficult to roll that aside, pry up the floorboards, and deposit the body beneath.

The stone in his stomach grew heavier.

Apart from a solitary wooden dining table chair and a disused fireplace full of rubbish, the room was bare. At least the sunlight that glared in through the large window and net curtains lit it well.

He took himself to other side of the room, directly opposite the open lounge door. He slipped his gun from his belt and sat on the floor. From here, he had a good view of the window, should anyone decide to look in and, of course, the door—the only entrance into the room. After a few moments of sitting there, with the gun on his lap, his nerves settled.

His thoughts drifted back to Yorke, about how he'd taken him under his wing when he'd joined the force, how he'd been best man at his wedding, and how fond he'd been of Frank. He'd also been a great help when Jake had concocted the grand idea to take a three year-old to St Mary's stadium. Most mates would have baulked at the idea. Yorke was happy to sit, with Frank on his lap, while everyone around him jumped up and down. Jake smiled as he recalled apologising to Yorke for making a trip to the footy hard work. Yorke's response was to suggest they come to the next home game. His words: *'Having a little one on my lap keeps me calm when they're attacking our goal, Jake. Keeps it all in perspective.'*

Jake, who'd been a bag of nerves after Southampton had been reduced to ten men and had to ward off Everton's late charge, had been envious of Yorke's zen-like attitude.

He'd also realised on that day that he'd never have a better
mate again.

≈

IT WAS dark when Jake opened his eyes. He pounced to his
feet, cocked the gun in his hands, and recalled why he was in
this unfamiliar place.

*You dickhead! Anything could have happened! Didn't you get
enough sleep on that fucking flight?*

Remembering Lacey's narrative around the psychopathic
Dr Holden, and her warnings regarding Carrie, Jake darted to
the net curtain and peered outside. Only half the streetlamps
seemed to be working, but it was enough to give him some
vision of Sycamore Street. Other cars were stationed around
Lacey's vehicle now, but all that told him was that more people
had returned home from their day jobs. He didn't know what
car Carrie or Dr Holden drove, so he had no idea if he was still
actually alone in the house with Lacey.

Shit.

*All three of these Looney Tunes could be in here with me
already!*

He wiped his brow with the back of his hand, then
checked his watch again and sighed.

*More than anything else, we need to get a bloody move on, put
the plan into action—*

A long, low moan came from another room, and Jake felt
an icy whip of fear. He readied his weapon and aimed at the
open lounge door. He held his breath and listened.

Nothing.

Refusing to believe it was the sound of wind or the noisy
hinges on an old door, Jake kept his weapon raised as he
moved forward.

There it was again.

Long, low, and pained.

The sound of human suffering.

With his heart thrashing in his chest, he took some deep breaths as he stalked towards the lounge door.

He heard it a third time.

Male. Most definitely male.

Had they finally gotten hold of Dr Holden? Was this the sound of the twisted man's agony? Dare he interrupt whatever the vipers were doing to him?

He looked behind himself at his former resting place by the fireplace.

And do what? Hunker back down? Since when had he been reactive?

Never. And he'd got this far! Proactive, then.

Go to it.

He'd had some firearms training and had honed some of those skills during his time in New England, where guns seem to be more readily available and, rather terrifyingly, a societal norm. So he turned out of the lounge with some ability, quickly manoeuvring his gun in different directions: the front door, the stairs, and the door to his right.

The kitchen.

Carrie's artwork.

The moan was continuous now, dipping up and down in volume.

He looked up the stairs. Maybe he should go to Lacey. Then he remembered she'd told him not to. Mind you—he looked back at the kitchen—she'd told him not to go in there either.

The moaning continued. It demanded attention. Jake *needed* to know. Not wanting to leave himself vulnerable to the other direction, he slid along the wall towards the door. His shirt dampened, and he had to rub at his brow several times when sweat crept into his eyes.

At the door, his left hand fell to the handle, and Lacey's voice from earlier sounded in his head: *'You know how precious people can be about their artwork.'*

He pressed his ear to the wooden door.

The moaning was incessant.

He pushed the handle, flung open the door, fell into a squat, and took aim.

~

*A*RTWORK*?*

In what world could such a thing be considered artwork?

'Carrie's working on something in there.'

Was she ever!

'She mightn't appreciate anyone seeing it until its finished.'

Jesus wept! What the hell did *finished* look like?

Although the man tied to the chair was blindfolded, he knew someone was there. He may have heard Jake come through the door. He was now moving his head from side to side, probably trying to catch some changes in the light or a silhouette. Jake briefly recalled pin the tail on the donkey as a child, and the fact that if you really tried hard enough, you may just be able to make out some of your surroundings, and then orient yourself from memory.

The man couldn't speak because his lips had been stitched together. Attempting to communicate would make a right mess of his face. Although, in all honesty, that was the least of his concerns.

A table had been positioned directly in front of him, close enough to kick. Of course, he couldn't do this, because both his feet had been removed, and it would cause him severe pain to lash out with cauterised stumps. When Carrie removed that blindfold, then the man on the chair would get to see his feet floating in formaldehyde, one per jar.

And he wouldn't just get to see his feet.

No, that would have been merciful compared to this. Jake put a hand over his mouth and gagged.

The tortured man would get to see his hands, too. And his ears, and his nose, and his ... surely not. Jake gagged again. He swallowed back bile and took a deep breath. *God, yes.* The patches of reddened, raw flesh on each side of the man's chest confirmed what he'd first thought.

That his nipples were also in formaldehyde.

Jake's third gag was louder, and the man in the chair most certainly heard him. He moaned his loudest yet, and Jake feared he may just cry out for help and tear his knitted lips to pieces. The man yanked his head back and forth, trying to see something. Then he suddenly waved his cauterised stumps about frenetically. It was both pitiful and surreal. Jake shook his head, the sight of such human misery over-whelming him.

Did this man think Jake was about to rescue him? That his time of torment was about to come to an end?

Jake shook his head.

The poor man was kidding himself. Looking at the state of him, he couldn't be rescued. It was too late. His torment would never end.

Feeling lightheaded, Jake steadied himself against the doorframe as he scanned the countless jars, not just on the table but underneath it and around the chair where the man sat.

All those different pieces of him.

A cheek, perhaps? A buttock, maybe?

He thought about Lacey, the killer he'd asked for help. He

knew she was different and that her capabilities were distasteful, but this seemed a whole new level of savagery.

The stitched scars on the man's torso suggested also that Carrie had already ventured inside him. Did some of these jars contain internal organs? Snippets of him, perhaps. Bits he could live without—at least in the short term.

He wondered briefly what Yorke would've done if confronted with this human jigsaw puzzle.

A good man. The best.

How did such a man respond?

Jake didn't know; he was at a loss.

But probably not like this. Jake aimed his gun at the man. *But we were never the same, Mike, were we? That was always the problem. No, you wouldn't do this, but that doesn't make you right —or wrong either, I guess.*

Some things just transcend any idea of right or wrong.

Like this.

Jake shot the man in the head.

∾

LACEY NEVER DREAMED.

Yes, everyone's mind needed to play outside reality at some point—it was healthy to do so—but, of course, that was what the Blue Room was for. So, when she was asleep, it was as if she ceased to exist. No matter the events preceding her rest, no matter how diabolical or bloody, she'd drift off to sleep calmly, ready to be reenergised. And when she was refuelled, she'd wake just as gently as she'd gone off.

As a result, she *really* didn't appreciate a gunshot awakening her. Especially not when she was lying low in a dishevelled house, awaiting the next move of her psychopathic foe. She also had to get moving before any more shots were fired.

After all, one shot could be written off as a car backfiring, perhaps. Potentially keeping the blues and twos from their door. But a second gunshot? Well, that would be Goodnight Vienna.

Moving quickly and gracefully, not how you'd expect someone who'd been dragged disorientated from a slumber, she plucked her hunting knife from her bedside table. As she exited the room, she crouched, knife at the ready in case of ambush.

She paused ... listened.

Nothing.

She started on the stairs, sliding against the wall, her fist to her chest, turning the blade of the hunting knife outward, ready for engagement.

Jake, looking washed out and confused, appeared at the bottom of the stairs, gun at his side.

What have you done, Jake?

My one?

The thought of her dead lover tightened her grip on the knife handle.

Her one's death would be unacceptable.

Unforgiveable.

'Where's Carrie?'

Jake shook his head. 'I don't know.'

'Who've you shot?'

Jake steadied himself against the banister 'There was a man in your kitchen.'

'Fuck! I *told* you—'

The front door opened near Jake.

Jake turned and ensured both hands gripped the weapon.

'My one?' Lacey said.

'Yes, Lacey.' Carrie entered, head lowered, sensing Jake, perhaps, but not seeing him behind the open door.

'Jake is here, and he's just about to lower his gun,' Lacey said. 'Aren't you, Jake?'

Carrie stepped forward and closed the door behind her. She turned to face Jake, who was looking more unstable by the second.

'You're bigger than I imagined,' Carrie said. She creased her brow. 'Why're you pointing a gun at me?'

Jake didn't respond.

You were warned, Jake, Lacey thought. *Could I have been any clearer?*

'I thought I heard a shot,' Carrie said, 'a moment ago. Was that you?'

Jake nodded.

Carrie looked towards the kitchen, and her expression started to change.

Lacey shook her head. *Watch where you tread, I said.* 'You need to put down the gun.'

'Have you lost your fucking mind?' Jake hissed.

No, I think that it's you who's done that.

Carrie started towards the kitchen.

'My one,' Lacey said. 'Please stop. Please come to me first.'

Carrie stopped and looked up at Lacey. Her expression was solemn.

Good.

Lacey nodded down at her and descended the stairs.

When Lacey was level with Jake, Carrie had refocused on reaching the kitchen.

Lacey pushed Jake's gun aside, staring up at his pale face. 'Fool.' Lacey turned around the banister and marched after Carrie, who had opened the door to the kitchen.

Carrie froze in the doorway. Lacey stopped too. She knew how Carrie would be feeling in this second, making it dangerous to get too close.

She needed a moment.

Take control, my one. I understand your disappointment, but there are others. There will always be others. Don't let any emotion get the better of you. Take control—

Carrie stepped into the kitchen and slammed the door behind her.

Lacey sighed.

Really? Is this what it's going to come down to? A choice between the two of you?

LABOUR AND TOIL

While Dr Stewart Holden waited for news on who Lacey's special guest was, he watched his new man, Vinnie.

Back when Felix had splashed the cash on having the Victorian prison renovated into Holden's stone dominion, one of the many challenges had been to fit a large refrigeration unit.

Felix had never asked the reason. In truth, Felix had stopped asking questions a long time ago. The answers he received usually disgusted him. He simply did right by his brother as per the oath he'd made to their long-dead father. Holden often wondered if Felix regretted his decision to accept his father's wealth on such peculiar terms. Maybe he now considered it Faust-like, perhaps? The selling of one's soul to the devil for riches?

It had been pointless on Felix's part not to ask the question regarding the refrigeration unit anyway, because one day, he did find out—on the very day Holden had asked him to stock it.

And not with dairy either.

Holden needed corpses. Without them, how would he entice his guests? Or tease them, as was the case with Keith 'Corpse Rustler' Burston?

Anyway, Holden didn't fully understand Felix's outrage over this. It was a win-win, as far as he could see. It gave his brother somewhere to dispose of the bodies. In his line of work, as a property-developing gangster, there were always people who needed rehoming.

Holden had selected the corpse of a slim man for today's observation. He could've gone for a fat man; in fact, he could've gone for a *very* fat man, but that may have been time consuming. Holden didn't know when he'd have to make a move regarding Lacey, and he was curious to see as much of this process as possible.

Vinnie was proving a stubborn bastard and really didn't seem keen on putting on a show.

Holden took solace in the fact that Keith had been like this to begin with but could now rustle corpses with the best of them.

The slim corpse was on the stone floor by Vinnie's mattress. A sharp skinning knife rested on the dead man's belly. There was also some strong cord so he could tie the limbs while he laboured, as well as some plastic bags for bagging any guts and internal organs if the skinner took it that far.

But, for hours now, Vinnie had simply sat, cross-legged, staring at the corpse.

A few times Holden had hit a button to fire up the intercom in Vinnie's cell. He'd offered him bribes: a tasty meal, the promise of a trophy from this skinned victim, a television wheeled into his room for a film of his choice. Nothing shifted him.

Holden checked his watch, saw that he was fifteen minutes

from having to step outside and contact Felix to find out what was going on with the big man at Lacey's house, and sighed.

Time to write it off for another day.

He wasn't too despondent. This was scientific investigation, after all. And scientific investigation was notoriously slow.

Still, it was healthy to have a little frustration. It kept you coming back for more. He hit the button again. 'Okay, have it your own way. I thought we may just get off to a better start than this. You did a fine job last time, but it keeps me healthy to have some trust issues, so let me talk you through how it works *again*. Secure your wrists to the cuffs protruding from the stone wall at the back. There's a sensor on them, so I know when they're secure, so there's no point in trying to trick me. Then I'll bring my trolley for old Nigel there. If you won't skin him, I'll just have to pass him along to Keith to relieve himself. He'll think it's Christmas. I've starved him of intimacy for close to a month now, so it might be good idea to remind him what he's missing.'

Vinnie dived from the bed and weaved the cord around dead Nigel's legs.

Holden's eyes widened. *Attaboy! Well, that was out of the blue. Seems you don't want Keith to sully your fresh meat.*

Vinnie sat on Nigel's stomach, facing his trussed legs, and made a shallow, circular cut just above the left ankle. He paused to examine and appreciate the precision of his work, then grabbed Nigel's skin at the cut and tugged it towards himself, stripping it from the flesh. He used the knife to loosen stubborn parts of the skin to stop himself cutting too deeply and damaging the meat.

Holden's phone buzzed. His alarm. It was time to go outside to take a call from Felix.

Not wanting to miss any of the show, he double checked

that the monitor was recording and, when satisfied, headed outside to take the call.

~

Felix had always struggled to keep his emotions in check, but it'd been a while since Holden had heard his brother raging like this. 'What the absolute fuck?'

Felix leaned against an oak tree beside the entrance to his stone dominion. 'I'm assuming the photograph yielded unexpected results?'

'Unexpected? *Unexpected*? You've initiated a fucking storm!'

'Sorry?'

'You've got me involved in something I really don't want to be involved in. What's the point in me helping you out if you're going to bring my whole fucking world crashing down!'

'Are you going to get to the point?'

'Shut the fuck up and listen. The man's called *Jake Pettman*. It'll mean nothing to you. Apparently he used to work for some of those upstairs. A bent cop. The alarm bells I just set off with that inquiry ... Jesus wept, you've no fucking idea. You can probably fucking hear them ringing from there!'

Interesting. And I just thought he might be an irrelevant toy she was planning on playing with. The plot really is thickening, after all. 'Jake Pettman, eh? Well, be interesting to know more about this—'

'No. You're not *fucking* listening. Not at all. This isn't about you. Or me. They want to *know* where he is, and they want to *know* why I'm inquiring after him.'

'You'll be fine, big-shot property developer like yourself. You've been feeding them long enough—'

'No! How many *fucking* times? Everyone is expendable.

Everyone.'

'So, what will you tell them, then?'

'That I feed my psychopathic brother other evil, fucking psychopaths and that Jake Pettman's current squeeze is my brother's latest fantasy.'

Holden grunted.

'Or not. You prick. They'll cut me loose.'

'Might do you some good to be cut loose, you sound—'

'Cut loose doesn't mean a severance package or early retirement. You really think I'm that important? The way they're expanding? I'm a drop in the fucking ocean!'

'With the obvious established, brother, could you try answering my question seriously now? What will you tell them?'

'I'll say that Jerry saw him skulking around one of our new Sunrise developments and that we followed him to this house on Sycamore Street, curious to know who he was.'

'Sounds doable.'

'But I need them to put this Pettman down before they ask too many questions. I'm waiting on the call now for his location. But then they'll give it to the best kill squad they have. The man is hard to put down, apparently. But I've got to hope they put him down before he talks. Before he denies ever being anywhere near my development. Anyway, the address, I need it. Give it to me.'

Holden sighed.

'Stewart?'

'Listen, brother, I need you to hold off until—'

'Don't you fucking dare!'

Holden felt a rare surge of irritation. 'I don't want Lacey killed in some kind of cross—'

'Listen carefully, brother. I. Don't. Care.'

'You need to.'

'This is bigger than you and your psychopaths! I'm in a do-or-die situation; there's no point in worrying about a pact with our father! if we don't give up his location, then both me and you will be sleeping in your refrigeration unit tonight.'

'Calm down. For such a successful man, I do wonder sometimes. Do you think rationally? Surely, you must've done in the past?'

'There's nothing to think about.'

'Of course there is! Yes, they want him. Okay, no problem. They can have him. Just a bit later. Why kill you? Then they'll never find out anything.'

'These people aren't patient.'

'Listen, take a deep breath, brother. I'm prepared to give you the location at ten o'clock tonight, not a second before.'

'That's too long; they want it *now*!'

'I'm sure they do but tell them Jerry has it and that you can't get in touch with Jerry. Whack him round the head with something blunt and heavy. Pretend he was in a car accident and was off the grid for a few hours; that'll do it. Now, take another deep breath, and soak up those words. *Ten o'clock*. You phone me back, and the location is yours.'

'This is suicide. Give me the *fucking*—'

'You're convincing, brother. Just check that Jerry is on the same page.'

'Nobody is convincing when it comes to *these* people. *Nobody*. After everything I've done for you, and you're fucking hanging me out like this?'

'Stop exaggerating. You're underestimating yourself. You're worth millions, and worth more to them alive rather than dead. And you did look quite the part in that new suit today. All shiny and that. Now, if you'll excuse me, I need to get back in. I suspect Vinnie might be trying on his new clothes, and I wouldn't want to miss that for the world.'

YOU WON'T SEE ME COMING

*S*till stunned by what he'd seen, *what he'd ended*, in the kitchen, Jake wavered at the bottom of the stairs. He stared at the gun in his hand.

Okay. That's enough. Snap out of it.

Lowering the gun to his side, but ready to raise it again at a moment's notice, he approached Lacey, who stood with her back to him midway down the corridor. He decided to stop a metre from her. The hunting knife in her hand was pivotal in that decision.

But was he really in danger from Lacey? After all, she'd already had the chance to strike as she turned around him at the foot of the stairs and hadn't taken it. He took that as a good sign that their relationship could be salvaged.

God, he hoped so.

He *desperately* needed her.

Steps needed to be taken—steps he'd struggle to negotiate, alone. Yes, he could kill, but his move regarding Article SE required something more. Something specialist.

'Lacey?'

Lacey nodded towards the closed kitchen door. 'Do you value your balls?'

'I don't have time for any of this. We don't—'

'Carrie castrated someone at Princeholm, and now she'll want to have another go.'

'Why? Because I put a half-dead husk of a man out of his misery? Have you seen what she did to him?'

'When Carrie was a child, that beast in there raped her mother, then raped her.'

Jake shook his head. 'That's awful. But doesn't it make it even less of an issue that I killed him? She'd already destroyed him. I mean, where could she go next?'

'She had ideas.'

Jake scrunched his face. 'What she was doing was just perverse, inhumane.'

'Out in nature, do you judge predators by your rules of morality?'

'I'm not out in fucking nature.'

'Oh, but you are. You very much are. And have been for a while, by the sounds of it. Now, don't move, and I'll attempt to save your balls.'

Aren't you forgetting who has the gun around here? 'You've got to choose between us.'

Lacey looked back. 'I already have.' She opened the kitchen door.

Carrie stood beside the dead rapist, running her fingers through his hair, then moaned—a moan not too dissimilar to the one that had brought him to that scene of carnage in the first place—although this wasn't a response to physical pain. It was most certainly anguish.

He heard Scott's voice in his head. '*Told you.*'

Oh, fuck off. I needed her. Still need her. Later, when she gets me what I need, you'll see. Everything will work out.

'Even without your balls?'

Jake sighed.

What had Lacey suggested earlier? That Carrie had evolved?

Into what exactly?

He eyed the gun in his hand. *Would putting an end to this situation be such a bad thing? Could Lacey stomach it?*

Carrie saw Lacey and turned to approach her. Her head was lowered, and Jake couldn't tell if she was weeping, but the moaning had stopped—at least for now. The scalpel glinted in her left hand; she must have picked it up from her display table.

Jake sensed they were about to fight.

Lacey had the bigger weapon, and the years of experience, but Jake wasn't prepared to risk it. He needed Lacey. He gritted his teeth, preparing to make a move at the first flash of steel.

Instead, the two women embraced.

Did that mean …?

A sudden rush of adrenaline made the gun in his hands feel less steady.

Don't you do it, Lacey. Don't you fucking turn on me.

In his mind, it played out like lightning. Two more shots. Two more dead bodies.

Then him sitting with three corpses. Four if you count the one under the lounge floor.

On his own again. Article SE chasing him down.

Welcome home, Jake.

Did you ever believe you could win?

Lacey whispered something in Carrie's ear. Carrie whispered something back.

Jake couldn't hear over the hammering of his heart.

Lacey turned. She mocked surprise over seeing Jake ready to fire. 'I thought I told you I had it in hand?'

'No, you said you'd attempt to save my life. It didn't sound that convincing.'

'I told you I'd made my choice.'

'Do share.'

'The world is more interesting with both of you in it, and I chose not to remove either of you. Lower your weapon.' She raised Carrie's scalpel. 'My one is holding up her side of the bargain.'

'What the hell were you whispering to each other?'

'I told my one that you wanted to save your son. She appreciates that.'

Jake guffawed. 'As if that makes a difference!' He nodded towards the kitchen. 'Look what she's done. Look what she *is*.'

'*He* wasn't innocent,' Lacey said. 'Frank is.'

Jake's heart dropped. *You didn't have to use his name, Lacey. Why did you go and do that?*

'I *like* children,' Carrie said.

'Do you?' Jake said. 'Well, do them all a favour and stay the hell away from them.'

Lacey raised her eyebrow. 'Play nice and lower the gun.'

He lowered it. 'Okay, but I'll keep it close for the moment, if it's all right with you?'

'Fine, but you're safe,' Lacey said.

'Am I?' he narrowed his gaze at Carrie. 'Am I really?'

Carrie turned to survey her dead *toy*, sighed, then looked back. 'Look. It's forgotten.'

Bullshit.

'Come within a metre of me and I'll kill you,' Jake said.

She smiled, as if to say, *Like you'll see me coming.* But instead, she said, 'Nice to meet you, Jake Pettman.'

∽

'I'm so glad you guys hit it off,' Lacey said as they drove away from Sycamore Street and towards Salisbury.

'Having seen what she's capable of,' Jake said, 'I'd watch your own back if I were you.'

'I admit, she's creative, yes. *Very.* But you seem to have forgotten what I'm capable of.'

Jake shook his head. 'Oh, I haven't. Not at all. Your infamy stretches far and wide, which is precisely why I contacted you.'

'Infamy, eh? I like it. Well, it's about to be put to the test. But just remember your side of the bargain. I help you with this, then Holden is next on the agenda.'

'Best hope I stay alive long enough in the company of your girlfriends, then.'

'*Girlfriend.* Singular.'

∽

Jake watched Superintendent Joan Madden pound the treadmill from the shadows of her personal gym.

The last time Jake Pettman had seen this bent copper he'd been battered and bruised in a wheelchair following an altercation with the hitman, Borya Turgenev. At least that altercation had, against all the odds, left that steroid-ridden Russian prick dead.

On that day, Madden had pushed Jake around the hospital gardens in a wheelchair, warning him that Article SE had him trapped. *'Make no mistakes, there'll be others. Others just as evil, if not more so. Which is why you can't run.'*

The moment Jake had left that hospital, he'd put her claim to the test and fled.

Unfortunately, she'd been right.

Some of those evil fuckers who had caught up with him in

New England were indeed worse than Borya. It hadn't been pretty, either. He had a lot of scars, physical and mental, as evidence.

Jake could even hear her puffing and panting over 'Born Slippy' by Underworld, which blared from her expensive sound system. She'd covered one wall of her renovated garage with a mirror so she could watch herself work out. In the reflection, he watched the sweat run down her face.

'It's been a while,' Jake said loudly, stepping from the shadows, keeping his gaze on her reflection.

Her eyes widened. She hopped and parted her feet so they were on either side of the tread.

Madden's hands moved towards the control panel, and Jake raised his gun. 'Easy does it.'

'I'm turning it off, and the sound.'

Jake nodded in approval.

The tread stopped, then, using a remote, she killed the music.

'Why the hell did you come back?' Madden asked, looking at him in the reflection. 'You'd made it, for fuck's sake!'

'Hardly. But I don't have time for those tales.'

He saw her eyes wander upwards in the reflection, sighting the door at the back of the massive garage, close to Jake—the door he'd come through before she'd come in the front way via the electric shutter door.

'Nice setup in here,' Jake said. 'You probably should look at security, though.'

'You *know* who I'm protected by. I don't need security.'

'I don't see anyone here now.'

'Ha! Both me and you know they're everywhere. What do you want?'

He inched forward, keeping the gun trained on her back,

while maintaining eye contact with her via the mirror. 'The truth?'

'The truth?' She guffawed. 'An interesting concept. About what?'

'About our last meeting together before I left. You told me that I was your friend, that you'd be there for me.'

She raised an eyebrow. He could tell she was weighing up whether to laugh him out the room. But she glanced at the gun and didn't chance it. 'It was the truth. I wanted to help you.'

'Do you still want to help me, *ma'am*?'

Madden turned. 'And how could I do that? You chose to run. I told you that you'd die for such a decision. You didn't listen.'

'Yet I survived?'

'Yes. A fucking miracle, which is why you should have stayed gone.'

He paused and gestured her with the gun. 'Look at you. Not a trace of body fat. Guess it pays to invest in a personal gym. Must have cost you some serious money, *ma'am*.'

'Quit it with the *ma'am*. For fuck's sake, what do you want? Are you trying to get us both killed? Is it money you're after? Is that why you've come back?'

He shook his head. 'No. Not money.' He maintained eye contact with her for a time until she became uncomfortable and looked away. 'Just help. That's all. Help to get my life back.'

She snorted, shaking her head. 'Impossible. And you know it. I gave you your chance to keep your life that day, to stay. There're no second chances in this game. Waving a gun at me won't solve your situation. Shoot me now if you want, but all you'll do is alert them to the fact that you're back, and then it'll be a matter of hours before ... well, I think you know. You made a mistake, and it's you, and you alone, who must now live with the consequences.'

Jake pounced forward, thrusting the gun towards her, spittle from his mouth glowing under the gym spotlights. 'Have you ever held a dead *child* in your arms?'

Madden showed him the palms of her hands while eyeing the shutters—a potential escape route.

Jake shook his head and sucked in two deep breaths through his nostrils to steady himself. 'You won't make it.'

'No. But someone might hear. You're best leaving.'

'You're living in the middle of fucking nowhere. Your own little patch of land. I mean, does no one ask any questions about where you get it from?'

'Inheritance.'

'Yeah, right. Is nothing beyond Article SE? Did they manufacture you a wealthy uncle who suddenly dropped dead?'

'Something like that. Look, I understand you're scared, but this isn't the answer. Your way out isn't here. Not with me.'

'No, it most definitely is. You've plenty to offer. I bet you're a treasure trove of intel. And the sooner we start looking through it, the better. *You're* my way out.'

'Delusional. Fucking delusional. What could I possibly have that would bring *them* down?'

Jake moved closer, jabbing his gun at her, as if it was his finger. 'I watched you, *remember*? Collecting things for them from that squat. The photographs of ex-GRU agents on that USB stick? I put that there and watched you collect it! You're Article SE's go-to for information. And I *need* that information.'

She shook her head aggressively. 'And then what?'

'I get that they'll kill you for leaking information. But I won't let it happen. The information will compromise them, don't you see?'

She snorted. 'You think Article SE responds to threats?'

'No, but I think they deal in common sense. What I'll present to them will be common sense. And that buys me, and you, freedom.'

'Oh, Jake.' Madden shook her head, feigning a sympathetic expression. 'You've got it all wrong. This won't go how you think.'

'Right or wrong, that's the play. I need you to accept it. *Live* with it.'

'It won't work. This isn't about you and me. It can never be—'

Jake raised his voice again. 'No. It's about my son. It's about the fact that they killed Sheila, and they'll kill Frank next.'

'Just give yourself to them. They'll make it quick, and I'm sure they'll spare your son.' Madden didn't seem to care that Jake was waving a gun anymore. She just seemed increasingly frustrated.

He'd never believed for a second she'd back down. He'd always known his next move would be necessary. But he'd wanted to try, desperate to keep as much dignity and integrity in these events as possible.

Jake sighed. 'I've seen what these people are capable of. Up close and personal. What's to stop them from executing my son in front of me? A final *fuck you* before they shut me down. All I have is this leverage that you're going to give me. That's it. And we both know it.'

'You can't make a deal with these people. That's not how they work.'

Jake stepped towards her. 'There's *always* a deal to be made.'

'You're out of options. What're you going to do? Kill me? It won't serve any purpose, and, as I said before, it will draw more attention to yourself. Personally, I'd take a bullet from you anyway rather than put myself in *their* crosshairs.'

'Maybe I don't kill you. Maybe I just hurt you ... a lot ... and for a long, long time.' He narrowed his eyes, keen to be convincing.

'Ha! You serious? I know you really fucking well. You may be impulsive, you may also have a ruthless streak, but torture? No.'

'It's different now. I've seen things. Done things.'

'Haven't we all?'

It was useless, but he gave it one last try. 'You shouldn't underestimate—'

'I'm not *underestimating* you. Take it as a compliment. It just isn't you. Takes certain personality traits—or rather a lack of them—to deliver someone to the depths of suffering. A certain skillset.' She grabbed a towel and dried the sweat off her face, then her shoulders. 'You, like me, would have a line.'

A knock sounded at the door that Jake had come through.

Madden flinched. 'Who's that?'

Jake stared hard at her.

'Who the fuck is it?'

'Someone without a line.'

'I don't understand.'

'You were right. I knew it would take something unique. Like you said, it takes a special person, someone with endless skill, to deliver someone to the depths of suffering. Break them without killing them. I'd have caved before getting you there.'

Another knock.

Madden looked right at the shutters and reached behind herself for the remote control.

Jake raised the gun again. 'Be warned that shooting you in the leg isn't one of my lines.'

Madden panned from the gun to Jake's determined face.

No question he'd do that, and she sensed it. She pulled her hand back without the remote.

'Come in,' Jake shouted.

The door opened, and Lacey Ray popped her head around the door. 'About time. There's a cat out there on the fence, wondering what I'm doing standing between her and the bin.' She regarded Madden. 'I value my eyes. I often think about what I'd miss the most, and it would be those. My eyes. Yes, most definitely. What would you miss the most, Superintendent Joan Madden?'

All the colour drained from Madden's face. 'You ...' The towel slipped from her hand. She backed away and stopped dead against the control panel of the running machine. She looked at Jake. 'You can't be serious?'

Jake nodded. 'You're in good hands.'

Lacey entered and closed the door behind her. She looked at Jake. 'Are we ready to get started, then?'

~

ON THE WAY back to Southampton, Jake stared at the USB stick.

'Are you sure it's *all* secure?' he asked Lacey.

'Every morsel. Yes. On *three* different clouds.'

Jake nodded. 'Okay, and there's nothing to worry about with the deliveries?'

'Can't see how. The emails are scheduled to go to SEROCU, the MET, and MI5. Also, if any of the deliveries do fall foul of a firewall then I added a bonus one. The local radio station in Salisbury! Details of at least one cloud is included in each email. If we don't hit abort, they haven't got a leg to stand on. Or a pot to piss in.'

'And no chance that Madden can undo your work?'

'What do you think this is? Amateur hour? Not only did I wipe all history, passwords, etc., but I also smashed the bitch's motherboard to pieces with a hammer.'

'The *same* hammer that you ...?' Jake creased his face.

'If it ain't broke, don't fix it. So now we're just relying on the bitch to set up the meet.'

'She will. She has nothing to lose now. She stays alive if our bargain works. If she doesn't contact them and those emails go out, Article SE is in a whole world of pain. And what you've just done to her will be the least of her worries.'

'I hardly did anything,' Lacey said. 'It was ridiculously easy. Even you could have managed it.'

'Doubt it. The first time she screamed, I had to step out for air.'

SHIT HAPPENS

*C*arrie couldn't believe Joe Wheaton was gone.

There'd been so much of him left, so much potential, so many thresholds to reach ....

She stared into the glass jar that contained the part of him Joe had violated both her and her mother with. She moaned. To have him taken away so soon was cruelty. Nothing but savage cruelty.

Still, at least she'd something to look forward to.

Jake Pettman was a large man, and it would take a long time to divide *him* into pieces.

She felt anticipation grow.

There was a knock at the door.

Swooping for the scalpel that she'd have used there and then on Jake if not for Lacey's plea, she marched down the corridor towards the front door. Taking a deep breath, she saw a hanging letter, its corner caught beneath the flap of the letterbox.

She looked through the peephole. Whoever had knocked and posted it was gone.

She pulled free the envelope.

Lacey was scrawled across the front. No address.

Intriguing.

Carrie turned over the envelope a few times, saw nothing else out of the ordinary, and opened it to reveal a photograph. Eyebrows raised, she studied an image of a boy, no older than ten or eleven, chained to a stone wall.

Tobias.

It was unmistakably him. That empty look in his eyes. The pale, gauntness of his face. Lacey had shown Carrie many images of her boy. He was, of course, the apple of Lacey's eye, and she often talked of being reunited with him one day.

Standing near to the boy, but not close enough to put himself in any danger, was another familiar figure. A grinning shitbag of the highest order. Dr Stewart Holden. When he'd challenged Lacey to play, he'd not been bluffing.

On the back of the photograph was a single word: *Ready?* —followed by a time and a set of coordinates.

Carrie checked her watch. Less than one hour.

Talk about short notice!

She took her phone from her pocket and located Lacey's number, but her finger froze before she hit CALL.

Lacey was in the process of helping Jake. Now, at some point, Lacey may be irritated about being kept in the dark regarding Tobias, but the ending of Jake's problem was in everybody's best interests, *especially* if Carrie solved Lacey's problem in the meantime. Because once Lacey and Jake were both safe, both their guards would come down. And then ... she looked back towards the kitchen and its display. She wet her lips with anticipation. *Her chair.*

With Jake surplus to requirements and Carrie having achieved the incredible, the saving of Tobias Ray, would Lacey resign herself to the correct choice? Plump for the right side?

Jake had to pay for what he'd done. Of that, there could be

no debate. It was just taking Lacey a little longer than usual to see sense.

So, feeling certain in this approach, Carrie punched the coordinates into Google Maps, and a pin fell onto a carpark on the outskirts of Southampton, about a twenty-minute drive. She headed upstairs to throw on some of Lacey's clothing and a headscarf, then slipped into some of her expensive boots.

No one would know the difference between her and Lacey until she was within striking distance.

Checking that her car keys were still in her cotton trouser pocket from earlier, she took the scalpel, not only with the intention of slicing and dicing should the necessity arise but with an overwhelming urge to take complete control of this situation.

Power was everything.

And when she had power, Jake Pettman would die.

Slowly and majestically.

～

THE BROAD LANE carpark had been shut down two years back when a carjacking went wrong and a newly married couple, Kyle and Eva Lowe, ended up in intensive care. Kyle never woke up, while Eva's injuries were so life changing that Kyle was regarded as the lucky one.

The council had done their best to shift the carpark on to a private business, but no matter how far they dropped the price, no one bit. The land was considered cursed. Eventually, the council decided to flatten it to build another recreation centre. But even though the intention to make good a dire situation was there, the money wasn't. These were tough times, after all. So, the intention was never realised, and the three-floor carpark fell to ruin over many years.

A joyrider had wiped out the shutters that led into the ground floor a long time ago, and although the council had tried to replace them in the first instance, they weren't willing to throw good money after bad when it happened again. Access to the carpark led to the ground floor becoming a quick stop for drug dealers or doggers, while the first and second floor became a destination for long-termers: the junkies and homeless.

Currently, Harry Watson was kicking back in his Audi TT, listening to Johnny Cash, while he waited for an update from his employer. He hated Sam Lane. Not because of the private investigator's questionable morals, and not because of the salary either—he was actually paid quite well—he disliked Sam for the same reason he disliked most people. Because he spoke to Harry like he had special needs.

Harry had a metal plate reinforcing his skull which he'd smashed in a car accident when he'd been younger. The large scar that ran the entirety of his head, combined with his slow drawl and strong accent, had everybody speaking down to him, like a small child.

The reality was that he was sharper than nearly all these fuckers combined.

Sam's name flashed on Harry's mobile. He answered. 'All good?'

'Okay, Lacey's left. She'll be coming to you in a red Merc.' Sam gave the license plate. 'Remember how perilous she can be? Remember what I told you? You know? About the hospital. Just make it crystal clear that if she harms you, she'll never set eyes on Tobias again. And you must, under no circumstances, harm her. Holden wants her alive. Do you understand? Otherwise—'

'Aye.' *I understand English, you twat.* He refrained from criticism, reminding himself that the money was good. Very good.

'All right. Say it back to me, then,' Sam said.

Fuck off. 'Yer breaking up.'

'Must be because you're in a carpark.'

'Can't 'ear you ...' *Dickhead.* He hung up.

He listened to a few more Cash songs, then opened a pre-packaged soggy sandwich from a supermarket fridge. He spat his first mouthful into a tissue, lowered his window, and threw out the whole sandwich. 'Fuck that.'

Two cars slid past where he was parked.

Drug dealers, probably.

He raised the window and spied his gun in the door pocket. Just a precaution. He didn't feel threatened. This place was considered a godsend by many, and nobody had an appetite to piss on anyone's chips and have theirs pissed on in return.

A red Merc slid past him. He glimpsed someone wearing a headscarf in the driver's seat.

Lacey Ray, I presume. He smiled. *Perilous, I believe.*

He couldn't see anyone else in the vehicle, unless they were concealing themselves. It'd be better if this were the case. There was no quicker route to a shitshow. And with a shitshow came no guarantees. If Lacey fell, Dr Stewart Holden, Sam's employer, would just have to swallow it. Harry was paid well, yes, but not well enough to take a bullet.

The red Mercedes had turned and reversed in so that it was parallel to him.

Lacey slid down her passenger window, and he opened his driver's window.

He grinned at her. Headscarf and sunglasses—who did she think she was? Fucking Angelina Jolie dodging the paparazzi?

'Lacey?'

The woman nodded.

'Good.'

'Where's Dr Holden?' Lacey asked.

'Not workin' like that, luv.' He reached to the passenger seat for a water bottle and threw it into her car. 'There's 'bout two gobs left. Neck that, gimme five to make a call, and when you start to feel knackered, 'op in 'ere.'

She grabbed the bottle, held it eye level, and swirled it.

'Ain't nuffin' to see, luv. We're druggin' yer up proper. Yer a dangerous critter! I ain't lettin' ya come near me after I saw those snaps earlier. Yeah, I saw 'em. 'Ow many times did yer slice that poor bugger in Prince'olme?'

'And if I don't drink it?'

'Then I drives off, and yer never again clap eyes on that lil' 'un of yers ...' The name escaped him. He eyed his notepad on the passenger seat. 'Tobias.'

'Seems you have it all thought out.'

'Aye. Neck it.'

'Bottoms up!' the arrogant broad said.

Fancy trollop.

She drank it.

'Good. Now gimme five.' He wound up his window and phoned Sam. 'She'll be kippin' in a short while.'

'Okay,' Sam said. 'You sound with the location?'

'Aye. Satnav primed.'

'You know about the blocked turn off?'

'Aye.'

'Just confirm which one it is?'

Prick. 'Shit, yer breaking up again—' He hung up and turned to look into her vehicle again.

Gone.

'What the fuck?'

This was all he needed.

He lowered his window. 'S'riously? One call an' yer lil' 'un be gone.'

Nothing.

'Ou' you come, an' I'll let you go to kip nice 'n' easy on the back seat.'

Still nothing.

'Al'igh', suit yersel', then.' He reached for his gun in his door pocket. When he didn't catch hold immediately, he glanced down, panicking that it had gone. Of course, it hadn't. His hand closed around the butt, and he looked up.

He saw the bitch's eyes just beneath that fucking head-scarf, then he saw the glint of metal.

At first, his cheek stung; a millisecond later, it felt like it was on fucking fire, and he wailed.

∽

CARRIE SIGHED as the scalpel bisected his cheek.

Like a sunbeam through morning mist.

She came against his teeth and was just about to slice upwards and disfigure him further when the stupid bastard did it of his own accord by wailing.

Now you've got a scar to rival the one on your head.

The bastard swung a gun upwards, knocking away her hand, and pulled the trigger. Her car's front passenger window exploded.

That was lucky.

Carrie swiped at his face again.

She dodged it, but, instinctively knowing he wouldn't miss again, she let herself fall and roll over the bonnet as the second gunshot sounded.

Stupid girl, she thought, regaining her footing.

She sprinted, inwardly cursing her naïve plan to simply

cut him until he blabbed. She *should* have anticipated a gun. She sighted the stairwell ahead. *Best not be locked, or I'm fucking dead.*

A third gunshot rang out behind her. 'Last chance, bitch!'

Warning her?

Stood to reason. Holden wouldn't want his goods soiled.

She threw herself at the stairwell door; it glided open under her body weight.

You'd have been better off shooting me, dickhead.

All carpark stairwells stank of piss, but she'd never been up one that stank of rotting meat, too. That fluid she'd thrown back from the bottle, then deliberately dribbled out the corner of her mouth, had left a foul taste. She tried to pay no attention to the nausea crawling over her as she sprinted up the stairs, especially when she heard the stairwell door on the ground floor crash open.

When she reached the top step, she opened the door onto the second floor and chanced a look over the railing. She caught the fat lug watching her from the floor below. His face was a bloody mess. 'Yer ain't got no place ter go—'

'Follow me up here, then,' Carrie said. 'But if you do, I'll cleave back open that fucked-up head of yours.'

He raised his gun. She darted backwards, listened to the gunshot, then burst onto the second floor.

This floor was out in the open, but it didn't matter to the many junkies and homeless people scattered about. She wondered why the gunshots below hadn't sent them scattering. Maybe they were used to them and were past caring. Maybe they were just too out of their minds on drugs.

It was a hot summer, and even in the evening, the air remained balmy. She clocked, with dismay, the lack of vehicles, and her hiding options were limited.

Concealing herself behind some people would be her best

bet. She sighted a small group huddled behind two shopping trolleys.

When she was close enough, she saw the individuals were out of their minds. Their eyes were rolled back, and they were drooling. One of them held a flame under a piece of tin foil, inhaling the vapour through a tube.

The door from the stairwell crashed open. Carrie dived into a crouch behind the only functioning junkie, albeit not for too much longer, judging by how eagerly he was chasing that dragon. Any faster and he'd be overtaking said dragon, and his heart wouldn't respond to any amount of adrenaline, injected straight into his heart or otherwise.

Even though many of the occupants of Broad Lane carpark level two were physically here, most of them were off in another world. Consequently, the sight of a man with a wonky head, with his face cut in half, pissing blood and holding a gun, didn't cause as much panic as you'd imagine.

Some murmured their discontent, and some scurried away, scared, but all in all, the entire event was rather subdued —and so felt quite surreal as a result.

He scouted for her through the waifs and strays, and Carrie realised it was only a matter of time; after all, she'd done herself up in Lacey's Sunday best and would stick out like a sore thumb.

Time to take back control.

Still in a squat, she reached for the handle of one of the two shopping trolleys. It was heaped high with one of the junkie's worldly possessions, concealing her well, but also carried some weight. She peered above it and saw the gunman was just drawing level—

Carrie pounced while thrusting. At first, the trolley rocked slightly, and she was worried it might tumble, but it righted itself in time. Keeping her hands on the trolley handle, she flew forward, excited to see his eyes widen with shock. She kept both of her hands on the handle as the trolley ploughed into him.

He fell backwards and grunted as he hit the floor, the gun slipping from his hand.

She yanked back the trolley and drove it towards him again. This time she *did* release it. The front wheels crashed into him but didn't mount his bulk, casting the junkie's worldly possessions everywhere.

She regarded the groaning gunman.

Right now, retreat would be an easy option, but she was still none the wiser to Dr Holden's location. And Holden's location was en route to that beautiful finishing line—the one formed in the image of Lacey's unwavering loyalty and Jake Pettman divided among many jars.

The man rolled onto his front, spotted his gun, and wormed towards it through old clothes and torn books.

'I don't think so.' Carrie kicked his already disfigured face. She slammed her boot into him again and again, before brushing the gun farther from him with her foot.

'Stop, please ... *Stop ...*' he said, spitting out blood.

She knelt closer to him, readying the scalpel. 'I want to know   '

He grabbed her ankle and pulled her foot from under her. 'Stupid bitch.'

On her back, she saw the prick staring at her. He could've been smiling, but she couldn't tell; his face was too fucked up. She drew back the foot he wasn't holding and prepared to kick out.

He was too quick and brushed her foot aside. Then, he started to crawl up her body.

Shit! Carrie really needed more practice and experience in situations such as this. She slammed the scalpel into the side of his arm.

Grunting, his eyes widened, before he continued moving up her.

With his weight building on her, she needed to move fast. She slipped the scalpel free of his arm and drove it into his side.

The idiot threw back his head, wailing and opening the split in his cheek further.

She yanked the scalpel free, and when his fist crashed upon her, she thrust again. After a flash of white, she felt the force of the concrete against the back of her head. She opened her eyes to see the fist returning. This time, the white seemed to burn brighter and longer, and she knew she was at risk of moving onto the losing team.

She didn't open her eyes for the next punch; instead, she focused on drawing out the scalpel and plunging it into his side for a third time. Flooded with adrenaline now, she thrust her weapon in repeatedly, desperate to avoid another crippling blow. She couldn't prevent it, but at least it was his final hurrah.

Afterwards, he lay still on her.

Strangely, even though she didn't have the energy to open her eyes, her hand continued to plunge the scalpel into him. Eventually, her arm joined her brain in exhaustion, and it flopped to one side. The tinkle of her scalpel on the concrete seemed to come from far away, as if in another world.

She took long, deep breaths, trying to steady the disorientation.

Get yourself together.

After a short time that she found impossible to measure, she felt the throb of pain in her face and the back of her head and knew she was coming back round. She opened her eyes, and everything spun. She closed them.

Shit ... Come on ... You got this.

She tried again, forcing them to stay open long enough to focus. Clocking the dead eyes staring down at her, she gritted her teeth, fought the pain and dizziness, and wriggled herself free of his bulk.

She struggled to sit upright. 'Fuck.' *You really made a mess of me.*

Eventually, Carrie made it into a sitting position and drew her knees to her chest. She kept her hands on the concrete to prevent herself from falling backwards or sideways. Then after another short period, in which her vision seemed to stop swimming, she worked her way to her feet.

She eyed the dead man, flat in a pool of blood.

Now what?

She turned in a full circle. Although the pain in her face was intensifying, things were becoming clearer. All the waifs and strays were still hunched together in little groups. Some watched, but it seemed no one had the appetite to get involved, even the one whose worldly possessions were covered in the dead man's blood.

'Sorry for the mess.'

She stumbled towards the gun, and when she was close enough, she leaned forward, inviting another sudden rush of dizziness. She put her hands on her knees, sucking in deep breaths.

Take control ... Take control ...

When she was certain she wouldn't pass out, she grabbed the gun and refocused on the bloody corpse.

Any ideas?

Still moving cautiously during her recovery, she rustled through the dead oaf's pocket until she found his car keys and his phone. She lifted his head by his hair, causing a sucking sound as his face withdrew from the blood. She spent a few moments desperately trying to get his phone's facial recognition to clock his oddly shaped mug and open, but the software refused to see past the blood dripping from his jowls.

Sighing, she let his head drop into the blood and pocketed the phone. She'd give her right arm for painkillers, but she was more than grateful that her faculties were still in one piece.

Carrie walked away, no longer stumbling but feeling stronger by the second.

~

IN THE DEAD gunman's car, Carrie caught several breaks.

First, she found some paracetamol in his glove compartment, which she chewed on despite the rancid taste. Second, she saw that the dumb idiot had entered the coordinates of his next destination into his satnav. Judging by the map, it was way off the beaten track. In fact, it suggested it was in the middle of a field.

She checked her bruising face in the rear-view mirror. It was puffing up at speed, and it wasn't the most attractive look, but it wasn't as bad as she'd first feared. Her head was clearing nicely, too. She'd be able to drive.

As she set off in her victim's vehicle, she wondered if there would be access roads to wherever she was going not displayed on the satnav. She certainly bloody hoped so. Lacey wouldn't appreciate her hiking across fields in these expensive boots. Mind you, she probably wouldn't appreciate the bloodstains on them either!

But, you know, shit happens.

BEST LAID PLANS

*H*olden paused the footage of Vinnie skinning Nigel to answer Sam's call. 'Yes?'

'Doctor Holden, there's been a complication. I'm sorry.'

'I hate apologies.'

'Ahh, sorry … Shit.'

'Just get to the point.'

'I got it wrong. Lacey's *still* at Sycamore Street.'

Holden sucked in a deep breath through his nose. The air whistled as it moved past his deviated septum. 'Are you sure?'

'She's just arrived with that Pettman fella from earlier.'

Ahh, well, Holden thought, exhaling and shrugging. *The game was never meant to be easy, was it? Better to play some before the victory.*

'I really don't know how this happened,' Sam said. 'I was *certain* I saw her leave.'

'No. You saw *someone else* leave, I presume. Maybe Amelia? That devious little nurse who castrated Stan. She must've acted on behalf of Lacey, eh? So, what did your man at the carpark have to say?'

'Nothing. Harry's not been in touch, and I can't contact him. Do you think she might have ... have ...'

'Killed him? Wouldn't surprise me. She, too, could be on her way back to Sycamore Street.'

He smiled. *Amelia ... Now she was proving an enigma.* He'd love to have her here. He looked at his three boys on their respective screens: Vinnie, Tobias, and Keith—*mice in comparison.* 'In a way, I wouldn't blame you for the mistaken identity. What I do blame you for, though, is this ... If Lacey and Pettman did leave earlier, why didn't you see them?'

Silence.

'Sam?'

'I—'

'Because you abandoned your post. Didn't you? The post I pay you an absolute fortune to hold.'

'I was starving.'

He snorted. *Another mouse.*

'Yet I called my brother not thirty minutes ago to give him that address. The news made him happy. So very happy.'

'Doc—'

'But now we've a problem. I couldn't care less what happens to Pettman, but nothing—I repeat, *nothing*—can happen to Lacey.' He gazed at her future cell, currently unoccupied. 'Not without me there. We don't have any choice now. You'll have to go and warn them. Get them out of there. Sooner rather than later.'

No response.

Mouse.

'Sam?'

'I'm not sure I—'

'I advise you to think carefully about refusing what I ask.'

'I understand you're paying me well, but—'

'Sam,' *mouse*, 'money shouldn't be your concern right now.

It won't be a consequence. You need to use your imagination. You can be sure I'll be using mine.'

Silence.

'You go and warn them. Now.'

'But ... but ...'

'But she might kill you? Yes, I'm aware of that. *Acutely*. But we've no choice. And that, my young friend,' *mouse*, 'is down to you not packing your lunch.'

'I—'

'Go *now*. Or, trust me, Lacey Ray will be least of your concerns. And we both know who's favourite to win this game; don't we?'

After the call ended and Holden had resumed his home movie, he envisioned what'd happen next. Lacey would extract the location from Sam, no problem, and she'd come here. Then they could finally play together again.

REUNIONS

*H*unched in the corner of the lounge, wide-awake, Jake daydreamed. First, there was Frank waving tearfully at him in the crowd after scoring the winning goal for his team. Then, there was Piper Goodwin's smile widening and growing clearer as he drove towards her.

Lacey interrupted at the door. 'What're you doing?'

'Dreaming of reunions.'

'Dreams are elusive.'

'Hopefully not for much longer,' Jake said, eyeing the USB in his hand.

'Are you still hoping? Are you not yet convinced?'

Jake shrugged. 'It's hard to believe when you've been running for so long.' He looked at his mobile phone on the floor, willing it to ring, willing Joan Madden to deliver the news.

They'll meet you, Jake. And they'll deal.

Was this also an elusive dream?

And if so, what chance did those other dreams really have?

'Anyway, where's your girlfriend?' Jake asked.

'Good question.'

'If she brings anyone else back here—'

'She won't.'

'But if she does?'

'Then she'll have lied to me. And she'll no longer be a problem for—'

A knock sounded at the door.

Lacey turned and looked at it.

'Carrie?' Jake asked.

'Why would she knock?'

Jake grabbed his gun and approached Lacey. 'Let me answer it.'

Lacey stood aside. 'Be my guest but use the peephole first.'

'Of course.'

A thin, little man on the other side, wearing jeans and a t-shirt, hopped from one foot to another, hands rammed in his pockets.

Using the door chain, Jake partially opened the door and peered out. He kept the gun in his right hand, hidden behind the door, but ready. 'Can I help?'

'You need to leave now.' The man looked terrified. Not a good sign. It made Jake's blood run cold.

'Who're you?'

'A friend. Just leave, *please*. You're in danger.'

This had to have something to do with Madden and Article SE. *What else? But how?* He was yet to give Madden his address. And no one had followed them; they'd been very careful.

'Please,' the man said. '*Listen.*'

Jake dropped the security chain, opened the door farther, and pointed the gun at the little man's head. 'Not until you tell me who the fuck you are.'

The man paled, took his trembling hands from his pockets, and held them up. If this was a soldier from Article SE, he was an incredible actor. 'Sam Lane. I'm nobody. A private investigator. I'm not a danger to you, but if you stay here, then—'

'Who do you work for?' Jake asked, his voice rising slightly.

'I-I …'

'*Who*?'

'I can't tell you that.'

Jake looked back and forth. Seeing no one observing this strange conversation but knowing it was only a matter of time before someone did, he said, 'Get in here.'

'No, I shouldn't—'

Jake stepped out the door, aiming the gun at Sam's head. 'Get in the fucking house and keep those hands up.' He sidestepped to allow Sam room to pass him. 'Search him,' he said to Lacey, then scanned Sycamore Street. *Good*. Still no one observing. He entered the house, keeping the gun locked on Sam as Lacey patted him down. He closed the door behind him.

Having finished the search, Lacey stepped backwards, smiling. 'You're lucky. Previous dickhead who stopped by didn't get a chance to explain himself.'

Sam's mouth hung open and he had tears in his eyes. He didn't look capable of speaking just now.

Despite Jake's size and the large gun in his hand, Sam couldn't tear his gaze from Lacey. He stared at her as if she was a famous rock star and he was completely in awe of her.

It isn't me he's worried about.

He was completely terrified of Lacey. 'Did Holden send you?' Jake asked.

He nodded.

'Interesting,' Lacey said, inching forward again.

Jake saw *that* look in Lacey's eyes. 'Stop,' Jake insisted. 'Let him speak.'

'Oh, he'll speak all right,' Lacey said, a wry grin on her face. 'Regardless of how the next couple of minutes play out. Why're you here?'

Sam started to speak, but suddenly stopped, as if he might be about to vomit.

'Come on now. I'm all ears.'

He took a deep breath and tried again. 'Holden asked me to warn you. He made a mistake, you see. Or I made a mistake. Well, a combination of both—'

'*Rambling*,' Lacey said, faking a yawn. 'Get to the fucking point.'

'Okay.' He closed his eyes, steeling himself, trying to get control. 'I was employed to watch you. Just watch. I'm not *like* that man ... Holden. I'm not interested or involved in the nitty gritty of whatever he does or this peculiar war with you.'

'Game,' Lacey said. 'Please. Have some decorum.'

'Game.' He glanced nervously at Jake. 'I sent a photograph of you earlier to him. I didn't expect it to have such ... such ...'

'*Consequences?*' Jake said, not liking the direction of the conversation. Not one little bit.

Sam nodded. 'Holden has a brother who works for some real cases. Gangsters, people in the underworld, that kind of thing. You know what I mean?'

'Oh, I know what you mean all right,' Jake said.

'So when he approached them to find out who you were, well ...'

'They expressed an interest,' Jake said, feeling panic kick up in his stomach. *They know where I am.*

Sam sighed. 'Yes ... very. I'm sorry.'

'How long have they known?'

'About thirty minutes.'

How were they not here yet? Jake took a deep breath. *What did this mean? Should he run?* After all, he needed to meet with them anyway. He just didn't need Madden to point them in the right direction anymore. But could he be sure Article SE knew about the leverage? If they didn't, it could end badly. A kill squad may just shoot him on sight.

He looked at Lacey, the panic in his gut intensifying. 'I think we should go.'

She held up a hand to steady Jake. She didn't look too concerned. Mind you, she never did. 'Why take so long to warn us?'

Sam looked down.

'We're not blessed with time. And that includes you. Also, be aware that Jake has a very itchy trigger finger.'

'The mistake, well ... the mistake I was talking about before,' Sam blurted out before looking up with desperate eyes. 'Shit ... shit ... I've children. *Young* children.'

'Sam, we're not here to discuss fatherhood,' Lacey said, inching closer. 'The mistake?'

'Holden has Tobias,' Sam said.

Jake's gaze darted to Lacey. He watched all that usual contentment drain from her face, and she stepped backwards. Jake suspected this was a *sincere* emotional reaction, and it stunned him, because he'd never seen such a thing before. Her head lowered.

With one hand, Jake kept his gun pointing at Sam, but with the other, he reached for Lacey's arm.

Before he touched her, she swatted him away and raised her head again. She then moved even closer to Sam.

Watching Lacey lose composure, momentarily, had been fascinating. But seeing how quickly she regained it was equally, if not more, captivating.

'Yes, I'd agree, that's a mistake,' Lacey said. 'A very big one, in fact.'

'It has nothing to do with me. I didn't even know until Holden asked me to drop a photograph of Tobias here.'

Lacey squinted. 'Photograph. What photograph? I haven't seen any photographs.'

'That's the actual mistake.' Tears ran down his face, and he was visibly shaking. '*You* didn't get the photo, except I didn't know, because I wasn't aware you'd left the house. There were coordinates on the bloody back of it. Then, after I delivered it, I thought I saw you leave, but it wasn't you. It must have been Amelia.'

Jake recalled that this was Carrie's previous identity.

'Except she doesn't look like me,' Lacey said. 'So, that was rather dim-witted.'

'She was wearing your clothes, sunglasses, your headscarf.'

Lacey looked at her footwear. Her Gucci boots were missing.

'She went to get Tobias then, so where the hell are they?' Lacey asked.

'The coordinates she was given were to a different location. A carpark. You were to be restrained there before being delivered to Holden.'

'And?'

Lacey was an inch from Sam now.

Don't do anything impulsive, Lacey ...

'And I don't know,' Sam continued. 'Harry, the man I employed to deliver you, he hasn't been in touch. And he isn't answering his phone. Amelia isn't with Holden, and I have no idea where she is. She might be coming back here. But you must leave. Holden doesn't want you harmed.'

'I agree,' Jake said to Lacey. 'We should get a move on. They'll send a kill squad. The fact they aren't even here yet is unbelievable. We need to scarper. We don't know if they're aware of our leverage. Imagine if they come in guns blazing?'

Lacey took a step back. She held up her palm towards Jake to request his silence while she thought.

Jake could feel his anxiety morphing into frustration. Lacey needed to get a grip. Staying here might get them killed.

Lacey tiled her head from side to side, still thinking.

'We *go* now,' Jake said.

'Fuck Article SE.' She looked at Jake. 'The plans have changed.'

Jake shook his head. 'No. It's suicide. We leave and we wait on word from Madden.'

Lacey pointed at Sam without looking at him. 'Aren't you listening to what *he's* saying?'

'I am,' Jake said. 'And we'll handle it. Of course, Holden wants you to charge over there; that's the point. We're stronger together, controlling the situation, not running off half-cocked.'

Lacey stared at Sam. 'Where *are* they? Holden and Tobias?'

Sam paled.

'What're you waiting for?' Lacey pointed at Jake as she addressed Sam. 'Didn't you just hear what *he* said? Holden *expects* you to tell me. He knows well enough that you won't refuse me.'

Sam nodded, but he still looked sick over the thought.

'Oh, don't worry yourself! I plan to kill him. You never have to worry about that rat ever again.'

'Lacey,' Jake said. 'I'm leaving now. This second. I prefer you with me, but if you're going to stay, I can't help—'

Lacey raised an eyebrow at Jake. 'He's my *son*.'

No, he's not.

'I'm going with Sam to get Tobias back and rid this world of Holden.' She looked back at Sam. 'Isn't that right, Sam?'

Sam nodded again.

Jake said, 'Your choice. I'm going to grab my bag—'

A knock sounded at the door.

Too fucking late.

~

THROUGH THE PEEPHOLE, Jake saw three armed men standing on the doorstep; a smartly dressed man flanked by two much larger men. Behind them was a black van with shaded windows parked on the road.

Only three?

From the back came the sound of smashing glass.

Or not.

Jake gulped. He'd fought himself out of a few one-sided situations before, but this encounter would certainly be a step too far.

'We're about to get squeezed from both sides,' Jake said. He put his gun on the floor and looked at Lacey. 'But be positive, we still hold the cards.'

'You may want to point that out before they turn this place into a bloodbath,' Lacey said.

'*Jesus*! Whit the absolute fuck?' A deep Scottish voice from the kitchen.

Jake immediately thought of the carved-up corpse. 'I think your girlfriend already has the market on bloodbaths cornered.' He pointed at Sam 'You keep your fucking mouth shut. And best you say nothing, Lacey.'

'Impossible.'

At least she was honest. Still ... 'Let me put this to bed, then we'll move on to Holden.'

Lacey blew him a kiss. 'I'll try.'

Jake opened the door, showing the three men at the door

his empty hands. 'Unarmed.' He gestured at the floor. 'My weapon is at my feet.'

'Kick it out,' the central man said.

Jake did, and the larger man on Jake's left swooped for it.

Jake heard the noise of the other men arriving in the hallway behind him.

The central man, who wore a freshly pressed suit and had a perfectly formed black quiff, said, 'Jake Pettman?'

'Yes,' Jake said. 'Come in and I'll put the kettle on. You need to hear what I've got to say.'

'Ye dinnae want to go anywhere near the kitchen.' The strong Scottish accent again. 'No unless ye've got a keen interest in human anatomy.'

Jake turned toward the hallway and surveyed another large man wearing army fatigues. There was another man behind him, making the group five strong.

'Can my friends leave?' Jake asked. 'And then we'll talk?'

'Talk about what?' the smart man asked from behind him. 'Talk about why you've been skulking around Sunrise Properties?'

Jake exchanged a confused look with Lacey, then turned back to regard the smart man again. 'I don't know what you mean.'

'Sunrise Properties? No? Well, you've been spotted lingering about there, so I hope whatever your reason, it was worth it. We would've been here hours ago if the person who made you hadn't gone off the grid for a while.'

'Car crash,' the Scottish soldier said. 'We should probably have a gander at that.'

Sunrise Properties. Was that somehow connected to Dr Stewart Holden? What line had the good doctor been spinning?

Jake looked back at Sam, who avoided eye contact.

Shrug off these peculiarities, Jake, for now. All that matters is that you have Article SE at the door, and you have leverage.

'On your travels, you also paid a visit to Superintendent Joan Madden,' the smart man said.

And there it was. Madden *had* gotten word out.

'I wondered why we weren't dead,' Lacey said.

Jake glared at her. She'd been right, it was impossible for her to stay quiet.

'Don't worry,' the smart man said. 'There's still time. But the decision isn't with me. Unfortunately.' He grinned.

The two larger men who flanked him raised their guns.

'So, let's go inside and speak to the one who makes the decisions, eh?'

∼

THE SMART MAN ORDERED JAKE, Lacey, and Sam to sit on the shitty carpet in front of the window.

Jake remembered that the body of Dr Holden's kidnapper was rotting beneath the floorboards and wondered if he, Lacey, and Sam would soon join it.

The Scottish soldier had drawn the curtains, shutting out the lamplight from the street. A single flickering bulb hung from the ceiling at the centre of the room. The smart man stood beneath it, holding the back of the solitary dining room chair, looking between the faces of his three captives.

The Scottish soldier was down on his haunches, setting up a laptop on the chair. He was in the process of tethering it to his phone.

The other three members of the squad hung back, holding their guns, ready to execute if ordered to.

Once the laptop was set, the Scottish man cleared Jake's line of sight and on the screen, he saw a middle-aged man wearing a pin-stripe suit. The man, who was unfamiliar to Jake, sat staring at them from the comfort of an office.

'Jake Pettman. I'll be honest; we weren't sure this day would ever come. And we were really convinced that you'd burned with all those rednecks in Mossbark. Sounds like you went through a living hell out there. Not the quiet retreat you'd hoped for?'

'It's not exactly quiet here either, though; is it?' Jake said.

The man nodded. 'No, I guess not. So, why not stay out there? Lost in all that emptiness. We'd have been none the wiser. But the one thing you can't do on this tiny island is hide. What drew you back anyway? Homesickness?'

'Do you care?'

The man shrugged. 'It's actually my job to care. About everything. Thoroughness keeps us anchored.'

'There you have it!' Jake said. '*Thoroughness.* The reason I came back. I just couldn't be sure how far you cold-hearted bastards would take your vendetta against me.'

'You're referring to your concern over Frank, aren't you? Your son?'

Jake's chest contracted, but he worked hard to maintain a sturdy demeanour. 'Wouldn't any father?'

'No, sadly, I don't think every father would ... mine wouldn't have ... I respect that you came back to protect your son.'

Fuck you. I don't want your respect.

'But you didn't need to. That's not how we operate. We don't kill children.'

'Really?' Jake raised an eyebrow. 'Tell that to the family of Paul Conway.' Jake tried to keep the distress from his face. It was hard whenever he relived the moment when debris from that car bomb caught Paul.

'But Paul wasn't the target. Alexander Antonovich was. Paul was just ... unfortunate.'

'*Unfortunate*?' Jake raised his voice and sensed movement from some of the soldiers behind him. *Stay calm. Remember the leverage.* He'd be dead already if they didn't want to deal. He felt a surge of confidence after reminding himself of this. He straightened up. 'Who're you? Are you the top dog?'

'Top dog of what exactly?'

'Of Article SE?'

The man leaned forward at his desk. 'Article SE, eh? The name that bureaucrats gave to an extensive, unified group of criminal organisations in the Southeast of England. How they love their abbreviations. Their simplifications! We're far more sophisticated than that. As if our network is really limited to one top dog!'

'Who're you, then?'

'My name is Walter. I'm a lawyer. Nothing more.'

'Did you order Sheila's death, Walter?'

'Your ex-wife?'

'Yes.'

'What makes you think that?'

'The gas explosion.'

Walter shook his head. He wore a saddened expression. 'Unfortunate.'

'Another *unfortunate*! You're a well of compassion.'

Walter didn't respond. He just offered a sympathetic smile.

'Anyway. I'm done with *unfortunate*. You just stay the fuck away from my son—and me, too, while you're at it.'

Walter nodded. 'I think there's something you need to hear. It may contextualise things for you. I'm an influencer. Some would argue that there is none more powerful than an influencer. There needed to be changes in our organisation. Subtle ones, but they were no less important for being so. If not for my changes, things may have been different with Frank. Killing children and sophistication doesn't have a place in our vision any—'

'Sorry,' Lacey interrupted. 'Look, I don't want to come between a CEO and his vision, because I'm sure it's all very inspiring—making dreams a reality and all that, *fascinating* stuff—but can we cut to the chase, Walter, influencer, dream maker, sophisticated guru—whatever you want to be called—because I couldn't really give a fuck. I've been sitting here, with my mouth shut for a while now, but this is really starting to drag.'

The smart man nodded, and the Scottish soldier circled around Lacey and put his gun to the back of her head.

Lacey laughed. 'Is this your idea of sophistication? Blowing my brains out? Execution? A real gentleman's sport—'

'Lacey *Ray*,' Walter said. 'I know you don't fear, but I need you to be quiet.'

'Sorry. I didn't think we'd met,' Lacey said.

'How could I not know who you are?' Walter said. 'As I said, we're thorough. And let's not forget that you stole Simon Young's child. At the time, that created a lot of work. And Simon was one of our best contributors *before* you killed him. It's something we've been meaning to catch up with you about.'

Jake kept his expression steady. It'd been him, after all, not Lacey, who'd killed Simon Young. Hopefully, if the leverage worked, that'd become an irrelevance anyway.

'How is Jane Young?' Lacey continued, undeterred by the gun to her head. 'Did she adjust to her life as a widow? To be honest, she was much better off without your fucking contributor.'

'Ah, you don't know? Jane is dead. Tobias killed her. The

reality was that Jane was a generous and kind soul. She tried everything with her boy after you twisted him up inside. Her reward was a knife in the chest while she slept. And now Tobias has disappeared.'

Jake looked at Lacey. Like before, when Sam had announced that Tobias was with Holden, something clearly stirred within Lacey. She'd be struggling to handle Tobias senselessly murdering a woman. After all, Lacey possessed some kind of code when it came to victims, whether she cared to admit it or not. An innocent female couldn't be further from Lacey's MO.

No doubt, she'd be assuming that Holden had killed the mother to gain possession of Tobias.

Jake looked back at Walter. 'Enough.' He nodded at the Scottish man with the gun to Lacey's head. 'Tell him to lower his gun, and let's get to the point.'

Walter smiled. 'You heard the man.'

The Scot lowered the gun.

'So, to *this* point, then, Jake?' Walter prompted.

'If you let me reach into my pocket for the USB stick—'

'Why? I already know what's on it.'

'Okay, then you'll—'

'You think you're the first person who's tried to bring us down?'

Jake shrugged.

'I handle threats like this daily. Wake up. This is the age of information. Everybody can be compromised by what exists in a cloud.'

Jake gritted his teeth. *Don't buy into his confidence. They wouldn't be having this conversation if he was genuine.* 'I want to make a deal.'

'A deal?'

Jake smirked. 'Yes. Keep it sophisticated. How you like it.'

'You stole from us. That isn't sophisticated. And now you ask me to make a deal with a thief? You think I can do that? You think I can carry on influencing by making such a compromise?'

Jake sighed. 'Well, you burned down my house and killed my ex-wife. Doesn't that even the scales?'

'You act so confident.' Walter laughed. 'But how do you even know that what you have will destroy us?'

'I don't. Maybe come next week, SEROCU, the MET, MI5 will all receive access to a cloud full of VAT invoices and petrol receipts. But I'm happy to take my chances.'

Walter nodded. 'I see.'

'And you have my word that while my son, myself, and my two friends here live, then I'll guard that information with every fibre of my being.'

'Better than Joan Madden?' Walter said, raising an eyebrow.

'She lives too. Okay?'

Walter sighed. 'You think that because you're still breathing, I've already made my decision, but I haven't. In fact, I'm still not even close. I think we could weather your *haul*, although I admit it does come with a fair amount of risk. However, sparing you following your disrespect also creates risk. I appreciate that time is of the essence for all of us. Allow me another five minutes to make my decision.'

Walter's camera went off.

Jake exchanged a look with Lacey, who shrugged. He glanced at Sam, who was deathly pale and had tears running down his face. Then he revisited those daydreams from before.

The goal-scoring hero Frank ran into the crowd and into Jake's arms. Piper Goodwin pressed her lips against his.

Walter reappeared on the screen. He glared at Jake for a moment. 'You stole from us. You disrespected us.'

The smart man was screwing a silencer onto his gun.

Jake tasted bile.

'As did you, Lacey. Yes, you hold some good cards, but I cannot make a deal with people who owe us so significantly. Do you understand the costs of such weakness?'

The smart man put the gun to Jake's head.

'So I have made my decision,' Walter said. 'And here it is.'

GUCCI BOOTS

*D*r Stewart Holden lived in a perpetual state of curiosity. To satisfy this, he travelled down the most obscure of paths and chose the most complex subjects for study. Keith 'Corpse Rustler' Burston and Vinnie 'the Skinner' Russell were perfect examples of this.

Currently, he was reflecting on another of his subjects: Tobias Ray.

He longed to give Tobias a pseudonym, but the boy was completely inactive. He'd eat and drink, slowly and sporadically, but that was all. The rest of the time, he just stared dead ahead.

Tobias 'Catatonic Fucker' Ray, perhaps? Or the more media friendly: Tobias 'Dead Behind the Eyes' Ray?

While considering this, movement on one of the monitors caught his eye. It was the one fed from the camera at the entrance.

Curious.

He touched the screen as the security light came on and revealed a tall brunette, heavily made-up, wearing next to nothing.

Who are you?

Holden rose and, being the curiosity-driven individual that he was, journeyed off for the answers.

～

ARMED with one of his brother's guns, because to not be so would be folly, Holden entered the keycode, listened to the clunk of the lock release, opened the sturdy door, and pointed the gun in the brunette's face.

The whites of her eyes shone bright against her heavy black eyeliner.

'Who're you?' Holden asked.

She stepped backwards. 'Sorry. I–I ...'

'*Who?*'

'Princess Honey.'

'You're a princess? I've never met a princess. And do princesses usually wear such dark makeup?'

'Sorry.' She backed farther away now.

'Why're you here?'

'I just do what I'm told.'

He stepped out, still pointing the gun at her head. The door shut behind him. He heard the clunk. 'What've you been told?'

'My boss said to come here. You *called* for me.' Her voice cracked. The corners of her eyes filled with tears.

Curious. 'I didn't call for anyone.'

'You gave your name.'

'Go on.'

'Dr Holden.'

Curiouser. 'I'm afraid you're wrong. I made no call.'

Holden glanced in the dark distance, he couldn't see far,

but he discerned a red Audi. 'Are you part of the game, Princess Honey?'

Tears streaked her face. 'Please, I'm sorry—'

'Shut up and kneel.'

As she obeyed, she regarded him with desperate eyes. 'I've got a child. I only do this to support—'

'Shut up.' He looked around. He could decipher trees in the darkness but little else. 'Amelia?' he called out.

No answer.

'Lacey?'

Unlikely. It hadn't been that long since Sam's call. So more likely Amelia then.

Unanticipated. Clever girl. He licked his lips. *There's room at the inn. Now to draw her in.* 'You do know that Lacey's in danger though, don't you?' He raised his voice in case she was very far back in those trees. 'Jake Pettman has brought all manner of shit to your home! I thought I'd gotten her out of harm's way, but it seems I've fallen foul of a case of mistaken identity.'

Princess sobbed hard.

He pressed the muzzle of the gun against her head. 'Shut up!'

Princess's hand flew to her mouth to stifle her screams.

Holden looked up and around again.

Nothing.

Slightly concerning, but no need to worry yet. 'Okay, *Amelia*, you pulled me out. Here I am. Show yourself.' He held his gun in the air. 'And I won't hurt you.'

He waited.

Silence.

Princess's sobs broke free again.

'*Shut up*!' He struck her across the face with the weapon, and she slumped back.

Okay. Let's up the ante.

'Let's play! This was your move; somehow, Amelia, you've got my location from the man sent to babysit Lacey, and you've called up a prostitute to come to these coordinates to see if I'm here. *Surprise, surprise.* But you're too late to deliver the good news back to Lacey because she'll be already on her way. So, now my move.' He pointed the gun at Princess, who was curled up on her side, weeping. 'An innocent woman. On your shift.' He snorted. 'I guess the thought doesn't turn your stomach or you wouldn't have risked her. But how would Lacey feel? Would she accept this? Unless I see you soon, Amelia, your girlfriend mightn't be best pleased.'

He waited, giving her a chance.

She didn't take it.

Interesting girl, aren't you? You must've anticipated this. The possible loss of life. Ah ... I see. You're testing Lacey's resolve for you, aren't you? Her commitment. How much she'll endure for you. Fair play. Glad to be of assistance. Let's see if you've the guts to see it out.

'I'm going to count to five, and then ... well, I think we know what'll happen then, don't we? Ready? Good. One.' He watched the trembling woman. 'Two.' He surveyed his surroundings. Nothing. 'Three.' He refocused on Princess, who stared at him, her face streaked with black makeup.

'Please ...' she murmured.

'Four.'

Seems it isn't just you and me that enjoy playing, Lacey. Amelia, too, has a taste for it!

'Five.' He shot Princess in the face. He looked up and around. 'I imagine that will raise a heated discussion in the marriage bed, but then I guess you knew that already, didn't you?'

Princess was gurgling.

He surveyed the trees and dirt tracks around the prison. *Nothing.*

Shit!

Had she gone?

Was she ever here?

Princess continued to gurgle.

He looked down at her and noticed his bullet had entered beneath her left eye. She was still breathing, staring up at him. Then he felt a surge of cold, hard anger—something he was unaccustomed to. He emptied the remaining bullets into her face until the gun clicked empty, then turned. He closed his eyes. Relief settled over him. Then he marched to the door and punched in his keycode.

'You really should do something about that temper of yours.'

He took a deep breath and turned with his gun raised. 'Amelia.'

Amelia, glamorously dressed, looking remarkably different to how she'd looked in her scrubs, stood over Princess. 'Actually, it's Carrie now if you please.' She stared down at the body. 'Look what you've done to her.'

'That was *your* choice, *Carrie,*' Holden said. 'And I'll make sure Lacey knows that.'

'Needs must,' Carrie said, eyeing the body. 'I needed you outside. You didn't have to make such a mess of her though, did you? That was *your* choice.'

'Still, you think Lacey will forgive you for leading an innocent woman to her death?'

Carrie contemplated it for a moment. 'Yes. Confidently so. I'm her special one.'

Holden shook his head. 'Just like Jake Pettman? Just like Tobias? How many *special ones* does Lacey have?'

Carrie glared at him. 'Not the same.'

Holden snorted. 'It's *exactly* the same.'

'Her affection for me is different.'

'No, her affection for you is a pretence, just like it is for the others. A shared lie!'

'Not true.'

'*Exactly* true.'

'We'll see.'

'We will. Remember who's the doctor around here. You're not as important as you believe yourself to be. No one can be in Lacey's world. As soon as you fall from Lacey's view of the ideal, which you soon will do, my dear, then you'll become expendable. Maybe you should consider this before you move forward.'

Carrie shrugged. 'You make interesting points. Claptrap, of course, but *definitely* entertaining.'

'No,' Holden said, smiling. 'You *hear* what I'm saying. *Think*. You're still in a strong position. You still have an opportunity.'

'For what? You're pointing a gun at me.'

He looked at it, remembering it was empty, then back at her. 'Yes, but I don't have to. Not if you see sense.'

She reached behind herself and appeared to be fiddling with the large leather belt that pinned her dress around her waist. When her hand emerged, she was holding her own gun.

His stomach sank. He didn't *fear* death, but the prospect of *losing*—well, he didn't like that one bit.

'Belonged to a man with a lop-sided head who tried to drug me,' Carrie said. 'Do you know anything about that?'

'Drop it, or I'll shoot you,' Holden said.

'Go on, then. But I was just over there.' She pointed to a mound of stone several metres away. 'And I could've sworn I heard your gun go click.'

'I reloaded.'

'I didn't notice. How long did you give Princess?'

Holden narrowed his eyes. He didn't feel beaten, not yet, but the fact that his stomach was turning over suggested to him that the threat was very real.

'Tell you what. I'll give you those same *five* seconds to reload and gun me down. How about it?'

'Listen to me. Think about everything I said before. *Expendable.*' He touched his chest. 'To me, you're anything but. I admire you. There's no way I'd throw you onto the scrap heap.'

She smiled. 'Yes, I've heard what you like to do with people who interest you. I'm guessing you have no bullets to reload with, then? So let's change the rules of the game, shall we? I'll give you five seconds to get away.'

'Don't be foolish.'

'One.'

'If you won't be shared, she'll turn on you.'

'Two.'

He turned and ran for the door.

'Three.'

He entered his keycode and heard the clunk of the bolt.

'Four.'

He opened the door.

'Five.'

He heard the bang and felt a sudden force in the back of his leg. He went down, face first, over the threshold. A burning sensation kicked up in his calf. The door was trying to close on him, which made it a struggle to turn over. When he eventually did, he hoisted his leg to his stomach.

Carrie stood over him, smiling and holding open the door.

'You're making a mistake,' he said, wincing. His calf felt like it was on fire.

She laughed. 'I think you'll find it's you who's made mistakes. I need you to lead me to Tobias.'

'How do you expect me to walk?'

'Lean against the wall and limp. Or crawl. To be honest, I couldn't give a fuck either way.'

THE SWEETENER

'*I*t's hardly the bargain you hoped for,' Lacey said to her passenger, keeping her eyes forward on the black van they'd been instructed to follow.

'But it's a bargain that keeps all of us alive,' Jake said.

'Sam is *still* at gunpoint back at the house. If he dies, I lose Tobias's location!'

'They won't shoot Sam. And after, when I've done what they've told me to do, we'll find out where Holden and Tobias are.'

'And Carrie?'

If we must! Jake took a deep breath. 'Yes—do you actually have any idea where she is?'

'How? I've told you already her phone is going straight to voicemail.'

Jake sighed.

The van indicated. Lacey followed suit. 'What're we doing trusting this lot?'

'We're not. And stop harping on about it! It was the only deal available, and I made it. The ball is in their court, but I think we're good. Look, if they kill me, the information is released. And by doing what I'm about to do, Walter is saving face. I can't see why they'd renege on the deal.'

'There're always things you can't see though. You know that better than anyone.'

Jake carefully recounted the offer Walter had given him while the smart man held the silenced gun to his head: *'I can't make a deal with a thief or a traitor. You must understand that. Rather I let you bring the whole organisation to its knees than sacrifice my integrity. Still, maybe there's a way for you to absolve yourself of your sins. A way to strip off those negative labels. I mean, why do you have to continue to be a thief and a traitor? Just pay back what you owe. Offer your service to us until your debt is clear —and that debt includes what Lacey owes us, too. Your girlfriend cost us by killing Simon Young. Then after your debt is cleared, you may, if you so wish, continue to work for us. But that decision is for another day and will be a considerable time from now. It's the only deal I have for you. The only one. I can promise you that servitude won't include children. It's not part of our vision. But can I promise you that your hands won't become bloody? No. But you'll have your life back. Lacey, hers. So do we deal, Jake? Do I have Russ lower the gun?'*

Lacey followed the van around a roundabout. 'You should've called his bluff. Told him it was your way or the highway.'

'And my brains may very well be all over your face.'

'No. I think you had him. You let him retake some control.'

'I couldn't risk it. If I was dead, then I'd be left with no control whatsoever. Until I know one hundred percent that this is over and Frank never pays the price for my past, I need to keep air in my lungs.'

'You think these megalomaniacs will ever let it end? *Really?* You think that they'll ever let you walk free?'

'I have to believe.'

'You're a fool, and you're back on their fucking lead.'

～

LACEY PARKED behind the black van and looked at Jake. 'I should come.'

'Walter was clear. Me alone.'

'Really?' She mimicked Walter's voice. 'Just a sweetener, just a sign of good faith. Seal our deal in blood.' She returned to her own voice. 'The man is a riddler. And my golden rule? Never trust riddlers.'

'I thought your golden rule was to never trust men?'

'It's the same thing. Why does he want you there and not me? What's he worried about?'

'Your unpredictability?'

'Fuck him. Who wears pinstripe suits these days, anyway?'

'Please, sit tight. We do as Walter says. Let me help these meatheads take out these—'

She smiled. 'So, you've no hesitation about executing a house full of people? Are you ready to admit that I was right about you all along?'

'*They're* terrorists. And they blew up innocent people, including a child.'

'And your best friend.' She raised an eyebrow.

Jake nodded. 'Let's get this done. Then back to Sam, and onto Holden.'

'And Tobias?'

Jake inwardly sighed.

'You've a problem with that, don't you?'

'What if he did kill his own mother?'

'It's a lie. It was Dr Holden.'

'But *what* if he did?'

'*Holden* killed Jane Young himself and made it look like Tobias.'

'You haven't seen Tobias in years. Do you have any idea of what you might find?'

'The same *lost* child. I was helping him to understand himself, and I'll help him again.'

Helping? You were teaching him to kill. 'Look,' he nodded forward. 'They're getting ready.'

Four members of the kill squad were outside the black van, getting ready. Russ, the smart man and leader, was back at the house, minding Sam.

Apparently three members of the terrorist cell occupied this house. Jake hoped to God that the intel was good. Walter had been adamant it was. He'd gone through his rationale in detail: '*We had the cell number at seven. We've now confirmed that the police shot four of the group trying to sabotage one of our factories. With only three left standing, now, tonight is the best time to strike. Finish them off.*'

Jake took the gun from the glove compartment.

Finish off the men who killed a six-year-old boy and his best friend.

And his freedom was confirmed.

It wasn't such a bad deal regardless of what Lacey said. He opened the door.

'You better come back,' Lacey said.

'I will. And you better be waiting.'

'Of course. Where am I going to go? I've no idea where Carrie is.'

∽

THE PLAN WAS SIMPLE. Although it seemed to him that all the risk fell to one man.

Him.

'Ye git the first kill,' the Scottish soldier said, pulling on his balaclava.

Or be the first kill, Jake thought.

The Scot adjusted his mouth hole. 'Drop whichever fucker opens the door an' *go* to ground.' He pointed at one of the other men. 'We'll pop the other two dragged oot by the commotion. A'richt, Stevie? If any retreat, Jay and Ray will snare them oot back.'

The Scot handed over a hi-vis jacket with *DHL* on the back and an orange gap. After putting them on, Jake took hold of an empty cardboard box.

With his left hand atop the fake delivery and his right hand beneath it, concealing his readied weapon, Jake set off alone down the street. He passed a dog walker, who was fortunately more engaged with scooping up his pup's mess than paying attention to Jake. Jake kept his head low as he passed beneath lampposts so no potential witnesses could get a good view of his face.

He turned onto the driveway and approached a rather modest two-floor detached house. Every light in the place looked to be on.

I hope you got this right, Walter. More than three men in there and this could get dicey.

He didn't want to move the fake delivery to reveal the gun, so he kicked the door with the side of his foot. Seconds later, the frosted glass panels darkened. Jake kept his head down, pretending to read the details on the box. The cap would partly block his face. The person on the other side of the door was most certainly scrutinising him through the peephole.

'Who is it?' someone called from inside.

'DHL. Package.'

'For whom?'

'Mr Thompson.'

Frederick Thompson was one of the terrorists whom Walter and his team had recently identified. It was Frederick's slip up that was about to cost these brutal individuals their lives. Frederick had spent a drunken night in Southampton, boasting to a night worker about some of his past exploits. She'd shared the information with her pimp, who'd been acutely aware of where to share that information for a good price.

'Just leave it on the doorstep, please.' The voice was *very* familiar to Jake.

He shook it off. Adrenaline was fucking with his mind. 'I can't, sir. Signed for only.'

'Well, you'll have to take it to be picked up from the post office, then. Mr Thompson isn't here.'

That voice ... The adrenaline intensified. *Ridiculous, Jake. Get with the programme; these prolonged silences will give the game away!* 'Anyone here can sign for it. Besides, it won't go to the post office; it will go into circulation. Best to just grab it now.'

Silence.

Shit! Have I blown it?

By now, behind him, the Scot and Stevie would be loitering in the shadows beyond the driveway, camouflaged by balaclavas and dark clothing, ready to pounce. Jay and Ray would be around the back.

And I've fucked up this one responsibility by wavering, because his voice sounded familiar.

He sighed. *One last throw of the dice.* 'Okay. I'll throw it back in circulation. Says *perishable* on it, though. Such a waste. A quick scribble and—'

He heard the clunk of the door lock. He readied his trigger finger.

As the door glided open, the man said, 'Where do I sign?'

God, it sounds just like him.

Jake lifted his head. The air caught in his throat when he saw Yorke standing in the doorway. He heard movement behind him.

The Scottish soldier and Stevie were on the move.

THE PEARLY GATES PART II

The day of the terrorist incident ...

Yorke felt the gun press against the back of his head. The bastard must have circled around him.

He closed his eyes. He couldn't feel fear. Only despair.

Images flew through his mind.

Sonia's three young children. Rob's proud parents.

Matthew, in pain.

His own family.

'At least tell me why,' Yorke said. 'At least give me that.'

The gunman didn't oblige.

A single gunshot cracked loudly over the shouting, screaming and sirens.

The pressure from the back of Yorke's head lifted.

Yorke, feeling alive but completely bewildered as to how that could be the case, wavered on his knees before falling forward onto his hands.

Shock. Fight it.

But shutting the world out had never felt so appealing, and his spinning mind felt compelled to accept it.

A hand clutched his shoulder.

He took a deep, sudden breath, opened his eyes, and looked up.

'Mike? Are you okay?'

Robinson?

Yorke opened his mouth to reply, but no sound came out.

The terrorist behind him—

Whacked by adrenaline, Yorke spun into a sitting position.

The terrorist lay in a crumpled heap.

In the distance, flames pouring from the scene of devastation licked the gate.

Sonia ... Rob ... Matthew ...

Yorke took several deep breaths, fighting off shock and disorientation, and managed to clamber to his feet. He turned to face Robinson. 'How?'

'Dave Matty.'

'Who?'

'At the cathedral entrance behind me, the best shot there is.'

Yorke looked at the cathedral. The glow from the blazing catastrophe at the gate behind played havoc with the shadows, making it seem as if there was movement around the cathedral where there probably wasn't any. Eventually he sighted a man holding a long sniper rifle near the entrance.

With Sonia, Rob, and that poor child scarring his every thought, he struggled to make sense of it all. He stared at Robinson. 'How did you get here so quick? *Shit!* You knew, didn't you? You knew this was coming!'

Robinson looked away. 'No. Not this ... not *this* exactly.'

Yorke jabbed a finger towards Robinson but stopped an

inch from his chest. 'Not this exactly? Then tell me how you got get here so quickly?' He sighted another armed officer move from the flickering shadows to join Dave. 'With your team?'

Robinson cut open a short distance between him and Yorke, no doubt fearful he might swing. A valid fear.

'We knew they were bringing Matthew to the gate,' Robinson said.

'*When*?'

'The moment you did. I swear. Not a second before.'

'But how? I only called it in on the way here. Unless … Christ! *Really?* You were monitoring my phone?'

Robinson flinched. 'I'm sorry, pal, but you gave Rozalija Andris your personal number.'

The twenty-three-year-old au pair, Article SE's plant, potentially murdered by the terror cell. The poor girl who was desperate to return to her parents in Lithuania, the poor girl who looked broken and capable of hurting herself.

Yorke shook his head. 'I don't follow. How could you possibly know *that*?'

'*She* told us. We managed to crack her, after all. In the hours after the factory incident. I'm sorry I didn't tell you. But by giving her your personal number, you just felt too involved. I felt it was best to give you some distance.'

'By tapping my phone? Not that distant!'

'I had your best interests at heart.'

'Bollocks! What did you learn? What I worked out on my own? That she worked for Article SE!'

'Initially, yes. But that wasn't the whole story.'

The sound of the emergency services flocking to the chaos behind him grew louder.

'We haven't got long,' Robinson said.

'Best speak quickly, then.'

'Just as you called it, Article SE were paying Rozalija handsomely to keep an eye on Greg Brace and the Noracell factory. And that remained the case *until* this terrorist cell itself threatened to move on her family back in Lithuania. It was the cell who turned Article SE's plant into their own. Canny, eh?'

So Rozalija had been in the pockets of the cell/kidnappers. It made perfect sense. How had the kidnapper found it so easy to take Matthew Brace? Because Rozalija had monitored the movements of the family in detail, all while she was on Article SE's payroll. She'd have alerted the cell to Greg's trip out into the woods with Matthew.

Yorke sighed. His own reckless behaviour now had a spotlight on it. 'And that explains how the bastards at the cell got my personal number.'

'You see,' Robinson said, 'you left me no choice but to tap your phone. And it was fortunate we found out, otherwise, well, otherwise ...' He looked down at the dead terrorist.

'But *then* you left Rozalija to die! I mean, she wouldn't have had any chance with the cell *and* Article SE gunning for her. It could've been either one of them who killed her after all! Why did you not protect her?'

'We were planning to move her from that hotel to another location.'

'You took too long.'

'I know. But look at the web she was tangled in. Playing Article SE and the cell off against each other! We barely had time to think.'

'You could've done more.'

'We were going to relocate her family to the UK. Give them all new identities. It was on the cards.'

'You let her down.'

'We were moving as fast as we could.'

But were you, Riley? Or did you hang back on purpose? To catch the bastards lingering in the shadows, watching ...

'We don't have long, fella.' Robinson lifted his head towards the sight of the chaos. 'Emergency services are blocked, and they can't get to us, but they'll open the other gate shortly. Listen, we still have a chance to get something from this mess.'

'*Mess*?' Yorke said, struggling to keep his voice down. 'That's one word for it. Two of my officers are dead. Paramedics, dead. That poor boy, dead. Same age as my daughter! This is more than a fucking mess! You *were* here! You could've—'

'Get real! It was an ambush. They had our attention on tomorrow's drop at the park. Yes, we knew they were probably leading us up the garden path, but what choice did we have?'

'You knew they wanted fireworks. To make a point. Stitching a bomb into a child's stomach? They certainly made a point.'

Robinson paled. 'Jesus wept. *Really*?'

Yorke nodded. 'I saw it.'

'Fuck.' SEROCU's boss now looked visibly shaken. 'I'm sorry. I thought ... well, I thought they had more morality than that. But my hatred for Article SE has blinded me. These fuckers are no different. I should've done better. I just worked on a hunch that the kidnappers would be close after dropping him by the gate, so I covered the local area with as many bodies as I could in such a short space of time. I just thought that if we could get to him,' he nodded down at the body. 'Then maybe we could turn him, find out where the others are. Bring down Article SE. I never thought they'd be capable of this.'

Yorke looked down at the dead terrorist, then at Robinson

with a raised eyebrow. 'Turn him? Was Dave off-target perhaps?'

'Fuck you for even suggesting it! If this monster was still alive, I'd shoot him again.' He looked down, took a deep breath, then looked up, preparing himself for something.

Yorke noticed they were in the process of opening St Ann's gate so emergency services could access the cathedral and the dead terrorist.

'Let's get them,' Robinson said, looking up. 'Let's bring them down.'

'How?'

'There's a way. But it's down to you.'

'After what they've done tonight to that child, to my friends, you think you need to ask?'

'It's a big ask.'

'No, it isn't, but believe me, this better not be about Article SE, Robinson. This is all about this cell now.'

'You have my word.'

The gate was open. Yorke saw the flashing lights of an emergency vehicle. 'Run. Don't go home. Go to Dave, and he'll get you out of here.'

'Why?'

Robinson gritted his teeth and scrunched his face, willing himself to get his idea out. He looked down, clearly second guessing his plan.

'Why?' Yorke repeated.

Robinson stared at him. 'Because for this to work, you have to be dead.'

~

Two of Robinson's men, Dave being one of them, took Yorke out via De Vaux Place on the other side of the cathedral grounds. They then drove to a safe house on the edge of Salisbury.

Before leaving Robinson at the cathedral, Yorke had given his one condition. *'You phone Patricia, my wife. Immediately. I won't have her think, even for one second, that I'm dead. You tell her that I'm safe and that I'll continue to be so.'*

Now, before they exited the car, Dave, the man who'd saved his life, turned around in the passenger seat and looked at Yorke in the back.

'You're quite the shot,' Yorke said.

'Served in Iraq.'

'He was one of the best they had,' the other officer said.

'Impressive,' Yorke said.

Dave said, 'The PTSD I came home with is less impressive.'

'Sorry to hear that. But thanks.'

'That was one hell of a difficult shot,' the other officer said. 'I wouldn't have made it.'

'We know.' Dave winked at his colleague, then refocused on Yorke. 'I'm sorry, sir, but can we take your phone before we go in?'

'Why? I already switched it off. No one can contact me.'

'I'm sorry. it's what Chief Robinson wants, and we can assure you that your wife already knows.'

Dave switched on the radio. They waited until the news started. Yorke listened to the report on the terrorist incident at the gate. Although the report omitted names, it indicated that among the dead were three officers—one of which was a deco-rated DCI. Yorke's blood ran cold. He could only imagine how Patricia felt right now. He reached into his pocket for his phone. He didn't hand it over though. Instead, he contem-plated calling her.

'Sir, please.' The other officer turned and held up his

phone with a message from Robinson on his screen, offering Yorke further reassurance that someone was with his family, and that there would be no shocks or surprises.

'I don't know,' Yorke said.

'Chief Robinson is a man of his word,' the officer said, nodding.

'He's the best,' Dave said. 'And he speaks highly of you too, sir.'

'Shit,' Yorke said, looking at his blank screen.

'I can only imagine the temptation,' Dave said. 'And we can arrange for you to speak to your wife later.'

'Okay.' Yorke handed over the phone.

～

THE HOUSE WAS a newbuild on a housing estate. It was decorated but was yet to be furnished. Yorke didn't want to sit though and was happy to pace the lounge alone, thinking. While he waited, he wanted to reason out the purpose behind Robinson's play. He recalled the report on the radio. The journalist had said that the bomber had fled on foot.

The only reason Yorke could fathom for having his death faked was so the cell would believe the terrorist had succeeded and lived.

For now, Robinson might call in enough goodwill to keep Yorke's name on this dead terrorist's toe tag, but what possible end game was there? The cell would simply wait for him to return, and then he wouldn't? So what point did it serve?

He tried to stay focused. To understand. But his losses tugged at him.

Sonia's children had already buried one parent. Now they'd experience true grief all over again.

Rage bubbled inside him.

Rob, like his own boy Ewan, had had an entire life ahead of him. Gone with the push of a button.

He backed himself against the wall and slid down it, until he was sitting; it was either that or let the bubbling rage erupt, and what purpose would that solve?

Where're you Robinson? What's our play?

He thought of the terrorists out there—*whatever it takes, you'll pay for this; for Rob, Sonia, and Matthew; you'll pay*—and cried.

~

'Mike?'

Yorke regarded Robinson hovering over him. He looked sympathetic. Maybe he saw the puffiness around Yorke's eyes from earlier tears.

'Are you okay?'

'Just tell me how we're going to get them.'

Robinson sighed. He went to the lounge window. The sill was low and wide, and he perched on it. 'It's a long shot. I'm second guessing it now.'

'Too late. You've just rushed me to a safe house, took my phone off me, then told all my colleagues that I was dead. We take the shot.'

Robinson stared out the window for a moment. 'Maybe.' He looked back round at Yorke. 'Alan Kershaw.'

'Who?'

'The dead terrorist. That's how we get in.'

'He's got a hole in his head.'

Robinson nodded. 'There's more to the story involving Rozalija Andris. With emergency services closing in at the cathedral, I didn't have a chance to tell you, but Alan Kershaw was Rozalija's link to the cell. This is how she kept the cell fed with information that allowed them to kidnap Matthew so easily—such as the usual times Greg Brace took his dog and son out walking.'

'So, it was Kershaw who threatened her then? Told her that the cell would hit her family?'

'Yes ... but later he told her that the cell was threatening him too. That they were *using* him as a puppet.'

'You buy that?'

'Of course not. He just wanted to get her to trust him. It's a common play.'

'Did it work?'

Robinson nodded. 'Not a hard sell to someone that's vulnerable and at their wits end. In that situation, you take hope wherever you can get it.'

'And?'

'They began a sexual relationship.'

'Bloody hell. You're joking?'

'Wish I was.'

Yorke shook his head. 'Poor girl—don't tell me she developed feelings for him?'

'Uh-huh. And this went on for months. She believed he had feelings for her too.'

Yorke sighed. 'She really was bloody vulnerable.'

'Maybe. The more I think about it, the more I think there might've been some truth in it,' Robinson said, rubbing his chin. 'He told her things, you see, things you'd expect him to keep close to his chest. Let his guard down, so to speak.'

Yorke sat up straight, intrigued. 'Loose lips sink ships.'

Robinson nodded. 'She was convinced that Kershaw wasn't a member of the cell. Just a gun for hire who got in far too deep. We investigated his history, and it's murky and potted, as you can imagine, but there was enough there to suggest he's motivated financially and doesn't have affiliations to ex-Russian GRU agents. She told us that Kershaw became very open and honest about his distaste for the cell.'

Yorke shook his head. 'Nah. He was playing her.'

'Maybe. Yet we have Kershaw telling Rozalija that the cell was small and quite pathetic, and a host of other things. There's spitting bile to curry favour, and then there's real venom in what's said. It doesn't sound like Kershaw was a fan at all. And if he was a fan, I don't think he'd have let the following slip. The cell was hiding in two locations.'

Robinson took off his jacket. It was a hot night, and newbuilds like this held heat very well. In this instance, *too* well. 'And this is where it gets very interesting. Kershaw contacted Rozalija immediately after the failed factory bombing to tell her that he wouldn't be seeing her again. The cell had offered him another job. One of their two locations was now down on men due to those unexpected four deaths at the factory. They wanted Kershaw to make up the numbers at one of the locations once this kidnapping situation was at an end. I think Kershaw telling Rozalija that she was on her own pushed her over the edge and was the reason she broke so easily when we went to talk to her.'

'Shit!' Yorke said. 'Maybe it was Kershaw that killed her?'

Robinson sighed. 'It's possible. After all, he'd told her a lot. He could have thought it best to go back and silence her? But I don't know for sure. He may've found it impossible if his feelings were as strong as he'd already claimed.'

'So, did Kershaw *know* the locations?'

'No.'

'So how the hell do we get to them? I'm lost.'

'I recovered Kershaw's phone from his body. And, as I anticipated, once news of the successful terrorist attack broke and that he'd fled, the cell texted him a meeting point. He's to head there tomorrow at eight a.m. They think he's still alive.'

Yorke, full of adrenaline now, couldn't stay seated and rose.

Robinson smiled as he nodded. 'Yes, let that sink in, pal. What we just did *worked*.'

Breathing deeply, Yorke paced the room. 'So you're heading to the meeting point to swoop them up?'

Robinson's smile fell away. 'It wouldn't work. They won't be that sloppy, especially if he isn't really one of them. They'll send one man, maybe two at a push. And if we move on them and we don't break them, we're back to square one.'

Yorke continued to pace. 'But what else do you have? Unless Kershaw has a twin brother, what other options are available?'

Robinson took a deep breath. 'Well, actually, we may not need a twin ...'

'I don't follow.'

'Kershaw told Rozalija that he'd only actually ever met one member of the cell. His contact was one of the casualties at the failed factory bombing. It transpires that his previous contact had passed his number to someone else in the cell prior to his fall as an insurance policy. It was this other contact that reached out and told him he was required at one of the locations following the conclusion of the Matthew Brace situation.'

'And Kershaw told Rozalija this?'

'Yes, in that final call.'

'Maybe they were close?'

'Maybe, yes.'

'Still, wouldn't this other contact have a photograph of Kershaw?'

'Potentially. We don't know.'

'But the door is slightly ajar. We must take this chance,' Yorke said.

Robinson sighed. 'Easy for you to say. It isn't you who could be sending someone to their death.'

'It's my decision. The risk is all mine.'

Robinson looked confused. 'What're you talking about?'

'I'm happy to go to the meet.'

Robinson shook his head. 'You're not taking any risks!'

'Sorry, I don't understand. You just faked my death, didn't you?'

'Yes, but you were never going to the meet! Dave has volunteered. If this can work, you can be sure Dave will make it work. And if it doesn't, well ... shit, I'll have to live with that.'

'Fuck Dave,' Yorke said, feeling his face flush. 'This isn't up for negotiation. I'm going. I'm not leaving it to anyone else.'

'Why? You're being ridiculous. He's trained for this. You're not. You've done your bit, and that bit was no less important.'

What Robinson was saying made perfect sense, but ... his friends, that child, among the wreckage.

'No, I survived for a reason,' Yorke said. 'I'm finishing it.'

Robinson looked irritated. 'Listen fella, Dave doesn't have a wife and children.'

'I'm going. No one else is dying. This one is on me.'

Robinson hopped off the sill. 'No. This is my gig. You're not on my team. I can't expect—'

'Doesn't matter what you expect, sir. I'm the one playing dead, so I'm the one calling the shots.'

Robinson looked down, shaking his head. 'You know it doesn't work like that.'

Yorke stopped pacing. 'I don't?'

Robinson approached Yorke. His face looked like thunder. 'Mike, I suggest that—'

'I don't threaten to walk out that door?'

'That would be a start.'

'Why? It'd give my colleagues and friends a shock, but I'm sure they'll all breathe a sigh of relief.'

'Meaning we lose, and they win.'

Just hearing those words caused a painful gnawing sensation in the pit of Yorke's stomach. Yorke sighed. 'Yes, but at least I lose knowing I did all I could. Sitting here while *someone else* risks his life, experienced or not, won't wash with me today. I've lost enough.'

'Your picture will be all over the news shortly. It's too late for—'

'Nonsense. With your clout, sir? No name. No picture. You can call it off for days.'

Robinson shook his head.

'Suit yourself.' Yorke turned and walked for the lounge door. 'But I'm not bloody bluffing.'

'Wait.'

Yorke turned.

'You're the most stubborn bastard I've ever met.'

You haven't met Jake.

'You don't know the first thing about what you're doing.'

'Let's start with, I get access to the first cell, then once I find out where the second cell is held up, too, I get in contact with you.'

'You may be completely cut off. All alone. Unlikely they'll let you keep your phone. Is this really what you want? Think of your family.'

'I have. I couldn't look them in the eyes again if I don't make this right.'

～

THE MEETING POINT was near Moors Valley Country Park and Forest, well off the beaten track. Yorke took Kershaw's old

Skoda. They needed to keep it as realistic as possible. How much the remaining members of the cell knew about their gun-for-hire was anybody's case. Fortunately, Kershaw's build was similar to Yorke's, but their hair styles were remarkably different. For the first time in his life, Yorke had a shaved head.

SEROCU didn't follow Yorke. The cell would certainly take precautions, and any such attempt would be clocked. That didn't stop SEROCU from bugging Kershaw's Skoda though. Although, Yorke was warned that they'd probably transfer him to their own vehicle. Yorke also had Kershaw's phone. Robinson had been clear on this too: *'If they've any sense, they'll chuck it before taking you anywhere.'*

Yorke stayed positive. People slipped up. It was human nature.

It was a good half an hour before anyone arrived on the dirt road. Despite the hot weather, a light shower had made an appearance, and Yorke left his engine on so he could bat away the droplets with his wipers as he waited. He'd spent hours with a sickly feeling in the pit of his stomach, but it was yet to show any signs of abating, and as the minute hand of his wristwatch crawled agonisingly onwards, it seemed to intensify.

With anxiety came moments of doubt.

Maybe he should've just left it to Dave. Ex-sniper, nerves-of-steel, no-ties Dave.

But he *again* thought of Sonia, Rob and Matthew, and he *again* determined that it was right and fitting for him to do this.

He saw a vehicle up ahead, crawling down the dirt track. He took a deep breath.

Here you go. Keep your nerve.

A BMW pulled up in front of him.

Yorke swallowed back bile, desperate to keep his lunch

bubbling away painfully in his stomach rather than over his lap, because did he really want to explain his terror to a pair of trigger-happy terrorists?

Two men stepped from the vehicle, both similar height, with a similar build and slicked-back black hair. Both wore the same serious expression.

Yorke wondered if he'd ever see his family again.

He ran his hand over his head and was momentarily surprised by the stubble.

The rain stopped pattering the screen, and the sun burst from behind the clouds.

Yorke opened the car door and stepped from the vehicle.

'Stay there, turn, hands on the roof of the car,' one of the men said.

Yorke obeyed, wondering if he'd been made already. He suddenly felt moments from another gun to the back of his head.

This time, there was no one stop that trigger from being pulled.

They patted him down and took his car keys, phone, and wallet, which contained cash but no cards; Kershaw *hadn't* carried identification.

'Turn.'

Yorke, still willing himself not to throw up, obliged, trying to look as confident as he could, with no idea as to whether he was succeeding.

Describing the men's expressions as serious was an understatement.

They aren't convinced. Not one bit.

Yorke caught sight of the shoulder holsters beneath the jackets and thought of his family again.

The driver handed Yorke the phone back.

'Thanks,' Yorke said, immediately wishing he hadn't. His gratitude sounded pathetic.

The driver looked at the other man, who hoisted out his own phone and fiddled with it. He looked as if he was punching in a text message.

The phone in Yorke's hand beeped.

'I've sent you a message. What does it say?' the man with his phone out asked.

Yorke looked at the screen, which glowed under the direct sunlight, and waited for facial recognition software to kick in.

Thank Christ SEROCU had anticipated this play.

It didn't work.

Fuck!

The IT department had reset it, and he'd already tested it. *What the hell?*

'Assuming that's your phone, Mr Kershaw, what does it say?' the man repeated.

'Something wrong?' the other asked.

'Fucking phones.' Yorke grinned, trying to act confident, and steady his hand from shaking too much.

Yorke clocked the man on the right reaching for his holster. Yorke turned around to take the phone away from the glare of the sunlight.

The phone opened.

He read the message out loud. 'I come in peace. Take me to your leader.'

The two men laughed. Yorke laughed too as he turned back round. Not because he was amused, not because he was relieved—to be honest, he didn't know what the hell he was—but because it felt appropriate to join in.

One of the men clapped a hand on Yorke's shoulder.

Yorke's breath caught in his throat.

The other one grabbed his phone, dropped it on the ground, and crushed it beneath his boot. 'A precaution.'

You were right, Riley. As always.

Yorke nodded, and they led him towards the BMW.

He was on his own, but at least he was still alive.

So game on.

His task: learn the addresses of both safe houses and reach out to Robinson.

What could be simpler?

DEFANGED

*J*ake lifted his head. The air caught in his throat when he saw Yorke standing in the doorway. He heard movement behind him.

The Scottish soldier and Stevie were on the move.

'*Mike?*' It was Yorke. No question. The shaven head was fooling no one.

Yorke's eyes widened. Recognising the man sent to kill him had clearly stunned him.

Jake desperately needed a solution in a situation that so clearly seemed to be without one, and with no time to think. If *he* didn't put Yorke down now, those pricks behind him most certainly would.

Yorke said, 'What *are*—'

Jake thrust the fake package into Yorke's face and swung the concealed gun upwards. It connected with his friend's chin and threw his head backwards with a sickening crunch.

I'm sorry ...

As Yorke stumbled backwards, Jake moved in with a second swing, across this time.

Forgive me ...

He struck the scarred side of Yorke's face. There was a cracking sound, and Jake's blood ran cold.

Yorke fell sideways.

Jake snapped a look behind him. As anticipated, the Scot and Stevie were tearing up the drive, ominous in their dark clothing and balaclavas, guns at the ready.

At his feet, Yorke was face down. Unmoving ... surely unconscious.

Enough for the bastards behind him?

Unlikely.

God forgive me ...

He readied his gun, aimed, and shot Yorke.

Jake felt like every drop of air had been sucked from his body.

'Nae bad, pal,' the Scot said, grabbing his shoulder from behind.

The hand on his shoulder gave Jake a shot of adrenaline but didn't steady him. He felt frenzied, suddenly angry, and desperate to close his hands around the Scottish bastard's neck. He started to spin.

'*Get fucking down!*' Stevie shouted.

Mid-turn, Jake allowed his legs to give way, and as he went to ground, he caught the doorframe splinter from the corner of his eye and heard the shot that'd almost killed him.

Yorke cushioned his fall. Jake lifted his eyes to the two men of Article SE's kill squad and watched them unload their automatics simultaneously. Jake snapped his head left in time to see the terrorist, pinned against the wall next to the door he must have just burst through, taking bullet after bullet.

The firing stopped, and the terrorist slipped down the wall, trailing blood, eyes wide but unseeing.

'Two off the board,' the Scot hissed.

Stevie and the Scot stepped over Jake to enter the house,

moving strategically, guns raised, ready for the third and final target.

Jake slid from Yorke so that he lay beside him. The right side of his friend's blood-stained face was exposed, and his eyes remained closed.

Jake's gaze tracked down the left side of Yorke's lower back where he'd delivered the shot. Although he couldn't say for absolute certainty, he was confident he'd only nicked his friend's side, as had been the intention. Blood was blooming on his shirt, and the killers around him wouldn't look close enough to see that it was merely a flesh wound. Appearance was everything.

However, it'd all be irrelevant if Yorke opened his eyes.

'Are ye *fuckin'* comin' or whit, Pettman?' the Scot growled.

'No need,' a deep voice said, cutting through the open door that the dead terrorist had used to enter the room.

Jake sat upright and clocked Ray, by far the biggest Article SE soldier, filling the frame. He'd already rolled up his balaclava to expose his sweaty, scarred face. He was dragging someone in pain, presumably the final terrorist, by the foot.

Ray dragged his squealing victim to the centre of the room, grunted, and released him.

Using this moment of distraction, Jake checked his friend once again. After clocking, with relief, that Yorke was still unmoving, he rose, gun still in hand, and surveyed Ray and his catch.

Ray looked proud of himself. He glanced between them all, smiling. Then he pointed down at the terrorist. 'The slippery serpent tried to strike from beneath a table. Ha! Don't worry, I defanged it.'

Defanged?

Jake saw that the poor bastard's hands were smashed to smithereens, presumably by the butt of a gun.

No wonder he was squealing. If he survived, which he wouldn't, he'd never use those hands again.

'This is no time to play,' Jake said. 'Just finish it.'

Ray didn't stop smirking, but a sudden darkness in his eyes suggested he didn't appreciate Jake's interference. 'All in good time.'

The other member of the kill squad, Jay, entered the room via the same door. He also had his balaclava rolled up. 'All clear. Our intel was spot on. Three in total.'

Jake chanced another glance at his friend. Yorke's face twitched. *In God's name, stay down, Mike.*

'A'richt,' the Scot said. 'Dae whit Pettman said, Ray. Slay your serpent.' He winked at Jake. 'Naebody got experience like oor wee runaway o'er there, or sae I've heard, like.'

Ray knelt, lifted his army pants slightly, and slipped out a long knife. He twirled it in his hand, pulled the terrorist's head back by his hair, and pointed the blade at one of his eyes. 'Seems a shame to rush—'

'For fuck's sake,' Jake said, throttled by impatience and terrified that Yorke would come round at any moment. 'I thought this was a professional outfit.'

Ray glared at Jake, no longer smirking. 'It is. He killed a kid. I'm happy to make an exception.'

'I didn't,' the man moaned. 'I didn't know—'

Ray slapped the back of the man's head. 'Shut up while we discuss your execution, fuckwit.'

'I'm about to walk. I'm happy to explain to Walter why,' Jake said to the Scot. 'Or you could just control your team.'

'Fuck ye, pal,' the Scot said.

Then he heard the unthinkable—a quiet moan from beneath his feet. It was barely perceptible, even at his proximity, but if any of them heard it, Yorke was dead.

He studied the men. All eyes were on Ray and his next move. They hadn't noticed.

'Git it done,' the Scot said to Ray. 'We need tae shift.'

'There's time,' Ray said, twirling the knife. 'For an eyeball or *two*, perhaps?'

The moaning at Jake's feet *seemed* to be getting louder. He prayed this was his paranoia.

The Scot, glanced in Jake's direction. *Had he heard the moan?* He looked curious—or, again, was this just paranoia?

Jake readied his gun. He'd die before they moved on Yorke.

The terrorist wailed as the tip of Ray's knife burst an eyeball. Using the distraction, Jake checked his friend again.

Yorke was starting to move.

Nothing else for it.

Jake marched forward, raising his gun, kicked Ray's knife-wielding hand away, and shot the terrorist in his good eye. The man gurgled and folded up. 'I don't fuck around on my shift,' Jake shouted, turning. 'Feel free to do what you want on your own.' He strode towards the open door, spying Yorke, whose eyelids were fluttering.

'Bad move,' the Scot said.

'What was it you said before?' Jake hissed over his shoulder. 'Fuck you, pal? Yeah. Right back at you, *pal.*'

Jake *knew* Ray would rage at having his prize taken from him and that his play would be coming, but if he could somehow get them from the house and away from his waking friend, he could worry about that after.

When Jake reached the front door, Ray said, 'Turn around so I can see your fucking face when I shoot you.'

'No,' Jake hissed. 'You can shoot me in the back. Then when my emails go out and fuck your bosses, you can explain it away. You think Walter will stop with your eyeballs, then, dipshit?'

He strode through the open door, clenching his teeth, half-expecting to feel a thumping sensation in his back, followed by the fall of the black curtain.

The Scot shouted, 'Everybody oot.'

Jake stormed up the drive. Relief was still out of reach. They might not gun him down just yet, but they were still to pass Yorke. If they clocked his recovery, the next gunshot he heard would signal carnage, because Jake, sure as hell, would kill as many of these bastards as he could before they hurt his friend.

He still heard nothing as he approached the end of the drive, and he held his breath, preparing for the worst.

I'm a fucking idiot.

He should've killed the 'defanged' terrorist the second Ray threw him down; there'd been too much chat, too much posturing, too much time for Yorke to wake up.

When Jake reached the end of the driveway, he turned, half-expecting to see them all in the doorway, looking down on his recovering friend, Ray licking his lips in anticipation over fresh eyeballs. But, with immense relief, Jake saw the front door closing and all four men of the kill squad walking towards him—all of them, apart from Ray, had rolled their balaclavas back down.

As relieved as he was, his senses were acute enough to detect Ray's sudden movement when he drew close.

Jake swerved the bastard's fist and struck him hard in the side of the face. The gobshite stumbled to the side and went over some overgrown plant pots.

The Scot, Stevie, and Jay went to help him untangle himself from the shrubbery and convince him to calm down. Drawing attention to themselves outside a kill zone was a bad move.

Jake watched the four soldiers jog away, then he moved his

gaze over to the front door. *Mike, what the hell were you doing there?*

He wanted to go back in, but a police siren in the distance convinced him otherwise.

He broke into a jog and saw the black van driving past him and away. When he reached the spot where Lacey had been parked, he groaned.

Where'd she gone?

He continued running, desperate to be as far away as possible before the police arrived.

As he ran, he considered where Lacey may have gone. He could only summon up two potential explanations.

First, she could've returned to the house to retrieve Sam, knowing he had the location of Holden and Tobias. Where that would leave Russ, the smartly dressed man guarding him, was anyone's guess, but if she put him down, that would only cause more friction with Article SE.

Bad move.

He hoped she hadn't done that!

The other explanation was that Carrie had contacted her. Maybe she was in trouble and leading Lacey to Holden.

This also sounded like a bad move.

Ahh, Lacey, couldn't you have just fucking waited?

Wasn't my word good enough?

He had money in his pocket, so he went in search of a taxi.

THE SECOND FIREFLY TO THE DANCE

Three minutes earlier ...

Lacey's phone buzzed twice. *My one.*

Lacey opened the first message to reveal a photograph of Dr Holden taped to a swivel chair.

Unexpected.

The second message contained a photograph of Tobias chained to a wall, much older now than when she'd last seen him.

She sighed. *My son.*

The phone buzzed a third time. She read her one's message: *Time to dance, firefly.* There was a set of coordinates.

She started her car. *Sorry to leave you in the middle of nowhere, Jakey, but that really isn't an offer I can refuse.*

⤳

THE CORPSE WAS recognisable as female from her build and outfit but certainly not her face. Most of that was gone. At least, it wasn't her one; of this Lacey was certain. Carrie was much shorter than whoever this had been.

So, who're you? Were you beautiful, my dear? Before he shot off your face?

She eyed the modern entrance on the archaic stone structure, then glanced back down at the body, really struggling to understand what had occurred. Did Carrie have anything to do with this?

Surely not. Inconceivable.

Her gaze lingered on the body for a moment longer.

I bet you were beautiful. I bet you really were. She sighed. *For you to be left here to rot and fester like a dead animal isn't acceptable.*

As she approached the entrance, the oddity of the situation triggered other concerns. Tobias's mother.

Jane Young. Controlled by a man. A vile man Lacey had enjoyed plucking from the world.

Regardless of what Jake and Walter believed, it couldn't have been Tobias who'd done that.

Inside this peculiar stone structure was the truth, and she intended to get it.

She looked up at the security camera.

There was a clunk. A speaker crackled overhead. 'Forward, firefly,' her one said.

Lacey opened the door.

~

Lacey followed the trail of blood.

Dr Holden's? Is he still alive, my one?

The corridor was long, narrow, and stuffy. Not a drop of natural light was granted access to this stretch, so some light bulbs, obviously placed here in more modern times, drooped from the low ceilings.

For a moment, Lacey felt peculiar. She paused and took some deep breaths trying to identify the reason.

Trapped. Claustrophobic.

That was how she felt.

Peculiar. She hadn't been aware she was capable of such feelings.

As she continued down the corridor, the feeling intensified and her thoughts journeyed to her time in the convalescence room.

Paralysis ... molestation ...

Her breathing increased.

Was this panic? PTSD?

This really was out of the ordinary.

She took long, deep breaths and regained control. After, she shook her head.

Maybe you're not the only one evolving, Carrie?

Still, it'd be better if this could just be explained away. A drop in blood sugar, perhaps? She'd not eaten for most of the day, after all ... Better that this *feeling* didn't become a *thing*.

It soon became clear that she was in some kind of Victorian prison. She peered into some darkened cells on route. Broken furniture and little else. Eventually, she sighted Holden up ahead in the centre of the corridor, duct-taped to the swivel chair.

The game is almost up, Doctor.

Surprising, really. She'd never really anticipated it ending in such a fashion.

Not rushing, she peered in a few more cells on route just in case Tobias was in one of them. But all she saw was the debris of yesteryear, the remnants of people living and dying in soulless vacuums.

Holden wasn't struggling in his bondage. Blood dripped from one of his thighs into a small bloody puddle on the floor. More duct tape had been wrapped tight around the wound to stem the bleeding.

Carrie had trussed Holden up good and proper.

His ankles were taped together in front of the wheels, and his wrists had been attached to the arm rests. The tape was over his mouth so he couldn't speak, but nothing in his expression suggested he was desperate to do so.

He looked hard at Lacey as she approached.

She smiled, keeping up appearances, but inside she felt a growing sense of disappointment that it hadn't been her who had brought down Dr Holden. Surely, her one would've known this? Going off gung-ho like this, stealing her thunder? It wasn't just disappointment growing here, Lacey realised; it was also unease regarding Carrie.

'Not trying to get free?' Lacey stopped in front of him. 'Anybody else, knowing what awaited them, would be in a state of uncontrollable panic. Not you though, eh? Not pain's sweet observer. Not Hell's doctor, Stewart Holden.' She tore off his tape.

He didn't wince despite the ripping sound. He did flex his mouth and wet his lips with his tongue though. 'Pain's sweet observer.' He chuckled. 'I've never heard curiosity, science, *learning*, described in such a way.'

'I guess it's my move now. Looking at your situation.'

His pale, damp face was twitching. He was fighting back the pain caused by the hole in his leg. 'Always remarkable. Winning or losing, your tone of voice never changes. Confident. *Assured*. Like it never really was a game. Like the outcome was never in question.'

Lacey shrugged. 'It wasn't.'

'I degraded and humiliated you beyond all measure. I'd be lying if I said I wasn't impressed, my true malignant narcissist.'

She turned him around and around in the swivel chair as she spoke. 'You might want to tell me where your journal is. You'll need someone to write your final chapter. Your lament over losing. Your conclusions. Your wasted hypotheses.'

'On the contrary.' Holden closed his eyes so as not to grow dizzy. 'I've learned so much. I know now that only a chosen few in this world can truly endure endless pain, suffering, and torment. You and me are of that chosen few. Carrie, too, no doubt. You're wrong about winning, and about me, losing. It was never about a winner and a loser. I *always* envisaged it ending this way, with you watching me as I endure. Over the coming weeks, you get to make that prolonged agony you envisaged in your Blue Room a reality.' He smiled. 'I promise I won't let you down. After, you'll be just like me, and you'll understand.'

'Now, why does that sound completely and utterly unpleasant?' She stopped spinning him.

He opened his eyes.

'You only had to take my fantasy and destroy it, didn't you, Doc?'

'I *promise* it will be—'

'Please! Your voice is starting to irritate me.' Lacey stared down the corridor. 'Where's Tobias?'

'In one of the cells.'

'I hope you were hospitable.'

'He was disappointing.'

'Sorry to hear that. Because of his table manners?'

Holden guffawed, but then winced over the pain in his leg.

'Do you have others?' She raised an eyebrow.

'Yes. Similar to us. But they don't understand what they are. Not truly. Not like me and you.'

'Do you know what your problem is? I think you're just lonely. You have the usual, bog-standard, no-frills case of the blues. Your marriage clearly isn't working for you.'

'Lonely! Don't be absurd! I can't be lonely. I—'

'Are you sure?' She looked down on him like he was a confused child.

'Yes. I have you.'

Of course! It dawned on her. *Everything* dawned on her.

'What is it?' Holden asked.

'It's all suddenly clear as day. You say it isn't about winning?'

'That's right. It's about *playing*.'

'*Yes*, precisely. So if we play, you do, in actual fact, win. By engaging you, interacting with you, *playing* with you, I'm feeding you. Why didn't I see it before? I'm just simply letting you win. All of the time! It doesn't matter one jot to you who's on which side of the knife.'

Holden stared at her.

'So, for the first time ever, I'm going to have to abandon my plan. What a turn up, eh? The Blue Room won't be best pleased, but hey-ho, this has come quite out of nowhere, so—'

Holden narrowed his eyes. 'No. You *won't* abandon who you are. You can't.'

'Won't I? Can't I? I don't want to buy into this static, unchangeable idea that you relish. I always liked the word *adaptable*. It has a nice ring to it. I mean, who wants to be a stick in the mud like you?'

'I won't believe it.'

'See? Rigid in thought. Be more openminded. I know Carrie is changeable,' *terrifyingly so*, 'and potentially Tobias,' *also of great concern*, 'so change. It seems all the rage. I'm not going to torture you. Cut off a piece of you every day, as previously promised. For one thing, I don't have time. I've things to do, children to raise …' *discipline*, 'and partners to guide,' *tame*. 'But the main reason is, I'm not playing anymore. You can sit here and bleed out for all I fucking care.'

Holden was now shaking his head erratically. 'But that isn't who you are.'

'No, you've just failed to understand adaption. Needs can be met in other ways.'

'Like Carrie? Your special friend. Like the way she's changed?' He smirked.

Lacey shrugged and stretched out the piece of duct tape she'd taken from his mouth, preparing to reattach it.

'Do you know what she did? Did you see that young woman outside? That *innocent* woman.'

She resealed his mouth. 'Shut the fuck up now, Doc. The fact that I'll never hear your voice again is the only victory I need.'

The door beside her opened.

Lacey turned to her one, surprised to see her in her own clothes. She looked very different. And not because she looked more glamorous and attractive. Although, she did. But because something had changed in her demeanour again, and she appeared more confident and assured than ever before.

Her one stepped forward and embraced her tightly, then backed away. 'Do I look like you, Lacey?'

'Well, it worked. You fooled them.'

'I really like looking this way.'

'I prefer you the other way.' It didn't feel right seeing her like this, pretending to be her, *wanting* to be her, perhaps.

'We'll see,' her one said. 'Do you like what I've done for you?' She pointed at Holden.

'I'm glad it's over, but you know, I can't be grateful; he was my problem.'

'Surely then he was my problem too?' her one asked.

Lacey nodded. 'Still, it wasn't how it should've gone. And you should know that.'

Her one looked away. 'Yet I did so well.'

Lacey nodded. 'I don't deny it.'

'Do you want to hear how I did it? You'd be *so* proud.'

Lacey was more eager to get to Tobias, but she nodded anyway, curious over Holden's final attempt to unnerve her.

Her one explained the incident at the carpark.

'I felt like you. I felt how you must've felt all those times in similar situations.'

Lacey inwardly sighed.

'What happened with that girl outside, my one?'

She looked away. 'I didn't shoot her.' She pointed at Holden. 'That was him. Although, I shot him, just as you'd have done.'

'Yes, but how did that girl get here? Who was she? What was her name?'

'Princess Honey. A prostitute. I arranged for her to come. It was necessary to draw him out. It worked, too.'

'She was innocent and she's no face left.'

'As I said, that was *him*.' She pointed again. 'He *chose* to do that.'

'But you *chose* to bring her.'

'Necessary. You'd have done the same, I'm sure.'

Lacey shook her head. 'I'm struggling to recognise you.'

Her one narrowed her eyes. 'You weren't like this before Jake came back.'

You didn't sacrifice innocent women before Jake came back. 'It has nothing to do with Jake.'

'I *won't* share you with him.'

'That wasn't ever a consideration.'

'And I won't share you with a child.'

Lacey inwardly sighed again. The inevitable had

happened. Carrie's evolution was making her too dangerous. It'd have to be dealt with. It felt right to strike this instant, but Lacey was all too aware that impetuous moves weren't always the right ones. She saw now the end for Carrie, but she wanted to give her that final piece of respect.

Some thought to how she'd do it and then a trip to the Blue Room. For what she'd done for her in Princeholm, she deserved at least that.

'You won't have to share me.' *That won't ever be a concern now.* 'You should've known to come to me first. To *not* take matters into your own hands.'

'I love you,' Carrie said, putting her hand to Lacey's face.

Lacey touched the hand on her face. 'People say I don't have the capacity for love.'

'And is it true?'

'Who knows.' Lacey gently eased Carrie's hand from her face. 'But you've given me a lot to think about.' She turned and eyed Holden down the corridor.

Lacey took a deep breath. 'Which cell is Tobias in?'

'Cell thirteen, farther along this corridor. I unlocked the door from the control room. But don't you want to have some fun with Dr Holden first?'

'Who?' She smiled as his eyes darted back and forth. 'I don't know a Dr Holden. He doesn't exist.' She regarded Carrie. 'Make that so.'

As Lacey started down the corridor, Carrie called out after her, 'I won't share you. I *can't* share you.'

I know, Carrie, that's why you'll have to die.

≈

LACEY OPENED the cell door and stared at her son. 'You've grown.'

Wearing a dark hoodie and black jeans, the pale boy stood with his back against the far wall, staring off into space.

Lacey entered the cell, closed the door behind her, and leaned against it. 'It's me. Lacey. Your mother.'

She watched him for a minute or so, knowing he wouldn't change the direction of his stare. Now that she was with him again, she felt like she knew him *so* well, despite them only having spent a short time together. A smile crept across her face as she reminisced, only for it to fall sharply away when a cruel image interrupted her thoughts.

Tobias stabbing his sleeping mother in the chest.

She shook it off.

No.

It wasn't true.

She hadn't needed to ask Dr Holden to know it was a lie. It would have just fed the doctor's need to play further.

With her gaze fixed on Tobias, she crossed the cell towards him.

He didn't move once. Not his eyes, his face, or any of his body.

It was only when she was within a metre of him that she could see his chest moving as he sucked in air. She ran her fingers over the modern-looking clasp around his left wrist that chained him to the wall. It had a glowing red LED display that indicated it was locked. She wondered how to unlock it, then considered the control room that Carrie had referred to before.

She reached out to take Tobias's other hand, but after noticing it was in the pocket of his hoodie, she ran her fingers over the back of his restrained hand instead. 'Do you remember me?'

Tobias's eyes moved for the first time. Not towards her, unfortunately, but rather downwards to the floor.

'It's Lacey. You were with me for a time. We had some fun, you and me. Some *real* fun.'

Enjoying the sound of his breathing in the same way she'd done when he was younger, she'd an urge to slip her arms around his back, longing to bring the child who she'd started to nurture, before he'd been cruelly taken from her, closer to her. She held back. He may have had spirit, Tobias—she remembered it well—but he'd always had fragility, too. She didn't want to move too quickly. Unsettle him.

She touched the clasp and thought again of Carrie in the control room. 'I'll go and have this taken off.' She kept moving her head, trying to force his eyes to meet hers. It didn't work; he simply averted them. 'Do you recall any of our time together?'

There was, of course, no response. Sensing frustration, she willed herself to be more patient. He's fragile, damaged. Be sensitive. 'I remember so well, and I've missed you.' *My brooding, silent boy.* She leaned forward and kissed his greasy, jet-black hair and let her lips linger there for a time. She closed her eyes and again recalled hugging him when he was younger.

'I remember,' Tobias said.

Her heart was full!

She pulled her head back and looked at him. Although he hadn't yet moved his eyes to hers, she was certain she detected some softening in his expression. She slipped her hand around the back of his head and pulled it gently to her chest. 'I've dreamed of this day. I'm sorry about what that monster did to you and your birth mother.' *Because it was Holden, of that I'm now certain.*

'I remember,' Tobias repeated.

'I'm so glad,' Lacey said, kissing his crown again. 'So, so glad.'

'I remember.'

'I hear you.' She eased herself backwards, slipping both hands onto his shoulders and looking down at him instead. He still didn't meet her eyes. 'But you can relax now. I'll just go and get this clasp undone—'

'I remember.'

Something was wrong. 'Tobias?'

Still not looking at her, he said, 'I remember.'

'Okay, I'm going—'

'I remember.'

He sounded like a robot.

'I remember.'

A malfunctioning robot!

'I remember.'

She squeezed his shoulders. 'Tobias. You're safe—'

'I remember.'

No ... no good at all. Her heart raced—an unusual reaction for her.

'I remember.'

She pulled his head to her chest again.

'I remember ... I remember ... I remember ...' he looped.

Eventually, willing herself not to shout at him or shake him, to try to snap him out of it, she stepped backwards.

He may have sounded like a malfunctioning robot, but he didn't look like one. In fact, he looked more like a robot with flat batteries. Head hanging slightly, eyes wide and unfocused, slumped posture. 'I remember ... I remember ... I remember ...'

A long wail from somewhere farther down the corridor burst the surreal bubble.

Dr Holden?

'I remember ... I remember ... I remember ...'

The wail came again.

'I remember ... I remember ... I remember ...'

Lacey slowly turned her head from side to side, feeling something she'd never felt.

Lost.

Lost in a chaotic symphony of monotone repetition from her broken son and agonised cries of her torturer bouncing towards her along old, stone walls.

'I remember ... I remember ... I remember ...'

Wail.

'I don't know the answer,' she said.

'I remember ... I remember ... I remember ...'

Wail.

She put her hands to her ears. 'I don't know what to do.'

'I remember ... I remember ... I remember ...'

Wail.

'I don't know how to help you.'

'I remember ... I remember ... I remember ...'

Wail.

'I remember –'

'*Shut up!*' she hissed, finally succumbing and dropping her hands from the side of her head and shaking Tobias. 'Snap out of it. Snap the fuck out of it.'

Tobias looked up at her.

Stunned, she took a deep breath.

His expression remained the same, but his eyes were suddenly alive. Switched on, as if they were light bulbs.

'Tobias?'

'I remember,' her son said. 'You forgot.'

She caught sight of his hand bursting from the pocket of his hoodie.

A flash of silver. Pressure in her stomach.

And she staggered backwards.

'You forgot,' Tobias said.

Lacey saw the bloody knife in her son's hand and realised that her stomach was burning. She clutched it.

You forgot ...

And then it was clear.

Tobias felt abandoned. And when you felt abandoned, you either disappear inside yourself, or strike out against the world. Tobias was moving between both responses.

She looked at her bloody hands, then at her son. And thought again of Jane Young.

It wasn't Holden, after all.

You killed her, didn't you, Tobias?

She couldn't say the thoughts out loud. She didn't want to hear the truth.

But it was the truth.

Because why would this boy follow some code given to him by the bitch who'd abandoned him?

Holden's cries of pain reverberated around the prison. She glanced down at her wound. She was bleeding heavily.

She looked back up and saw that Tobias's eyes now looked more alive than ever.

He charged, knife raised, and Lacey, still in a state of complete disbelief, stood there welcoming the inevitable.

The inevitable never came. Tobias stopped dead, the chain attached to the wall at full stretch.

He waved the knife in the air, desperate to cut her.

She sighed, considering the situation.

There was only one thing for it: *enough is enough. Time to regain control.*

She steeled herself. 'I couldn't get to you.' She spoke loudly over Holden's tormented cries.

'You forgot.'

'I was locked away like you are now.'

'You forgot.'

Shit! His mind was thoroughly made up. 'So, your bitch of a mother dies, eh? Your betrayer?'

'You forgot.'

'And then what?'

'You forgot.'

'You spend the rest of your life on this planet breaking my code?'

'You forgot.'

Fuck this.

To the soundtrack of barbaric cries and true torment, she fled to the cell door and tugged at it.

Locked.

Shit.

Carrie, you bitch. I should've killed you when I had the chance.

The speakers in the room crackled. 'Check your pockets.'

She eyed the camera in the corner of the room. 'Open the door, Carrie.'

'Why've you started using my name? It has been *my one* for as long as I've known you.'

'I don't know what you're talking about. Please, open the door!'

A loud *clunk* sounded, and for a moment, Lacey suspected she'd seen sense and opened it. However, when she tried the handle, she realised that wasn't the case, and after hearing a noise behind her, she swooped to one side.

Tobias crashed into the door.

She glared at the camera and reached into her pocket. She knew it was a scalpel even before she pulled it out. She flicked off the protective cap with a thumb.

Tobias turned, holding up his blood-stained weapon.

'Tobias,' Lacey said. 'Please.'

'You forgot,' he said.

THE FIRST FIREFLY TO THE DANCE

Earlier ...

*H*olden did a grand job of shuffling down the corridor, using the wall to keep himself upright, but he couldn't manage all of it. Eventually he slipped down the wall into a sitting position. He pointed at the trail behind him. He was struggling to catch his breath. 'I'm pissing blood. I can't go on.'

'That's a problem,' Carrie said. 'I've no idea where I'm going.'

'Should've thought about that before you shot me in the leg.'

'A flesh wound. I'm no doctor, but if I'd hit an artery, wouldn't you be dead by now?'

'Listen. If you go straight ahead, a couple minutes max, past some locked cells, you'll see an open door on your left. There's a swivel chair on wheels.'

'Cells? What's this place? A prison?'

Holden smiled.

Carrie looked back the way she'd come.

'Honestly, what am I going to do?' Holden asked. '*Run*? You've seen how slow I am. You'll be back before I even make it to the door anyway.'

'Okay,' Carrie said, walking away.

His instructions proved accurate, and she found the door to the control room open. She scanned the many monitors on the wall. *Fascinating.* She counted three occupied cells. One of which held Tobias. *What're you up to, Dr Holden?*

Despite wanting to explore this box of delights further, she knew she was allowing Holden too much time to crawl to freedom. She checked a few drawers, struck gold with some duct tape, and pushed the swivel chair out of the room.

She found him where she'd left him. His eyes were closed. *Have you died? Now that wouldn't be good.*

She parked the chair, leant over, and slapped his face.

His eyes snapped open.

'You don't look the best,' Carrie said, backing away. 'Pasty.' She gestured at the chair with the hand not holding the gun. 'Your chariot.'

'Hold it, then.'

She plucked the duct tape from the seat and watched him struggle his way up the wall into an upright position. Eventually he hovered there, weight on one leg, gasping for air. She rolled the seat close to him so he could plonk back into it. He sighed with relief.

'Now, I'm going to tape you to the chair. Struggle and I'll put a hole in your other leg.'

'Do I look in any state to struggle? Besides, I'm not about to get myself killed. Next time you may just get that artery.'

Carrie laughed as she wound the duct tape several times around his left wrist, locking it to the arm rest. 'But surely you know? That you're going to die anyway? Why wouldn't you fight?'

'Because I don't fear death. What I do fear—or, at least, find inconceivable—is never seeing Lacey again.'

After Carrie had taped up his second wrist, she asked, 'Why're you so fascinated with Lacey anyway?'

'You wouldn't understand.'

'Try me.'

'No. There's no point, really. To understand, you'd have to be the same as her.'

'*I'm* like her.'

'No, you're not. Just because you wear the same clothes now and kill people, that doesn't make you alike. Not in any way.'

Carrie felt a surge of irritation, and she wound the tape around his ankles extra tight. 'What would you know?'

'More than you. I know also that you're going to die too. That Lacey won't accept what just happened outside.'

'You're wrong.'

'We'll see.'

She pushed him down the corridor. 'Who're the poor bastards in these cells?'

'Most of them are empty.'

'Some aren't. I saw on your monitors. And Tobias is in one of them.'

'So, you saw my collection. Or rather you saw how pathetic it was. If it wasn't about to end in this manner, I'd be adding both you and Lacey to it.'

'Me? I'm honoured! I thought I wasn't special.'

'You're special.' He snorted. 'Just not as special as your girlfriend.'

She angrily thrust him through the open door of the control room.

He yelled in pain when his leg banged into the frame.

'I'm going to enjoy watching you die,' she said, wheeling him to the monitors.

'Maybe. There's every chance you'll go first. Remember the dead prostitute out front? Also, there's the issue of power.'

'What're you talking about?'

'Have you ever had the power taken from you?'

'I don't know what you're—'

'*Think* about it. Has anyone ever taken your power?'

Her mind wandered to Jake and the case of Joe Wheaton. Joe had been hers. Jake had taken him from her.

'I see from the look on your face, that someone has. And how did it make you feel?'

Like killing them.

'I rest my case.'

She leaned on his damaged leg, and he squealed. 'Do I have to tape your mouth?'

'No, but I'd tape the wound. It's bleeding heavily. You might keep me alive long enough for Lacey then.'

She wound the duct tape around the wound again and again. He screamed as she did so. She stood and prodded at the monitor on the far left which showed an individual sitting beside a male corpse, lovingly stroking their hair with the hand that wasn't chained to the wall. 'Who's that?'

'Keith.'

'And?'

'He likes dead people. Passionate about them.'

'Tell me more.'

He did.

She nodded and pointed at other monitor, where a man had someone's skin draped over them like a blanket.

'Vinnie,' Holden said and told her about him, too.

'Interesting bunch.'

'They've their own unique needs, yes.'

She smiled. Her tongue brushed against her teeth. She wondered if their desires felt like her desires. 'What would Keith do to me if I went in there?'

'Well, for a start, he's chained to the wall, so nothing. But even if I released him, he'd barely bat an eyelid at you. You're the wrong gender. He prefers his victims male *and* powerful, like his father. More powerful than him, at least until he's moulded them into his subservient pets. Do you see the way he stares at the camera?' He smiled again.

Carrie looked at Holden. 'It's you he wants.'

'Of course. When he isn't playing with his toys, he stares at the camera, day and night, imagining what I *feel* like. Cold, inanimate—in his control. Look at him stare! He can't even see me. Not really. He must have an image of me, fully formed, burning in his conscious mind.'

'The way you talk, it almost sounds as if fate brought you together.'

'Fate.' He laughed. 'Fate doesn't play any part in my studies. I'm only interested in the observable. Choice and consequence.'

She tapped Tobias Ray on the screen. 'A ten-year-old boy. Tell me about *his* choices. Most children I've ever come across are impulsive and don't think a great deal about consequences.'

'Don't buy into the exterior. The lack of expression, the silence—that boy thinks, he reasons, and he makes choices.'

'And you've learned all that from watching this statue?'

'To some extent, but mainly from his profile. I picked it apart long before he came to me here. His past exploits with Lacey were very colourful. The things he did, the things she *taught* him to do. The roadmap she tried to give him.'

'Yes, she's told me.'

'I imagine she has, but I've *also* read the doctors' reports from the many years he's been back with his mother. And there are many. You want my conclusion?'

'Is it worth anything?'

'I'm as certain of this as I am of Lacey turning on you, dear.'

Carrie narrowed her eyes. 'Maybe I should just hurt you some more.'

'A waste of time. Where truth and reason are concerned, nothing will stop my tongue.'

'Even if it is no longer attached to you?'

'Best using tape; you wouldn't want to disappoint Lacey any more than you already have done. Although, it's too late now anyway.'

She took a deep breath. 'Go on, then. Give me your fucking conclusions.'

'You know already that Lacey and Tobias hunted together?'

Carrie said, smiling, 'She taught him well.'

'Taught?' He guffawed. 'Taught. That boy is no different from Lacey, you, or those men in my cells. The capacity for such actions isn't taught. Acquired. *It's innate*. Instinctual. And you know what? We smell each other out.'

'What? Like dogs?'

'If you like, yes. Lacey sniffed him out, just like she caught your scent, too. She merely tried to control his capacity, influence him. *Like she's done with you*. And you can't do that with one another, as you're starting to find out. Look at you. That young woman you sacrificed? Coming here in Lacey's place? Rebellion. You're rebelling. Likewise, Tobias, too, will rebel.'

'Hypocrisy! Look at you controlling everything around you! You clearly don't practise what you preach.'

'I'm a scientist. I observe, measure, and learn.'

'Until it backfires on you?'

'Maybe.'

'So, in your opinion, I'm rebelling against Lacey, and Tobias will too?'

'Yes. And there's something else.'

'Go on.'

'Well, those psychiatric reports, of which there are very many, indicated something extremely interesting. He felt betrayed, abandoned by Lacey. That feeling of betrayal combined with an insatiable need to retake power and control, well … you can imagine. And, you know, he killed his own birth mother. A woman. *Brutally*. Was that in Lacey's code? I think not. And if you still don't buy it, well, listen to this. Over the years, he'd drawn countless pictures of Mother Lacey.' He smiled.

'So?'

'In all of these pictures, Lacey was dead.'

Carrie flinched.

'Yes, dead. So I don't expect she'll be getting the reunion she anticipates.' Holden paused. His eyes widened, as if he was having an epiphany. His mouth opened slightly, and he exhaled a satisfying-sounding *ah*.

'What?'

'It makes perfect sense now.'

'What does?'

'Why you're here. Why you're retaking power and control.'

'We've discussed this. I'll cut out your tongue. I'll risk it. Tape up the stub like I taped up your leg.'

'No, listen. Genuinely.' His voice was filled with excitement. 'You're doing all of this because you feel betrayed too, just like Tobias!'

She flinched. 'You're barking up the wrong tree.'

'Am I?'

'You're just trying to destabilise me. *Us*.'

'No. You're too intelligent. You can hear what I'm saying.'

She leaned in and pointed the gun in his face. 'Stop it.'

'Tell me, how did you feel about that man, Jake Pettman, coming back into Lacey's life? That must've pissed you off.'

'He's a minor inconvenience.' *Not true. He'd been anything but minor.*

'And now the prospect of having to *share* her with the boy in that cell? What does that bring to your emotional table?'

She pulled the gun out of his face and turned away. 'Whatever makes Lacey happy.'

'And you. Don't you want to be happy too? Are you *that* subservient to Lacey's needs?'

'*Fuck you*! I know what you're doing. You're a clever little firefly, I'll give you that. But your dance is almost up.'

'As is yours. And as is Lacey's. You'll do well to listen to me. Before all of us are at an end.'

She backed away from the doctor, turning as she did so. *Think. He's in your head. It's what he's good at. He's just trying to manipulate the situation.*

But every time she thought through what he said, desperately looking for holes, the more accurate his assessment seemed to be.

She'd had enough of Lacey's control. Her decisions were forever backfiring. She was furious with Lacey's decision to reintroduce Jake into her life. And now this? A child. A child who was no part of her—and no part of Lacey, for that matter.

And would Lacey kill Carrie for her afront? For using that woman to lure out the doctor? For trying to control the situation herself and prove she didn't need to be led any longer?

In her mind's eye, she saw Lacey smile.

Yes, she fucking would.

'You know I'm right.'

But she had to hope. She had to at least *try*. She loved Lacey; she'd wanted to be like her for so very long. These days, she even felt like her. Before Lacey's escape, she'd fantasised about their time together often.

Both of them.

Against the world.

No Jake.

No Tobias.

No one else.

Just the thought of it warmed her inside.

She'd at least try. And failing that, well, couldn't she just become Lacey? Fuck the doctor and his assessment that he was too different. He'd be dead before the day was out anyway.

She leaned in over him, close enough so she could see the veins that crisscrossed his whitened eyes but not quite close enough that he could take a bite from her if he so wished. 'Enough talk. I need you to teach me how to use the control room. The cameras, the speakers, the remote locking of the doors. And the cuffs, how do they work?'

'All remote controlled too.'

'Good.'

'Can I hear your plan?'

'It's not so much a plan as a decision. And I won't spoil the surprise for you.'

'Intriguing, but—'

'You'll see her again. Lacey. That's all you need to know. It's all you really want.'

'Still, I—'

'Or you can die now, and I'll figure out these buttons myself. The reality is you've convinced me. And with that truth comes the knowledge that you're completely expendable.'

He nodded and showed her what to do, then she sealed his mouth with duct tape and rolled him into the corridor outside the control room. She went through every drawer in the office, seeing all manner of tools and objects. Some with blood or hair stuck to them. She found a knife and a scalpel with a protective cap. She pressed the button on the control panel to unlock the door for cell thirteen. Then she went to pay Tobias a visit.

'Lacey's coming to you, Tobias.'

The motionless boy stared off into space.

I know you're listening, Tobias. Somewhere in there, some part of you hears.

'Coming with the same intentions she had before. To control you, to *use* you. And cast you aside, like she's done before. Like she's done to so many others before.'

Like she'll do to me.

She stroked Tobias's face. 'So, Lacey's coming to you. But ... to free you? No, I'm sorry. Not to free you.'

She slipped the knife into his pocket and ran her fingers over his cold face again.

Still no change in expression. No movement of the eyes.

But you hear, Tobias. You hear ...

'Say goodbye to her. Say goodbye to her before she says goodbye to you.'

As she left the cell, she returned to the fantasy again.

Both of them.

Against the world.

No Jake.

No Tobias.

No one else.

Using the keycode provided to her by Holden, Carrie went

outside and texted the location to Lacey, along with a message: *Time to dance, firefly*. She returned to the control room and watched Tobias through the monitor. He hadn't moved.

I'm doing this for you, Lacey.

For us.

She looked at the scalpel that she would slip into Lacey's pocket when they embraced on her arrival. *One day you'll realise I did this for your own good.*

For our own good.

And if it all goes wrong?

Well, don't worry, Lacey, I'll be still here.

I'll keep your legacy intact.

∾

LATER, while Lacey was with Tobias in his cell, Carrie watched Vinnie work from the control room.

The control room! I bet you felt like a god up here, didn't you, Dr Holden?

Even though she'd turned off the sound feed from Vinnie's cell, she could still hear the screams. She recalled his words earlier: *'I'm a scientist. I observe, measure, and learn.'*

No, she thought. *You control. You play with them. A tweak here, a tweak there, and you've your very own show. Well, I hope you don't mind if I play too.*

Holden thrashed his head back and forth as his legs were stripped.

What do you think of this show?

Or perhaps, this one?

She turned her gaze to the other monitor, where Lacey was still conversing with Tobias. Unfortunately, they were speaking at a low volume far from the mic, and the sound wasn't being picked up clearly enough. She'd caught a few words but nothing too sensical.

At this point, the boy seemed to repeat, 'I remember,' as Lacey pleaded with him, but the manner of their conversation was confusing.

Can't you tell already, Lacey, that this is a dead end?

She sighed. Although the thought sounded clear and positive in her mind, she struggled to latch on to it and absorb the hope it offered.

She heard another loud scream and gazed back at the other monitor.

Keith, who she'd earlier led at gunpoint into Vinnie's cell, was gripping Holden's stripped, fleshy ankles while his arms were worked on.

Hearing the murmurings of *remember*, suddenly changed up for *forget*, redrew Carrie's attention to Tobias's cell.

Shit!

She'd missed it!

Lacey had backed away, clutching her stomach. Tobias had gone full stretch on his chain and held a bloody knife in his hand.

'I couldn't get to you,' Lacey said.

She had upped her volume levels; Carrie could hear it.

'You forgot.'

'I was locked away like you are now.'

'You forgot.'

'So, your bitch of a mother dies, eh? Your betrayer?'

'You forgot.'

'And then what?'

'You forgot.'

'You spend the rest of your life on this planet breaking my code?'

'You forgot.'

For fuck's sake, Carrie thought, *all this sentiment! Stop all this talk! You're Lacey Ray. He's a ten-year-old animal. Wild, untameable. You see what your hesitance and sensitivity has cost you? You have a gut wound! Use the realisation. Put aside these hindrances and do what you always do so well.*

Lacey darted for the cell door and tugged at it.

Yes, Lacey, I locked it.

She pressed the button for the mic. 'Check your pockets.'

Inside you'll find my gift to you when we embraced earlier.

Carrie saw Lacey's eyes dart to the camera in the corner of the room. 'Open the door, Carrie.'

'Why've you started using my name? It has been *my one* for as long as I've known you.'

'I don't know what you're talking about. Please, open the door!'

Carrie pressed the button that released the clasp on Tobias wrist. The loud clunk made the speakers buzz in the control room.

Lacey tried the handle.

Tobias darted across the room, knife raised.

Carrie held her breath.

Lacey rolled away over the door, and then the wall.

Tobias crashed into the door.

Lacey glared at the camera.

I know what you're thinking. You're thinking that you should've killed me already. Carrie sighed. *Maybe it would be too hard for Lacey to reconcile with this after all?*

Lacey retrieved the scalpel from her pocket and flicked off the protective cap with a thumb.

Tobias turned, holding up his blood-stained weapon.

'Tobias,' Lacey said. 'Please.'

'You forgot,' he said.

Carrie smiled.

Tobias approached her, blood-stained weapon raised.

It's for the best, Lacey.

Lacey backed away.

Just kill him, you stupid bitch! Carrie went for the button to instruct her to do so, then changed her mind. *No. This is on you. Prove yourself to me. What is it you really want?*

Lacey threw down her scalpel.

Silly.

Tobias charged, swinging the scalpel, and cut Lacey's outstretched palms.

Pathetic.

Lacey swooped and retreated backwards in another direction.

Tobias followed, slicing the air with his blade.

'You're Lacey Ray,' Carrie said out loud without pushing the button. 'Lacey *fucking* Ray. You're a killer. Don't you yield.'

Lacey looked at the camera as she backed away. 'Let me out, Carrie. I won't hurt him.'

Was this it, then? Was this really the end? Carrie banged the table. *Then die. Die for all I care. You aren't fit for that name anymore.* Carrie switched off the monitor and killed the sound. *You're both welcome to each other. Weeks from now, I will throw Jake's severed head into the cell, and all three of you can rot together. And I, the real Lacey Ray, will enjoy what you turned your back on.*

She looked back to the other monitor.

Still alive, just barely. Holden had been weakened to the point where Vinnie had considered it safe to release him from his bonds. The doctor was naked, face down on the floor, with large swathes of skin hanging from various parts of his body. Vinnie was sitting, with Holden's head between his knees; his hands were full of loose skin, and he was pulling it, working it off his victim's lower back. At the other side of Holden, Keith, who was naked, was in the process of leaning over the mutilated doctor, grunting as he rutted him.

Carrie switched off the monitor.

That was too much.

Even for her.

FREE PASS

*Y*orke sat alone in the hospital gardens. Despite the signs instructing him not to do so, he smoked. He was never usually one to break rules, but he figured that being pistol whipped and shot by his best friend entitled him to a free pass.

His last drag on the first cigarette was deliberately long, and he opened his lungs to full capacity so the flesh wound on his back would burn. The pain reminded him that he was still alive. After recent events, a little reminder wouldn't go amiss.

Jake.

When the hell did you get back?

Yorke blew out a cloud of smoke, shaking his head and smiling grimly.

It'd only been a short time since Yorke had called Jake in God knows where and told him about his ex-wife's death in the gas explosion. So did that somehow make it his fault that Jake had landed back home like a lightning bolt?

Yorke took another drag and blew it out.

No. That wasn't fair. What choice had he had? Not tell his best friend that Sheila had died in suspicious circumstances and that his child was now living with her mother? Roles reversed, he'd have expected the same phone call.

He recalled making that call and listening to Jake's fear on the phone. He'd been intent on returning home—seems he hadn't been bluffing. Couldn't he have done it more quietly, though?

Quietly?

He snorted.

Quietly? Jake Pettman? What planet are you living on, Mike?

Still, showing up with an Article SE kill squad had to rate quite highly on the all-time list of grand entrances.

He dropped the cigarette on the ground and stubbed it out.

And what'd Jake got himself into? Running with Article SE again?

Because it'd most definitely been them. Who else would've the motive and the means to hunt down and eradicate a cell like that?

Had they threatened Frank, Jake's son? Is that what'd pulled him back in again?

It was the only thing that made sense. Not that it made it right. I mean, who was Jake now? He certainly wasn't the man he remembered. Watching him shoot an unarmed man point blank in the face was something he could never unsee.

He put another cigarette in his mouth, lit it, took a deep breath, and closed his eyes. Patricia would kill him if she smelled it on his breath. But right now, he was so fixated on the image of Jake executing someone so mercilessly that he struggled to care.

He heard a cough behind him, threw down his cigarette, and stamped on it.

'Busted,' Robinson said.

Yorke sighed. 'Waste of a good cigarette.'

'How's the back?' Robinson asked, sitting alongside him.

'Stinging. I was just thinking how much I appreciated it. It makes me feel alive.'

'However, to ensure you definitely stay that way, they're supposed to observe you after a head wound.'

Yorke waved him away. 'I'll be fine.'

'Still, the nurse looked like he'd shat a brick when he found you gone.'

'Why? I made the bed,' Yorke said, looking longingly at his mashed fag.

Robinson eyed him incredulously. 'You're right. There's absolutely no way that you should still be alive. I mean ... *how*? Really? How the fuck?'

'Luck of the devil, I guess.'

'No. You were dealing with the devil. That's why you *should* be dead. No one survives Article SE.'

Not true. Jake did.

And now me.

Yorke shrugged.

'I mean, how could a member of one of their kill squads be such a bad shot?'

Yorke regarded Robinson. He looked immoveable. Why wouldn't he be? He'd spent most of his career on the frontline, fighting organised crime. No one walked from an organised Article SE hit. Not unless, by some miracle, those doing the hit copped it instead. 'I'd prefer not to dwell on it. Especially not tonight. It's all rather raw.'

Robinson nodded. 'I understand.'

Yorke knew he'd only delayed the inevitable; he'd have to engage in a more thorough discussion on it at another date.

'So, anyway, I was dropping by with an update.'

Yorke stared at him, wide-eyed. 'How long were you going to make me wait?'

'At least until you headed back inside. Shall we?'

'I really need the fresh air.'

Robinson tapped one of Yorke's cig butts with the toe of his shoe. 'Fresh air?'

'Nerves are shot. Hardly surprising. Hope it was worth it.'

'It was. The location of the other half of that cell, Mike. Priceless. Absolutely fucking priceless.'

'Yes. And I only had to spend three days pretending to be scum of the earth for it.' He lit another cigarette. 'So you and my wife can damn well put up with me having a cigarette or two.' He took a puff. 'Now, does this update relate to the *surviving* half of the cell going to jail for a long time?'

The other cell members had been holed up in Winchester. During Yorke's second day 'working' for this cell, he'd accompanied one of the terrorists on a visit to this other location. Because the cell had confiscated his mobile when they'd first taken him in, Yorke had no means to contact Robinson, and breaking away from such a close-knit group to get out a message had proved impossible. Still, as soon as the ambulance had picked him up from the bloodbath, Yorke had rushed the message to Robinson as quickly as possible.

Every remaining cell member was now in custody.

It wouldn't bring Sonia, Rob, or Matthew back, but it was something.

Justice was all that remained.

And the wheels were turning.

'*I wonder if Article SE knows there're more of them?*' Robinson had said to Yorke earlier. '*Surely? The members of the cell were never all going to be in one place—keeping all their eggs in one basket, so to speak!*'

'The update?' Yorke asked.

'The cell members were biddable. They're keen to deal—'

'Hang on!' Yorke's blood surge.

Robinson took a deep breath and sighed. 'Are you going to let me fucking finish?'

'We never agreed to deals.'

'For fuck's sake. Let. Me. Finish! We agreed that they'd face justice, and they most certainly will.'

Yorke's heart thrashed in his chest. 'But?'

'There's no *but*; they're going to jail, for a long time. No one is walking away from a child's death. The deal for their information on Article SE is a simple identity change and a relocation to a prison somewhere in the murky lands of the north.'

'It is a bit of a *but*.'

'Really? So we just let them be hacked to pieces in a canteen in a more local prison?'

'You live by the sword and all that.'

'This doesn't sound like you.'

Yorke sighed, threw down his cigarette, and rubbed his temples. 'No, I guess it doesn't. But remember, they didn't just kill Matthew. I saw what they did to him. Barbarians. This lifeline doesn't sit right.'

'If they're dead, they can't feed us information or testify if we ever need them. It's a win for us if they survive because we stop more of the bad guys.'

'Don't even begin to talk to me like a child.'

'Okay. Sorry, but you can be assured that they'll all serve every single day of their sentences.'

'And are they giving you what you need so far?'

Robinson smiled. 'And then some. It's going to be a week of raids. They know a lot, this cell. It seems the Noracell weapons factory is just the tip of the iceberg. We'll deal Article SE some savage blows. They'll reel from this. Fucking reel. Mark my words.'

'As long as the bastards on both sides of this are getting a kicking, it's all good with me.'

Robinson grabbed Yorke's shoulder. 'You swung it, mate.'

'I'm sure sniper Dave would've delivered too.'

Robinson raised an eyebrow. 'Would he?' Another suspicious reference to Yorke's miraculous escape.

'I'm sure,' Yorke lied. Deep down, he knew Jake, this newer version of Jake, wouldn't have spared a total stranger.

'Okay, I'm going to ask you one last time before I hold you at gunpoint. Get back inside. Once you're all warm and snuggly, I'll tell you more wonderful things the cell coughed up.'

Yorke winced as he stood and checked his watch. 'Okay, but you haven't got much time. Visiting hours are finished, and I've a phone call booked in with my long-suffering wife.'

'That's lucky. About the visiting hours, I mean. She won't smell the smoke on your breath.'

Yorke laughed. 'The fact that she's beautiful is what makes me lucky. Have you seen this scar on my face?'

'Jesus. Are you blaming me for that again?'

'Of course. I aim to flag it up in every conversation. Also, has the news actually gone out that I'm alive yet?'

'It's been reported as a media mistake. You were injured but didn't die, as first reported.'

'Good. One of the doctors who popped in earlier recognised me before clocking my name. He went as white as a sheet.'

DEAD SYCAMORE TREE

*J*ake knocked on the front door of the house on Sycamore Street.

Expecting Russ, the smartly dressed leader of the kill squad to open the door, he stepped backwards and waited.

The door didn't open.

He tried a second time, this time readying his hand on the gun beneath his jacket.

Still, no answer.

He chanced the handle. The door was unlocked and glided open.

He entered quietly, closed the door behind and engaged the thumbturn lock. If someone returned while he was searching the house, he'd like to hear them entering. In the case of Carrie, this could very well prove the difference between life and death.

He checked the entire house, including the kitchen which contained the carved-up corpse.

No one was here.

Walter had instructed him to return here, following the mission, to check in with Russ.

He wasn't overly concerned because news that he'd fulfilled his end of the bargain would get back to Walter regardless, but it was peculiar. Especially as he'd been minding Sam Lane.

Still, Walter had been explicit in his order to Jake to come back, so it seemed prudent to wait a short time in case Russ and Sam had made a short trip out.

Jake didn't want to ruffle any feathers after coming this far. But an hour before sunrise, he was gone. No longer.

This house was cursed.

He searched the house again and managed to recover a fresh burner phone from Lacey's room. He plugged into the socket by the front door and then sat down on the bottom step. Should anybody make a sudden appearance he would have the upper hand.

As soon as he sat, his mind returned to his concerns over Yorke. Not just over his health, although this was obviously a major factor, but over the fact that he'd been in a cell safe house, posing as a terrorist. Undercover? Surely.

He nodded. Had to be. Yorke didn't have a bad bone in his body.

As the hours slipped by at the bottom of the stairs, Jake gave careful thought to the situation with Lacey. At first, he thought it was just disappointment that she'd driven away, and he'd been unable to fulfil his side of the bargain. But then he realised that it wasn't only about that.

And he finally confronted what he'd been too preoccupied to confront before now.

Tobias Ray.

A ten-year-old boy. A *vulnerable and damaged* ten-year-old boy.

So, Jake's disappointment came down to two clear reasons. Firstly, without his help, Tobias was more likely to fall foul of this crazy doctor. And secondly, if Tobias was, by some miracle, rescued, he'd be under the care of Lacey and Carrie!

Jake was a lot of things, but could he turn a blind eye to that?

He thought of the carved-up corpse in the kitchen. *The home life of a ten-year-old?*

Leaving that to happen would make Jake something else altogether.

Tobias *had* to go back into the system, and Lacey wouldn't have that—not without Jake dead at her feet. Which kind of left him no choice really, did it?

He'd been lying to himself, and Lacey, all this time.

Jake sighed, now knowing, with no small degree of pain, what his next move was. He checked that the burner phone was charged and made it.

～

AFTERWARDS, feeling like shit over his betrayal, but knowing it was the only play, he threw his new burner phone, now on silent, into his rucksack.

It felt strange to think that his whole life existed within this rucksack. A change of clothes, some toiletries, the last of his dollars and pounds, but, most importantly, his photographs.

He reached in and took out the dog-eared photograph of Frank in his Southampton shirt. God, how different his lad had looked the other day on the playground. Taller than all the other boys.

In the same way I'd been.

With a smile, Jake recalled his boy bursting from the

others with the ball at his feet.

Better at football, though. I couldn't shoot for toffee.

He wiped away a tear. Was Frank *now* safe? Was this certain?

Jake had to be confident in everything he'd done.

The leverage from Madden, the threat of emails, and his vow to work off his debts. It was all there. In place. Which was kind of why he was so hesitant to leave Sycamore Street. Article SE may wonder where he'd gone; they might even *suspect* he'd run again. Unthinkable. But it was now almost four in the morning, and he'd given them long enough. They weren't coming back. He would reach out to them as soon as he'd found a place to lie low. Clear his debts once and for all.

And when that's done—he looked at the photograph—*I'll buy you the latest shirts, son. I'll take you to every game. I'll watch you score goals in every single one of your own matches.*

He pressed the photograph to his chest, knowing he was probably kidding himself.

You're a dangerous man, Jake. A magnet for the darkness in the world. Behind you are footsteps of blood. Many, many footsteps. Do you really believe that the ones in front of you will be any different?

He put the photograph of his son in the bag with the others and zippered it.

He had to hope. Without hope, what was there? Really?

He stood, threw the backpack on, then grabbed the gun that'd been sleeping beside him—

The thumbturn lock on the front door rotated.

Clunk.

Jake's breath caught in his throat.

Carrie or Lacey?

He lifted the gun and fought to keep the gun steady despite the adrenaline.

The door opened towards him, blocking his view, initially, but also keeping him hidden from whoever it was.

The person walked in, and Jake clocked their profile.

For a split second, he was confused. But recognition quickly dawned on him. Carrie in Lacey's clothing. She held a rolled-up plastic shopping bag in her left hand.

He kicked the front door shut behind her, then aimed the gun, making it very apparent he was on the verge of using it.

She smiled. He didn't like it. She had a look of victory about her. Also, blood stained her blue dress despite no visible injuries.

'Where's Lacey?'

'Didn't make it, I'm afraid.'

Jake's blood ran cold. 'You're lying.'

Carrie shrugged, grinning.

'Why're you *fucking* smiling, then?'

'She made poor decisions at the end. She had a good life. I'll see that she's honoured. I will take her identity.' She slid her right palm down the front of the blue dress. 'How do I look?'

Feeling panicked, Jake controlled his breathing. 'Tobias?'

'Same. Same. Holden, too.' She waved her hand. 'All gone. Just me now. Me'—her grin widened—'and you.'

The thought of Lacey and Tobias dead made his stomach turn. *It could be a lie. It probably is a lie. She's just trying to unsettle, delay the inevitable. Focus on the here and now. Just kill her. Do the world a fucking favour.*

'Soon to be just you,' Jake said. He slipped his finger around the trigger.

'You may want to rethink that,' she said, looking as calm as ever.

'I'll do my *thinking* when you're a corpse.'

'Yes, and you'll be filled with regret ... and torment *after* you open this bag. In fact, you'll probably put a bullet in your own head. I can't see how else you'll cope.'

He looked at the rolled-up plastic bag again. *She's toying with you.* 'Not interested,' Jake said.

She shrugged. 'Up to you.' She closed her eyes and pointed at the centre of her head. 'Ready when you are.'

He started to squeeze the trigger—

His eyes fell to the bag again. He loosened his finger.

Shit! She's bluffing. Just fucking do it!

He tried again but failed. He took one of his hands from the weapon and thumped the wall. 'What's in the bag?'

'Take a look.'

'I *said,* what's in the fucking bag?'

'And I *said,* take a fucking look.' She offered it.

This is madness ... End her ... just end her ...

He snatched the bag.

Keeping the gun on her, he held the top of the bag with one hand and shook it so that it rolled out. Heart thumping in his chest, he prepared to look inside.

'Some context first, Jake.'

He glared at her.

'Before you came into my life, I demanded that Lacey tell me everything about you. You could call it due diligence. Anyway, she did. She told me *everything* about you. And she *showed* me things, too.'

The sudden coldness in Jake's stomach was like nothing he'd ever experienced before. He looked at the bag he was about to open. 'What's in the bag?'

'She showed me your son. She showed me where he lived.'

The cold in his stomach moved quick, engulfing his entire body. He staggered backwards until he was leaning against the wall.

God, no?

Surely, no?

'What's in the bag?' he pleaded.

'Open it and see.'

His whole body seemed to be folding in on itself, and he wasn't even aware if he was standing or down on the floor anymore. The only thing on his mind was the plastic in his hand. He couldn't take his gaze from it. 'Frank?' Then, without even realising he'd made the move, he had thrust Carrie against the wall and pressed the gun against her head. 'I'm *going* to kill you. I'm going to *fucking* kill you!'

'It isn't your son. It isn't Frank.'

He scrunched his face in confusion and backed away from her, his mind racing. And then the disorientation momentarily freed him from its grasp, and he felt some relief. 'Thank God ... thank God.'

He tore open the bag to expose a syringe, alongside a severed finger, still wearing a familiar wedding ring and an engagement ring with a green jewel on it. '*What?*' He turned his head slowly from side to side, disgusted. '*Who?*' But then he remembered where he'd seen those rings before. 'Oh God.' His eyes widened as he stared at the finger. Then, he glared at Carrie. 'How could you? His grandmother? What kind of monster—'

'*Relax,* she's not dead! I just took that to prove I'd been there. If you didn't recognise it, well, I have a photo on my phone showing her all trussed up. And she didn't suffer. See that syringe? It's loaded with etorphine. I gave her a dose of that. She'll live to fight another day, albeit without her finger. Your son, on the other hand ... well, that depends on you.'

'Where the fuck is he?' He shook his head, the cold sensation consuming his body again. 'Where is he?'

'Alive ... safe. For now.'

'Why're you doing this?'

'Because you owe me.'

Still clutching the bag, he pounded his chest. 'I'm here. Take it out on me.'

'Oh, I intend to. And careful with that bag; you need the syringe.'

'But why Frank?'

'Just to get your attention. Nothing more. Look. Would I still be standing if I hadn't taken out that insurance policy?' She raised an eyebrow. 'I think we all know the answer to that! So here's the thing; I need you to inject yourself with that needle, then we can get to work.'

She turned her head, and he followed her gaze to the kitchen door.

Surely not?

His chest felt like it was closing in on itself.

'Now,' Carrie insisted.

'No. That's ridiculous.'

'I think you'll find it's you who's being ridiculous.' She checked her watch. 'Two minutes.'

'Until?'

She regarded him, dropping the smile for once. 'Frank dies.'

'What? How?'

'Tick tock.' She nodded at his syringe.

'Where is he? Outside in the car?'

'No. But take a look if you want. Waste some time.' She eyed her watch.

Jake felt like everything around him was melting away. 'What've you done to him?'

'He's safe for another'—she squinted at her watch—'one and a half minutes.'

'Fuck you,' he hissed.

'A phone call will put it all right. He'll be back to his life with Grandmother and her nine remaining digits.'

'Who do you have to phone?'

'None of your business. Do you want to know how much time you have left?'

'How do I know you'll make that call?'

'I guarantee it.'

'What's a fucking guarantee from you?'

'All you have.' She looked at her watch again. 'Tick tock.'

He glanced at the kitchen again. He had no choice.

It was for Frank.

He caught Carrie smiling, and before he knew it, he'd lost control of himself again, and had her down on her knees with the gun pinned to the crown of her head. He suddenly felt like he was outside the house looking in at himself through a window.

'In forty seconds your life will end in one of two ways,' Carrie said. 'At my hand or your own when you learn what has happened to Frank.'

Fuck!

'Tick tock.'

He pulled the syringe from his bag and removed the cap.

Madness. Absolute madness.

He sat on the step and pressed the tip to the fleshy underside of his arm. 'He lives. You promise.'

'Pinky swear,' she said.

'Fuck you,' he said and injected himself.

∽

JAKE OPENED HIS EYES. Bright light threatened to split his head in two. He squeezed them shut again, trying to come to terms with the pain. Then the memories flooded back, making pain the least of his worries. He willed his eyes to open and forced them to stay that way until they started to adjust.

'*Frank*!'

Everything was too bloody slow in reforming in front of him.

'*Frank*!'

The room stank of death, and he knew he was in the kitchen—a place of rotting flesh and body parts in jars. Carrie's souvenirs.

'*Frank*!' His voice sounded clearer in his own head. His senses were exploding into life. The room around him was knitting itself together at speed now.

'He's here,' Carrie said.

Jake retched. Vomit warmed his chin, then his chest. The gagging wasn't drug induced. It was panic induced.

His boy, Frank, was just in front of him, bound to a chair, trembling.

He coughed out more vomit and cleared his throat so he could speak. 'No. This wasn't what you *said*!'

'I said he'd live. And he will.'

Jake stared into his son's wide, tearful eyes; they spoke of terror and a world that'd never be the same for him again. He emitted a low moan, not from pain but from true despair.

He tried to reach for his child, to reassure him, but it was only at this point that he realised his hands were taped to the arm rests. 'Frank. Are you hurt?'

Frank shook his head. It caused tears to streak his face.

'Everything will be fine. I promise. Okay?'

Frank nodded. 'I'm scared, Daddy.'

Inside, at these words, Jake despaired, but he pressed it down and back, forcing instead a false calmness onto his face. 'I know. I've missed you.'

Forcing back tears, Jake looked around. The remains of the

man Jake had put out of his misery had been laid neatly at the far wall, the multitude of jars containing his pieces neatly stacked beside him. Jake already knew what lay on the table in front of him, between him and Frank, but he'd deliberately not looked closely. He turned his eyes to it.

Jars filled with yellowing liquid. Six wide, four deep. Enough for twenty-four souvenirs. Twenty-four pieces of him.

He glared up at Carrie, standing to his right and holding secateurs.

She was ready to burn his whole fucking world to the ground.

Now he was unable to hold in the despair. He started to rage.

He writhed in the chair and tried to pull both hands free of the arm rests.

Carrie stepped behind him and applied pressure to the chair to stop him toppling.

Eventually, gasping for air, he slumped down in the chair.

'You think it was easy, getting you from the stairs to the kitchen and up into this chair? I wasn't about to take any chances. That tape is tried and tested. Trust me on that one.'

'You let my son out of here.'

'No,' she said, standing beside him now. 'Your boy will live, as promised, but he stays.'

Jake suddenly felt as if he was sinking away. He shook his head. 'You can't.' He looked at his trembling, pale boy, then up at her. 'There must be something I can do.'

'No. I'm sorry. There isn't.' She worked her secateurs. 'These were Lacey's. She always spoke fondly of them. She also spoke fondly of you, even though I knew and tried to warn her that you'd eventually turn on her.'

Jake flinched. Carrie had been right. Still, at least, Lacey wasn't alive to experience his betrayal.

Carrie examined her secateurs. 'How fitting it will be to use them now. A tribute, if you'd like. The new Lacey using the tools of the old.' She grinned. 'Yes, I like that.'

Jake focused on his boy and shook his head, willing himself not to cry, or explode in anger again. His poor boy was shaking in his chair. How much would Frank have to experience before this was finally over?

'I'm pleading with you,' Jake said. 'Please.'

'Why should I listen? After what you took from me? Joe Wheaton destroyed so much of who I could've been.'

Jake gestured to where her victim rested. 'There was nothing left of him. You'd taken nearly everything!'

She snorted. 'I'd barely started, as you're about to find out.'

'But, my son. Please, I'm begging you. Take him home first.' He raised his voice. 'You take him—'

'I want him to watch. I want him to learn.'

The world spun around Jake again. 'You can't—'

'Lacey had a son, and she will again.'

Jake closed his eyes for fear of passing out; everything seemed to be dissolving.

'I'll take good care of him.'

He was in hell. There was no other explanation. And his words from earlier revisited him, pounding at his heart and soul.

You're a dangerous man, Jake. A magnet for the darkness in the world. Behind you are footsteps of blood. Many, many footsteps. Do you really believe the ones in front of you will be any different?

He shook his head. 'No. He's my son. You can't … please.'

'Open your eyes and look at him.'

'No, I—'

'Open your eyes and look at Frank or the first piece will be from him.'

Jake could feel the tears building behind his eyelids. 'No, I can't bear it ... I ...'

'No ... Don't!' Frank shouted. 'No ... please ... please ... leave me alone. Daddy, help ... help!'

Jake opened his eyes and saw that she'd slipped one of Frank's fingers between the blades of the secateurs.

'Stop! I'm looking,' Jake said, hot tears streaking down his face.

Carrie released Frank's finger.

Jake stared at Frank. 'I'm sorry, son. I'm sorry ... so, so sorry.'

Carrie walked back to Jake. 'When Lacey told me all about you, she didn't mention this.' She stroked his wet face with the secateurs. 'She didn't mention the weakness.'

He recoiled from the secateurs, but she just leaned in and moved the blade across his face to his nose.

'Destroy me, but not *him*,' Jake said. 'I beg you.'

Carrie nodded. 'I'll rebuild him. I'll rebuild him in my image. In Lacey's image.'

Jake spat a mouthful of tears in her face. 'Fuck you, monster.'

She rubbed the spit off her face, smiled at the saliva shining on her hand, then leaned in to take a piece of him.

Jake didn't want to scream in agony in front of his son, but he had little choice, especially when he saw his ear floating in the first jar.

～

EARLIER ...

.   .   .

Yorke had been instructed to stay awake until a certain time. Standard procedure when knocked unconscious. He read a fitness magazine, and, while doing so, vowed to take on a triathlon the following year.

Why not?

If he could survive Article SE and his psychotic best friend's rampage, he could survive a triathlon!

When a nurse came into his room, he expected it was because observation time was over, and he would be advised to grab some sleep. Little did they know that when they gave him the all-clear, he was jumping ship and grabbing a taxi.

It may have been the middle of the night, but he wasn't staying here any longer than necessary.

He'd grab some paracetamol first, though; the last ones were wearing off, and his back was really starting to burn.

However, the nurse wasn't here to tell him to get some shuteye. She was here to tell him that someone had called the hospital to speak to Yorke.

'On police business,' she said.

～

The nurse allowed Yorke to use one of the hospital offices, which stood vacant in the early hours. The call was patched through. Even before he heard the voice, he knew who it'd be. Who else would be forced to call Salisbury Hospital to speak to him? Jake didn't have Yorke's new personal number.

'Mike?'

'Don't worry, I'm alive.'

Jake sighed.

'That better be the sound of relief.'

'It is, yeah. I'm sorry,' Jake said. 'Are you all right?'

'What do you think? Still ...' He broke off.

'*Still* what?'

It was Yorke's turn to sigh. 'Ah, whatever. It's good to hear your voice, buddy.'

'Yours, too, mate.'

'Now, do you want to tell me what the *hell* is going on?'

'Hell.' Jake snorted. 'Now there's the right word for it. How about you tell me what's going on in your life, then I'll get to mine.'

Yorke guffawed. 'Maybe you should start! After all, you're the one who almost killed me!'

'You can't kill someone who's already dead, can you?'

Fair point. 'You talk first. I'm the one with the badge, and you're … well, shit, I don't know what you are anymore! Did I really watch you shoot someone point blank in front of me? I'm kind of hoping it was some kind of nightmare.'

Jake didn't respond. Yorke simply listened to him take a deep breath and exhale.

'Where're you anyway?' Yorke asked.

'I'll get to that soon. Look, I had to do that, back at the house. You were waking up. They would've killed you.'

Made sense. 'Okay. So, can I go back to assuming you're an angel, then?'

Jake laughed. 'Well, that's a stretch. Look, I'm the one against the ropes here.'

'As usual?' Yorke added sarcastically.

Jake grunted.

'Go on, then,' Yorke pressed. 'What were you going to say?'

'I need your story first. Just the way it is.'

Yorke guffawed. 'You're serious, aren't you?'

'I'm afraid so. I love you, mate, but really, who do I trust anymore? The world went to shit for me a while back.'

Bloody self-pity, again. Yorke shook his head. *Whatever. I'll go first.* If he finally got the truth out of Jake, it would be worth telling him what had gone down. Yorke told his tale. A few times he stood, ready to pace, then remembered each time at the last second that he wasn't on a mobile, and the phone wasn't cordless.

Afterwards, Jake gave his verdict. 'Fuck.'

'Insightful.'

'No, I mean, fuck!'

Yorke said, 'No ... sorry. Still not getting anything of value.' He drummed his fingers on the table. 'Want to try again?'

'You've been through it, mate. Sorry. Sounds awful!'

'Well, what did you think when you saw me with that terror cell? That I was on a weekend retreat?'

'I didn't know what to think, to be honest. I just didn't want you to die.'

Yorke swallowed. 'Well, I guess I should be grateful that you put some thought into that!'

'I'm so glad I didn't fuck it all up for you. That you got some of them in custody. What those bastards did ...'

'Yes. We don't need to go through it again. I was there, remember?'

'Must have been hard. Sorry.'

See, you self-pitying prick! It isn't just you who goes through the wringer. 'So, you trust me now?' Yorke asked.

'Never didn't.'

'You said—'

'I know. Probably just trying to delay the inevitable. Having to tell you everything.'

'Why?'

'Because you already think fuck-all of me.'

'Not true.' *There are some things, yes, but ...* 'You're my mate. So, come on. I've shown you my scars—given to me by you, I hasten to add—now show me yours.'

Jake told him.

As he listened, Yorke's anxiety levels spiralled, and he wished to God he could just have a fourth cigarette before normal life resumed and Patricia outlawed it until the end of his days.

Afterwards, Jake said, 'What? Not even a solitary '*fuck*!'?'

'I don't really know how to respond.'

'Go with your gut.'

'I'm horrified, but that's as much as I can verbalise! I don't know whether I'm horrified with you or just this situation in general. I just don't know.'

'Well, at least you have confirmation of what you always suspected.'

'Which is?'

'That I'm a killer,' Jake said.

Yorke noticed someone walk past the office and look in. They held up a hand in greeting and then, fortunately, moved on.

'I knew you were a killer long ago. You staked Borya Turgenev, remember? In my home?'

'Was forced into that one. There've been others. With some, I didn't need my arm twisting.'

Yorke felt a wave of nausea. 'How many?'

Jake sighed. He didn't answer.

Probably for the best.

'I take it that we're not meeting up for drinks, then?' Yorke asked, his heart heavy over the inevitable. If he ever saw Jake again, he'd have to arrest him. Best mate or not, it was who Yorke was. He couldn't change that. Jake would know this. 'Maybe you should just leave again now that Frank's safe,' Yorke said.

'Or you'll bring me down?'

'What kind of question is that?'

'Hmm ... what kind of answer is that,' Jake said. 'Don't

worry. I know the reality. I know the consequences of my choices. So, do you still want to know where I am?'

Yorke drummed his fingers on the table. *Good question.*

'Mike?'

'I don't know. Are you in danger?'

'No more than usual.' He laughed.

'Do you want to put me in this position?' Yorke asked.

'Listen. This isn't about me anyway. I'm about to give you some more dangerous fish to catch.'

'Who?'

'Lacey Ray and the nurse who helped her escape.'

Yorke stood, stretching the phone cable. Blood rushed to his head. 'Come again?'

'You heard?'

'You're with Lacey?'

'Sorry, did I leave that part out before?'

'Yep, along with the name of the bent officer who gave you the leverage. Is there anything else hidden? Secrets you want to share? Lacey Ray. Bloody hell! Isn't she more dangerous than Article SE?' Yorke snorted.

'We have an understanding. At least, we did, *until* this phone call. I'm going to give you an address. *Her* address.'

Jesus Christ. Yorke shook his head. Lacey Ray. Bad, bad news. So many police hours invested into finding her. And Jake knowing her location!

What was going on in the world?

'Now, you're going to need armed response there; do you understand me? Armed response. You know how dangerous she is, and the other one, Carrie, is worse. Mike, listen carefully. What you find here, it beggars belief! You take *all* precautions. There are at least two victims on site. One in the kitchen, and one beneath the floorboards in the lounge.'

'Sweet Jesus.'

'Jesus, or any other of His kind, isn't operating in Sycamore Street. I can assure you of that. But listen. You can't just come flying in, sirens blaring, when they aren't here. Lacey hasn't survived this long from stupidity, and trust me, this Carrie is wild and dangerous. If you arrive before them, it's game over. You must wait until they're both in the house before you come in.'

'I don't want you waiting in that house either then Jake, do you hear me?'

Jake grunted. 'I get that. Wasn't planning to! There's a ginnel opposite. Ten minutes after this call, I'll position myself there. Keep an eye on the house. Less conspicuous than you and a team. As soon as both your catches are indoors, I'll alert you; I'll need your personal number though. And make sure you get close enough to be ready but not so close that they could notice you. Okay?'

'I don't know.'

'They need to be back in custody. Pronto.'

'I get that, but it sounds—'

'Nothing to think about. It's the right move. There's one more thing.'

'Go on.'

'They might have Tobias Young with them. He's ten.'

'I don't understand! *Tobias Young!* Again, after last time? What have I missed?'

Jake told him.

'Bloody hell.'

'You got a pen?'

Yorke found one on the table and scribbled down the address that Jake gave him. Then, with his head reeling and his grasp on reality suddenly feeling tentative at best, he gave Jake his personal number.

'Now get out of that house,' Yorke said.

'Just about to. I waited around to see if these bastards, Article SE, would come back. They aren't showing.'

'Good.'

'So, I'll speak to you from that ginnel, okay?'

～

YORKE WOKE ROBINSON.

It was his best option. His own team were *only* just getting over the revelation that he was alive and in hospital. They would probably send a psychiatrist to check him out first before taking any of this news at face value!

There was no time for any faffing.

Robinson was his best bet and, in his opinion, still owed him.

Robinson was demanding full disclosure before he granted the use of his team though, such as: 'Where the hell is the information coming from? Who's contacting you to tell us when to move in?'

Yorke refused to say but advised him that catching Lacey Ray would be no minor development.

'Bringing in Lacey Ray *after* the cell, sir. You're going to be toast of the entire force!'

Robinson snorted, 'I'm too old and jaded to give a shit about a pat on the fucking back. How I got the intel to pull her back in will surely come under scrutiny at some point. Is there anything more you can give me?'

'I'm sorry, but if my contact comes good, I'll deal with it after.'

'If?'

'They will.'

'Sounds like career suicide.'

'Or a promotion if you deliver.'

'I'm about to retire.'

'They'll throw you a bigger party.'

'For fuck's sake … obviously, I can't say no, can I? She's a fucking serial killer. How do I live with myself if she got away again?'

'I wouldn't let you live with it.'

'I don't doubt it. You're not coming though. When you get the alert from your contact, just forward it to me.'

'In that case, I'll drive myself there and handle it.'

'Ah … for fuck's sake, not again,' Robinson said. 'Was our last stand-off prior to your undercover mission not enough for one lifetime? Do you ever give me a fucking break?'

'You'll catch plenty of breaks in your retirement.'

'With you on my back, I'm not going to make it. Listen. Come, but you're not going in; do you understand?'

'Understand.'

Robinson and his team picked up Yorke in one of two vans. Armed response had been quickly briefed on the mission. Throughout the journey, the officers were filled with adrenaline and talked incessantly. Yorke, meanwhile, suffered in silence with the back wound and a fair helping of paranoia that Jake was still too close to danger. Serial killers and gunfire weren't a predictable combination.

Robinson still had no idea about Jake's recent involvements. Hopefully he'd never need to know. But if he did find out, Jake would only have himself to blame for his downfall. No man was above justice, even his closest friends.

Still, Yorke knew it'd be an awful burden for him to bear. Watching Jake going into custody would be like watching a younger brother, or even a son, going to jail.

But still, wasn't this just selfish of Yorke? Weren't his feelings secondary to the wheels of justice?

If Jake was proven to be a criminal, he *should* suffer the punishment. That was the reality.

As per Jake's instructions, armed response parked several streets back and waited for the signal.

Yorke, ignoring various random conversations, stared at his watch. The second hand raced, and the minute hand marched, and all the time, he could taste bile in his mouth and feel his heartbeat in every part of his body.

Eventually, when he couldn't stomach conversations about reality television any longer, he exited the rear of the van, moaning about his weak bladder and the need to find a dark alley.

He sprinted down a ginnel that connected to an adjacent street. Midway, in the darkness, he dialled the number Jake had phoned him on earlier. No answer.

He listened for ringing in the distance. Nothing. But that didn't prove anything; it'd be unlikely that Jake would leave the ring on.

After finishing up on this ginnel, he tackled the next one, knowing this was surely the one that Jake would be on. Because this led straight onto Sycamore Street.

Midway down this ginnel, he tried Jake's number again. Again, no answer, and again, no sound of ringing phones in the distance.

Shit.

He ran to the end of the ginnel and looked out onto Sycamore Street.

Jake was nowhere in sight.

$\sim$

JAKE'S VISION PULSED, while the taste of blood grew richer, and the acrid stench of the carved-up corpse made him gag. Each stab of agony delivered by Carrie sent *every* sense into over-drive. But no sense splintered him quite like the sound of his boy, his *child*, crying and pleading for his father's life.

Carrie dropped another piece of Jake into a jar.

Jake looked at his left hand. Two fingers missing.

He wanted to scream, roar from the top of his lungs. The agony was insane, but he forced it back, *inside*. He didn't want to do that to his son. Whimpers and moans were all he allowed himself.

'Please ... leave my daddy alone,' Frank said.

'Enough ... enough,' Jake begged, looking at Carrie. 'There must be some part of you ... please ... some part of you that must know ... must *understand* ... how wrong this is. Let him go. At least do that ... I beg of you. Let my son go.'

She knelt in front of him, her head tilted slightly, examining him. She touched her chest with the bloody secateurs. 'A part of me? Elaborate. What part would that be?'

He dropped his head and realised it was useless.

She'd pick away at him until he remained nothing more than a fleshy husk.

And every single moment would be burned into the memory of his beloved child.

His mind wandered to Yorke. It was soul destroying to know he was so close, yet so far, waiting on a phone call that'd never come.

He felt sympathy for Yorke having to discover him this way. The sight of Jake's demise would tear out his heart. Yes, forget that Yorke would've slapped handcuffs on Jake the second he saw him. That was different. Arresting him would've killed a part of him inside, and he'd have lived with the trauma of his choice until the end of his days, but that was the price of justice. And Yorke would never turn his back on *justice*.

Finding Jake slaughtered, though?

In pieces?

Was there any coming back from that for Yorke?

Was there any coming back from this for his son?

'Come on,' Carrie said, opening the secateurs again. 'What part are you talking about?' She slid one blade up each nostril.

'Humanity,' he said and closed his eyes; the bite of the secateurs set everything on fire.

There was no suppressing this scream, no matter how much he wanted to for Frank.

Afterwards, out of breath, slumping in his bonds, he looked at the blood washing over his chest. 'Fuck you,' he murmured.

She pulled his hair and lifted his head back up. She showed him the open secateurs.

'Fuck ... you ...' The words dribbled out with blood.

This time she pinched his entire nose between the blades.

He closed his eyes.

He listened to Frank crying and pleading.

No more.

This was it.

He just wanted to die.

Put him out of his misery, but, more importantly, end this fucking show before it ruined his son's mind.

'Kill me,' he pleaded.

'All in good time.' The secateurs tightened. 'Now brace yourself, this one's going to be messy.'

∽

YORKE OBSERVED the front of the house on Sycamore Street. From the front of the house, the upstairs lights looked to be off, while the windows downstairs glowed.

When his phone rang, his heart almost stopped. *Jake? Thank God.*

He looked at the screen and sighed. *Robinson.*

'Sir?'

'How's the piss? Where the fuck are you?'

'Sycamore Street.'

'Which bit of 'stay the fuck in the van' was lost on you?'

'I'm going in.'

'Why?'

Yorke sighed. He was at a dead end—there was nowhere else to go. 'Because I think my best friend is in there. That's why.'

'Who?'

'Jake Pettman.'

'What? Your copper mate who disappeared—'

'Yes, he's back.'

'I don't understand.'

Yorke sighed. 'You didn't understand how I survived the kill squad. Now you know. He was part of it!'

'For fuck's sake! He's bent and still involved with Article SE and you're all on your own. Stand the fuck down, Mike. We're coming *now*.'

'Come now, yes.' He sighed. 'But I can't stand down. I'm not having him going down in a shootout. We're taking him in alive.'

'If he's bent, you don't owe him anything.'

Yorke recalled the night Jake had taken down Borya Turgenev and stopped Patricia from being murdered. 'That's where you're wrong.'

He hung up and crossed the road, wincing over the burn in his lower back, which had been kicking up a right fuss since his earlier sprint down the ginnels. He reached the other side of the road and touched the area of the wound, then looked at the blood on his fingers, confirming that the stitches were probably torn. 'Shit.'

He beheld the house again and considered. Knowing what Lacey Ray was capable of, he determined that the front door was suicide and slipped around the side of the house instead. Moving at a brisk pace, while maintaining caution, was difficult with a wound that throbbed to high heaven, but he gave it a go.

Ahead, at the rear of the house, was a glowing window. Beyond that, a side door. He crouched and peered through the corner of the glass at a sink and some scattered crockery—the back of a dishevelled kitchen.

Gritting his teeth against the pain in his back, he crawled beneath the window and eased himself up. An ear-piercing scream froze the blood in his veins. He sucked in a deep breath and peered in with wide eyes.

First, he sighted a bloody corpse cast to one side of the room, surrounded in some kind of clutter. Then he saw the back of a large man, presumably Jake. Opposite him was a young boy. Yorke's breath caught in his throat. *Frank?*

And who the hell was that leaning over Jake, messing with him while he begged and screamed? Was that Lacey? Or the other one? That nurse?

Yorke put a hand over his mouth, distrustful of his own reactions. A sudden cry of alarm, a shout of fear, a moan of despair—neither response would be a surprise in so bleak a situation.

Adrenaline raced through him, and a sudden desire to burst into the kitchen and help Jake and Frank filled him.

He darted for the kitchen door and gripped the handle.

Stop.

Lunacy, she could be armed.

Draw her out.

He knocked hard on the door, looked both ways, and went with his gut.

The rear of the house.

He covered the remainder of the side path and swooped around to the back garden.

Yorke's mind reeled from the atrocity, but he had adrenaline and used it to stay focused. He spotted a plank of wood among some debris at the edge of the garden and claimed it. Then he approached the brick wall at the back of the house, just beside the corner and the path.

He heard the back door opening. Sweat dripped over his forehead. He blinked it out of his eyes.

He waited, listening for a voice or footsteps.

Nothing.

Just the sound of moaning and weeping coming from inside that hellhole.

Come on ... come on ... whoever you are — just make a move.

Maybe she was very light on her feet? Maybe she was making her way towards him, and he couldn't hear her?

His heart beat faster, and he tightened his grip on the wood.

What should he do?

The urge to turn and bear down on the kitchen pulled at Yorke in the same way it had pulled on him to burst through the door before. But, like last time, he considered the possibility that she was armed. After all, Jake *had* been armed. So, Lacey or that nurse could now be in possession of his gun.

Shit.

But he couldn't just stand here all fucking night!

Five seconds, Mike. Five seconds. If she hasn't walked into your plank of wood by then, you go round. Otherwise, she finishes off Jake and his kid.

One ... two ...

Jake moaned louder still.

Three ...

He looked at the plank held high his hands. *Ready ...*

Four ...

'Who's there?' A woman's voice. Close. Thank God. She'd bitten. 'Lacey?'

So it was the nurse.

Another step ...

'I've *got* a gun,' the nurse said.

Inches away! Get this right, Mike. He spun around the corner, swinging the plank.

The wood crashed into the side of her head. Off balance, the shot she got off missed. She crashed into the brick wall.

A second swing. This time her hand. The sight of the gun spinning away in the air was satisfying.

Another swing. Centre of her head. She crumpled to the ground.

He raised the plank, ready if necessary.

It wasn't. Her eyes were closed, and blood had suddenly drenched her hair and forehead.

He cast the plank aside and swooped for the weapon. Holding the gun, he stared down at her, wide-eyed, wondering if he'd, in fact, killed her.

Then he pounced over her and burst into the kitchen.

In the presence of such atrocity, the stink was to be expected. With no time to fasten his top button, he felt that cold stabbing sensation at the bottom of his neck which always came in the vicinity of death.

'Jesus,' he hissed under his breath, surveying the mutilated corpse surrounded in jars of yellowing liquid. He kept both hands on the gun as he manoeuvred, knowing that Lacey could be somewhere here, too.

'Mike ... is that you?' Jake said. He sounded exhausted.

Frank was sobbing.

Yorke kept his voice low. 'Yes, I—'

'Tell me she's dead,' Jake murmured.

'I don't know. But it's okay. I have the gun.' Yorke pivoted and drew level with Jake's chair.

'No, it's not okay,' Jake hissed. His words fluctuated in volume. He was in a lot of pain and struggling to get his words out. 'You must go and finish her off.'

I can't do that. I'm not you. 'We'll be gone before she wakes up. Where's Lacey?'

'Dead ... apparently. Not here, anyway.'

Yorke moved backwards so he was almost alongside the small table between Jake and Frank. 'It's over ... listen ... I promise, it's over.' He drew level with the table and sighted the jars. One of his hands dropped from the gun to cup his mouth, the urge to vomit suddenly intense.

He looked up at Jake's face and gasped.

'It's worse than it looks,' Jake said. 'Just get us out.'

But was it worse than it looked? Really?

An ear was missing, and blood poured from his ruined nostrils.

'What's she done to you?'

'A lot less than she could've done ...' Jake paused to gulp some air.

Yorke cast a look behind him at Jake's trembling, pale son. *Poor boy.* He shook his head, trying desperately to not let tears fill his eyes. He looked back at Jake, who was panting heavily in the chair.

'I know, it's awful ... unthinkable,' Jake said. 'Just get him out. Whatever you do ... just get my boy out.'

'But Robinson, armed response, they'll be outside already. It's over. I can't protect you.' He leaned forward and touched Jake's bloody cheek.

Jake flinched. 'Just get my boy out.'

Yorke drew his hand back. 'I'm so sorry.'

'Don't worry. As long as Frank's okay, I couldn't give a monkey's.'

Yorke placed the woman's gun on the table beside the jars and selected a knife, forcing back his revulsion over the steel stained with red. 'I'll start you off.' He moved to the wrist on Jake's left hand and recoiled. 'Christ.'

Two of Jake's fingers were missing.

'No worries. I'm righthanded.'

Yorke felt the tears in his eyes again as he hacked through the tape.

After, Jake took the knife from Yorke. 'I can take it from here.' He nodded at his son. 'Frank.'

Yorke watched Jake work the blade onto the tape on his other wrist, squeezing his eyes shut as tears of pain streaked his face.

Yorke brushed away his own tears, took a deep breath, and grabbed a second bloody knife from the table, then faced Frank.

Frank seemed paler since Yorke had last looked at him; he was also shaking more.

Yorke worked as desperately as he could through the tape on Frank's wrist until he broke through.

Jake murmured, 'The things he's seen ... the things he could've seen ...'

Yorke looked back at him. 'I think it's best we don't discuss it anymore. Not until after. He's ...' He broke off before telling Jake he may have been going into shock.

'What's wrong with him?' Jake asked.

'He'll be fine,' Yorke said, not knowing if that was true at all. 'But he could do with fresh air and maybe some distraction.'

Yorke turned and moved the knife onto the second wrist. His phone buzzed in his pocket. He plucked it out and sandwiched it in between his cheek and his shoulder as he worked on Frank's second wrist.

'Update?' Robinson insisted.

'Thirty seconds max and we're walking out of here. There's three of us coming—me, Jake and a child, so keep your guns down.'

'Tobias?'

'No. Jake's son, Frank.'

'What the fuck?'

'I'll explain later.'

'Lacey and Amelia?'

'Lacey isn't here. Presumed dead. Amelia is around the side. Unconscious. I put her down with a piece of wood.' Yorke broke through the tape on the second wrist. 'She won't be getting up in a hurry.'

'Her name's Carrie,' Jake said from behind him.

'Apparently, she's called Carrie now. Look, no one will be armed.'

'Positive?'

'Positive,' Yorke said, now working on the tape binding Frank's ankles. 'You have my word.'

'Don't we need to worry about Jake?'

'No ... he's injured *and* unarmed.'

'God help you, and me, if you've called this wrong.'

'I've not, sir. *I've not.*'

He broke through the tape. Frank was free. 'Okay, less than ten seconds. Be ready to receive us at the front door. No guns, remember.'

'The moment we see you at the door, I'm sending Dave around to secure Amelia ... sorry ... Carrie.'

Yorke hung up, slipped his phone into his pocket, and

glanced at Jake, who was now on his feet. He nodded at the knife in Jake's hand. 'You need to put that down.'

Jake nodded and put the knife by the gun on the table. His empty hand lingered above the gun.

'Leave it. Your son is walking out with you. You take that gun you risk everyone's life.'

Jake withdrew his hand, stood up straight and nodded.

Yorke put his knife down and then eased Frank's arms around his neck. Although he was too shocked to grip, he was light enough to be carried. Yorke had one arm beneath his legs and the other around his back.

Jake opened the kitchen door, and Yorke slid past him, carrying Frank. He sighted the front door at the end of the hallway and broke into a slow jog.

When he reached the door, he allowed Jake enough space to go around him and turn the thumblock and press the handle. Jake opened the door and moved back to the foot of the stairs so Yorke could march out.

Three officers charged over to help Yorke. They eased Frank from his hands.

'He's in shock,' Yorke said. 'We need an ambulance.'

Robinson approached behind the three officers.

'I said he needs a *fucking* ambulance,' Yorke shouted.

Robinson said, 'Calm down, you're safe. Where's Jake?'

Yorke felt his stomach churn. He turned, hoping, praying that Jake was standing at the open front door.

He wasn't.

The front door slammed.

Clunk.

Locked.

'Go ... go ... *fucking* go,' Robinson hissed, then grabbed Yorke's arm to hold him back as four armed officers swooped around him.

Two went to the front door to knock it from its hinges, while the other two hit the path at the side.

$\approx$

Behind you are footsteps of blood.

Jake grabbed the gun from the table.

No more footsteps.

He pressed the gun to the soft flesh beneath his chin and closed his eyes.

Take him to his matches, Mike. Watch him play. I know you will.

His finger slipped around the trigger.

He let his mind linger on Piper for a moment, playing in the garden with Peter's dog. He smiled.

Sorry I never made it back. Take care of that dog. Jesus, Peter had loved that fucking dog!

He tightened his grip.

Laughter.

Carrie.

He opened his eyes.

She hobbled towards him, using the kitchen surfaces to hold herself upright, almost dragging one of her legs. She must've gone down hard on it when Yorke had struck her. A lot of blood ran down her face, too.

Jake pointed his gun at her.

She paused, panting, a metre in front of him, still laughing.

Before, that laugh had been insidious, now it was pitiful.

'They're going to cage you for the rest of your life,' Jake said.

'And you?'

He didn't reply.

She nodded at his gun and snorted. 'How can you fucking resist killing me? It's not like you haven't done it before. Go on I know how it feels. The *need.*'

He thought about the cruelty of others that came before her and what he'd done to end their scourges. She was right. But still. 'No. I'm tired. I think the cage will be enough.'

'It didn't work for Lacey.'

'Lower the gun!' someone shouted.

Jake sighted an officer in full body armour pointing his weapon at him through the kitchen window.

'Surprise. It's all getting serious now,' Carrie said.

'Looks that way.'

'*I said*, put down the gun!'

Behind them, Jake heard someone kick open the front door. *It was almost over.*

Carrie smiled. 'Lacey had a lot of fan mail in jail. I expect I'll have the same.'

'Your point?'

'I reckon I could get someone to help me.' She smirked again.

Jake nodded. 'Seems a cage won't stop you, will it?'

She shook her head, slowly. 'No, it won't.'

Jake dangled the gun from his finger and raised his voice. 'I'm going to put it down.'

'*Slowly ... down ...*' This time the voice came from behind him. They'd made it through the front door.

Jake started to kneel, slowly, dangling the gun. 'There's only one way to keep Frank safe then, I guess.'

'Better the devil, eh, Jake?'

'*Fuck* the Devil.' He raised the gun and shot her in the head. There was an explosion of bone and blood.

He felt weight on his back, pressing his face towards the floor.

Then he heard a familiar voice in his ear. 'Stay down.'

Mike.

The gun was pried from his hand.

'*Disarmed,*' Yorke shouted.

Jake looked up to watch Carrie slide down the wall with a hole where her left eye used to be. He welcomed the sense of relief that came from knowing his son was now well and truly safe.

And for that reason, and that reason alone, maybe it wasn't so bad that Yorke had saved his life after all.

CLEAN

$\mathcal{W}$ alter Divall, self-proclaimed influencer of Article SE, watched Felix Holden die at his feet.

It wasn't as quick as Walter expected and so didn't make for pleasant viewing. The gaze from Felix's twitching eyes remained on the lawyer throughout, seemingly pleading for mercy. *Pathetic and pointless.* His throat had been cut, so it was far too late to spare him.

Not that the lawyer would've changed his mind. No. After seeing those horrors on the monitors, there'd never been any chance of that!

The property developer's eyes stopped twitching, and Walter sighed again.

Such a waste.

Smart, successful, motivated ...

And what dress sense!

Everything needed for our sophisticated face!

Yet—he stepped away from the spreading pool of blood at his feet and surveyed the control room with distaste—*this!*

This is disgusting. So, in the end, you turned out to be just like so many of your predecessors. Weak.

'*My father's wishes!*' Felix had said.

Walter shook his head and stared at Felix's pale face. *You should've put a pillow over your father's face when you found out what he was, and you should've done the same to your brother. You were pathetic, and you've no right to drag us into the mire with* these—he eyed a monitor that displayed two men covered in blood, playing with a mutilated corpse—*atrocities.*

He faced Russ Jenson, leader of one of their most formidable units—another man who dressed well and projected decorum. *Strong. Unflappable.*

Still, hadn't he thought the same of Felix?

He sighed as he watched Russ use some Kleenex left on the desk to wipe clean the blade he'd killed Felix with. 'And Sam Lane?'

'In the van with Olly.'

'Bury him.'

Russ nodded. 'We will.'

'What a tale, eh?' Walter said.

'Wouldn't have believed it,' Russ said, 'unless I'd seen it with my own eyes.'

Walter said, 'No one can ever know. This *isn't* what we are. Well done for getting the truth.'

'Honestly? I barely touched the man. He seemed keen to get this off his chest.'

'No wonder. This kind of stuff can eat at you. Unfortunately, it *must* stay on our chests, for good.'

'It will.'

'See that your men clean.'

Walter pointed at the other monitor.

Lacey and Tobias.

All eggs in one basket.

'And just check that mother and son are dead.'

'Will do.'

'Good. I will go outside and get some air.' Walter turned for the control room door. 'This place sickens me.'

'And Jake Pettman, sir?'

Walter stopped and turned back. 'What about him?'

'Well, I'm assuming—'

'Assume nothing.'

'But—'

'He lives.'

'But we could find a way to neutralise that leverage?'

'Not the point.'

'I see. But surely it'd be better to—'

'He lives *because* I like him.'

Russ shook his head, bewildered.

Walter wasn't irritated. Russ had a right to his bewilderment. And Walter liked it.

Everyone should always remain accountable and open for judgement.

Even him.

Still, he knew he was right on this one. 'Jake Pettman is a wonder. A *passionate* wonder. Let him think he's won. One day he'll be one of our greatest assets.'

'Sir, I'm not sure—'

'It isn't your job to be sure. It's simply your job to *do*.' He was a bit irritated now. Time for Russ to let it go. 'That's the end of the matter.'

~

As Russ approached Ray, Stevie, and Jay, he heard them arguing over who should pop the two psychopaths.

They stopped arguing when they noticed their boss.

Russ gave them all an angry look, especially Ray, who he was particularly pissed off with. He'd heard all about his loss of control earlier. Delaying the execution of a target for pleasure was a definite no-no. Ray would have to be disciplined.

Russ smiled. 'If you hadn't been arguing, you would've heard the sound of their cell door unlocking.'

Their faces paled, and they threw an awkward glance at the cell door.

'Yes. Lucky for you, the crazies didn't notice either. Have you seen what they've done to that poor bastard in there? Felix was adamant it was his brother before we put him down, but really, how can you *even* tell?'

No one answered. They were too ashamed of being caught behaving like children.

'Jay,' Russ said, 'you take cell thirteen farther down the corridor. Lacey and Tobias. They're both dead already. But let's just make sure.'

Jay nodded but couldn't hide his disappointment, grunting as he trudged off.

'Ray, you wait out here while me and Stevie go into these two freaks.'

'Russ—'

'*Don't.*' He held up a finger. 'Don't even fucking dare.'

Ray nodded and stepped backwards.

Russ and Stevie entered the cell, guns drawn. The two men, one naked and the other fully clothed but drenched head to toe in blood, scurried from Dr Stewart Holden towards the back of the room.

'Fucking hell,' Russ said.

'I know,' Stevie said.

Russ had gotten a good look at the small monitor in the poky control room, but now, up close, such atrocity took on a whole new level.

'He's still alive, too,' Stevie said.

'Fuck off.'

'No, really. That's one of the things we were … discussing *before*.'

'You mean arguing about?'

'Yes.' Stevie flushed. 'We were taking turns to look through the slot. His chest. Look carefully at his chest.'

Russ leaned in, squinting at the red, raw flesh and the exposed rib. His chest was moving. Gently. Barely perceptible. 'Fuck. You can hear it, too. *Faintly*. The tiniest of whistles.'

'His eye, too.'

Russ studied Holden's skinned face. He'd lost one eye in the process, but one still poked out the pulpy flesh. Russ caught it moving, the smallest flicker. 'He's looking right at us.'

'Uh-huh. It's freaking me out. Not even an eyelid to blink with. Could you imagine? It'd irritate the hell—'

Russ glared at Stevie. 'You fucking serious?'

Stevie shrugged.

'I think that's the least of his fucking worries, don't you?' Russ turned back round. 'Ready?'

'*Very*.'

'What a house of fucking horrors,' Russ said, sighing.

They raised their guns and executed the three men.

~

DISAPPOINTED that he'd missed out on popping at least one of those monsters, Jay trudged down the corridor. And, as he neared the thirteenth cell, concern over the condition of Lacey and Tobias quickly grew.

What if they were alive?

Because it really wasn't Jay's bag, killing women and children. I mean, he'd killed women before, of course, under order, but that'd been different. These women had been part of the criminal life and had been trying to kill him. The prospect of killing a defenceless woman—a woman like his mother, for example—sickened him. Now, there was a woman who'd known how to love, to *nurture*—his mother; the world had been a colder place since she'd vacated it.

Still, Lacey was nothing like his mother, and far from innocent, so if push came to shove, he would do it. I mean, he'd have to. It was his job. But he hoped that she'd at least come at him first with a weapon.

The child, though.

If Tobias was breathing, it could be a real problem.

Because this was one line he just didn't want to cross.

So, as he opened the cell door, he really did hope the child was already dead.

He entered and raised his gun ... and then lowered it, sighing.

He needn't have worried.

Lacey sat by the cell door. Her skin was pale, and her hair hung limply over half her face. Her one visible eye was closed. Tobias, the young boy, was across her lap, lifeless and wide-eyed. With one hand, she'd been cradling his head, while with the other, she'd been stroking his face, until she'd stopped moving.

Both had contributed to the large pool of blood beneath them. Lacey's blouse was bloody due to a stomach wound, while Tobias's throat had been cut. A scalpel and a knife lay in the blood beside them.

Jay knew of some of the story surrounding Lacey and Tobias. Not naturally mother and son but rumoured to be in adoration of each other. He appreciated the tragic nature of the scene. How fitting they'd died together, their blood finally joining, unifying them.

Jay wasn't a poet, but he was considered a deeper thinker than most by the men he killed with, and he found some beauty in the image.

He also recalled his own mother holding him as a child, nurturing him. She'd done everything in her power to give him the childhood every kid deserved despite the impoverished neighbourhood they'd resided in, and the spiralling crime rates. Jay lowered his gun, gave a nod of respect, and moved for the door.

Lacey's visible eye opened.

Despite the state of her, he jumped out of his skin.

Still, why wouldn't he? This was Lacey Ray, after all. To say she had a bloody history was an understatement!

He inwardly sighed as he raised his gun.

After appreciating the bittersweet image and connecting it with his own childhood, he found the prospect of interfering in this scene sickening. But this was, of course, his lot. His obligation.

He waited for that eye to move upwards to sight him before he killed her. He wanted to gesture his appreciation over her attempts to try and care for this child, whom, Jay assumed, had been murdered by that monstrous fucker in the other cell.

On first seeing the remains of Stewart Holden, he'd vocalised his thoughts to the others. *'No one deserves that.'*

Now, looking at this dead ten-year-old boy, he decided that maybe Holden had deserved it after all.

Lacey's eye didn't move though. It looked downwards. Her attention was clearly on the child's face.

The tragedy intensified for Jay.

Here, faced with her own death, there was no fear, no concern, just a complete infatuation with her lost child. And here Jay stood ready to execute her, no better than some of the other barbarians they'd put down—like those in the terrorist cell, for example.

He sighed and closed his eyes, disgusted with himself. And then he was there again, in his mother's arms as a young boy, listening to her promises to always care for him, to elevate him from the world they lived in, to look on him with pride until her last breath.

A last breath that came all too early because of a drunk driver.

Fourteen years old was too young to lose a mother.

Especially when she was the only person who ever loved him.

He felt the tear on his face.

But this is your life now, Jay. This is your job. You must do what's expected of you.

He tightened his grip on the trigger, trying to force back the memory of his mother, which was so visceral that he could almost feel her fingers stroking his cheek as she sang to him. Up and down ... up and down.

He opened his eyes, took aim—

Lacey stroked Tobias's face up and down ... up and down. And when the first note of a hummed lullaby left her lips, Jay lowered his weapon.

Jay left the cell, wiping away his tears, and closed the door behind him so this mother could die in peace.

SUMMER LIGHTNING

*Y*orke thanked the officer at the door and entered the visiting room.

Jake held up a cuffed hand to greet him. The chains that looped down through the hole in the table rattled.

Yorke pointed over the table at Jake's long, unkempt beard and raised an eyebrow.

Jake creased his brow. '*What*? Earlier this year, you said it suited me.'

'Yes, I also said it took the attention off the missing ear.' Yorke put his backpack on the table. 'But when I start to worry about birds nesting in it, then I go back to preferring the missing ear.'

'How can you prefer something that isn't there? Doesn't make sense.'

Yorke laughed. 'Can't you at least put some shape back into the beard? Use some beard butter, perhaps?'

'What the fuck is beard butter?' He snorted. 'Actually, don't tell me. Prefer not to know what I'm missing out on. Besides, not as if I need to worry about being presentable for work, is it?'

Yorke sat down. 'And what about your visitors? Do we not matter?'

'Visitors?' Jake chortled. '*Visitor.*' He tried to maintain a brave face, but his smile soon fell away, and he looked down.

'Sorry, mate. Didn't mean to ...'

Jake waved his left hand, the one missing two digits, causing the chains to rattle. 'Pack it in. Not your fault I'm officially friendless. I managed to achieve that all on my own.'

'You're not friendless.'

'Sod off. You only come and visit me out of guilt.'

'Bollocks!'

'I'm everything you detest.'

'You have me all wrong, then.'

Jake smirked. 'Nah. I don't. You're a man totally facing in the right direction. You can't comprehend the things I've done. You blame yourself for what happened to me. It's guilt. You can't like what you've hated for so long. What you're *driven* to hate.'

Yorke looked down. *Was he right?*

Maybe. Who knows? He sighed. *Still, how many sleepless nights have you spent dwelling on this subject? You've vowed to stop thinking about it!*

Jake pointed at the backpack. 'Have you got the rock hammer in there so I can start chipping away at the wall behind my Southampton FC poster?'

Yorke laughed.

'How the hell do you even get a backpack in anyway?' Jake asked.

'High-security clearance.'

'On account of the new job?'

Yorke nodded. He unzipped the backpack and retrieved two flasks. He removed the lids and slid one to Jake.

'Is that what I think it is?'

'Green tea?'

'Piss off,' Jake said. 'Better be Hopback's original?'

'And finest.'

'Piss off again.' Jake picked it up with his chained hands and took a large mouthful. He closed his eyes and swallowed. 'Bloody hell, it is ... taste those East Kent Goldings hops. Yeah!'

Yorke also took a mouthful of Summer Lightning.

'Hate me all you want, man,' Jake said. 'I *fucking* love you.'

Yorke nodded. 'Happy birthday, shithead.'

Jake raised an eyebrow. 'You remembered?'

'Obviously. I'm not going to smuggle beer into jail on any old day, am I?'

'You've got a reputation to uphold now, I guess.'

Yorke shrugged.

'How's it been? The new job?'

'Being at war with Article SE? How do you think?'

'Stressful?'

'Yep.'

'Exciting?'

Yorke laughed. 'Guess so.'

'Head of SEROCU.' Jake slammed down his beer and pointed at his chest. 'My best friend. Who'd have thought?'

'It's not all that glamorous.'

'Oh, it is. Although, I don't appreciate these long gaps between visits.'

'Yep. That's the only problem. The job takes you all over the place.'

He took another mouthful of Summer Lightning. 'As long as you make it to see him once or twice a month. That was the deal.'

'It was. And I am. Without fail.'

'Evidence?'

Yorke reached into his unzipped backpack and extracted

a brown envelope. He tossed it over to Jake, who removed the photographs.

Yorke allowed him a few minutes to peruse the pictures of his son playing football.

'What's with that celebration?'

'They're all at it now,' Yorke said. 'Trademark celebrations.'

Jake took another mouthful, nodding. 'Good lad.'

'He's a cracker. Scores at will. Nothing like you ever were.'

'More of a team player?' Jake asked in a sarcastic voice.

Yorke inwardly sighed. 'He's just brilliant.'

'Music to my ears.'

Jake reached the last photo. His hands trembled slightly, and he laid it in front of himself rather than drop it. The photograph was of Frank facing away from the camera with his new Southampton shirt. He had a thumb over one shoulder, pointing down at his name: Pettman. Yorke had arranged this gift on Jake's behalf.

But Yorke knew that wasn't the reason Jake had tears in his eyes. Nor the reason he now held both his clenched fists to his mouth. It was the words that Frank had scribbled across the photograph that had surely set his best friend off.

I miss you, Daddy x

THE BLUE ROOM

*T*obias.

Now that we're here, I'm positive you'll understand.

Yes, I know it's cold, and I know the walls can sometimes feel like they're closing in on you, especially when they're this rich and deep in shade, but you'll grow accustomed. There was a time when I felt the same way. But there're good reasons for this place, my son.

My place.

Our place.

Blue means forever, my boy. Like the sky. Like us.

Notice how that pain you felt is lifting?

Come. Sit with me. It feels so good to have my arms around you again.

I never abandoned you, and now that the barrier those others put up between us is gone, you can finally believe this.

Ha! Tobias! Has that caught you attention?

I know, it's nice to touch, isn't it? Softer than other books. Leather bound.

That's my diary.

No, my silly cherub, you can't read it! A diary is personal. Very personal. It contains my thoughts, my dreams, my hopes ... and yes, because contrary to belief, I do have them, my fears. It also contains things in my life that I don't wish you to know about. Not until I've gone. Then my darling, you can sit here in this very room, bathing in the cold blue, and learn everything there ever was to know about me.

If there's such a thing as knowing everything there ever was about a person, which I doubt very much!

Yes, of course, I'll teach you to write your diary!

But, of course, it doesn't take much teaching, my pudding. You merely need pen, paper, and time. Not a lot of time, just enough, to turn your thoughts into words.

And because no one else will ever read it if you so choose, you don't have to worry about how it sounds or how it comes across to others. There'll be no judgement. Judge others, by all means—that's the point of the Blue Room, after all—but you'll never be judged by the words you write.

And because of this, it can be the most beautiful way to spend your days!

So try it, my chicken!

Here is a piece of paper; here is a pen. Sit over there and write what you feel.

My beautiful boy.

In the meantime, I'll continue my own. If you need me, just shout. I tend to get sucked in.

I love you too, Tobias.

So, where to start?

How about here?

Dear diary, I've so much to share with you ...

Coming 2024 – The Secret Diary of Lacey Ray.
Sometimes the darkest thoughts are best kept secret.
Pre-order now.

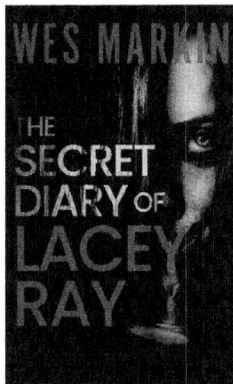

Scan the QR to
READ NOW!

ACKNOWLEDGMENTS

Writing Better the Devil was a daunting task! It'd been over two years since I'd last been in Yorke's world and had become firmly locked in Gardner's world up north in Knaresborough. Still, I was felt ready for the challenge, especially as I knew it would give me another opportunity to write about Lacey and Jake. But what a challenge it was! From the outset, it felt so stylistically different to the other Yorke books, that I felt compelled to take a step back and reassess whether this was the right move. Thankfully, I had the wonderful Donna Moffatt on hand, blogger extraordinaire and talented writer, to review the words I'd written down, and to convince me to continue on this particular journey.

And for that I'm grateful. Because, honestly, without her words, I don't know whether I would have continued, and I really like Better the Devil. I hope you enjoy it too.

Thank you again to everyone who had supported me. There are so many of you, and I really couldn't have done it without all of you helping me.

Will Yorke return? As the leader of SEROCU to take on Article SE?

Honestly, I don't know.

First up, Lacey Ray, and then we'll see what happens.

FREE AND EXCLUSIVE READ

Delve deeper into the world of Wes Markin with the **FREE** and **EXCLUSIVE** read, *A Lesson in Crime*

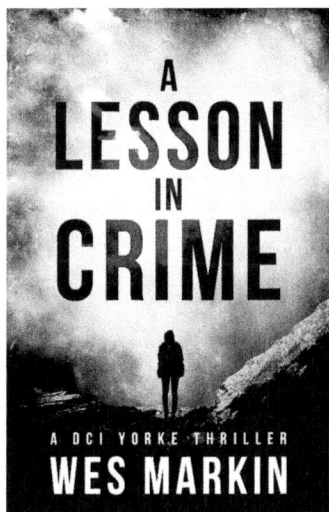

Scan the QR to READ NOW!

START THE JAKE PETTMAN SERIES TODAY WITH THE KILLING PIT

A broken ex-detective. A corrupt chief of police. A merciless drug lord.

And a missing child.

Running from a world which wants him dead, ex-detective Sergeant Jake Pettman journeys to the isolated town of Blue Falls, Maine, home of his infamous murderous ancestors.

But Jake struggles to hide from who he is, and when a child disappears, he finds himself drawn into an investigation that shares no parallels to anything he has ever seen before.

Held back by a chief of police plagued and tormented by his own secrets, Jake fights for the truth. All the way to the door of Jotham MacLeoid. An insidious megalomaniac who feeds his victims to a Killing Pit.

And the terrifying secrets that lie within.

A JAKE PETTMAN THRILLER

THE KILLING PIT

Some secrets are better left in the dark

WES MARKIN

Scan the QR to
READ NOW!

JOIN DCI EMMA GARDNER AS SHE RELOCATES TO KNARESBOROUGH, HARROGATE IN THE NORTH YORKSHIRE MURDERS …

Still grieving from the tragic death of her colleague, DCI Emma Gardner continues to blame herself and is struggling to focus. So, when she is seconded to the wilds of Yorkshire, Emma hopes she'll be able to get her mind back on the job, doing what she does best - putting killers behind bars.

But when she is immediately thrown into another violent murder, Emma has no time to rest. Desperate to get answers and find the killer, Emma needs all the help she can. But her new partner, DI Paul Riddick, has demons and issues of his own.

And when this new murder reveals links to an old case Riddick was involved with, Emma fears that history might be about to repeat itself...

Don't miss the brand-new gripping crime series by best-selling British crime author Wes Markin!

∾

What people are saying about Wes Markin...

'Cracking start to an exciting new series. Twist and turns, thrills and kills. I loved it.'

Bestselling author **Ross Greenwood**

'Markin stuns with his latest offering... Mind-bendingly dark and deep, you know it's not for the faint hearted from page one. Intricate plotting, devious twists and excellent characterisation take this tale to a whole new level. Any serious crime fan will love it!'

Bestselling author **Owen Mullen**

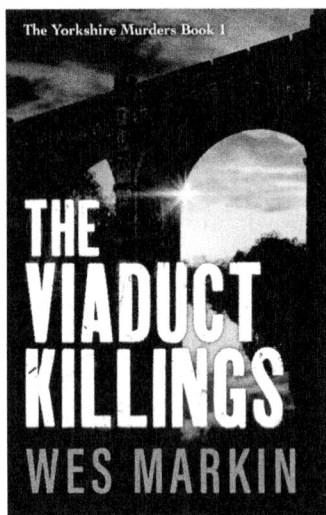

Scan the QR to
READ NOW!

STAY IN TOUCH

To keep up to date with new publications, tours, and promotions, or if you would like the opportunity to view pre-release novels, please contact me:

Website: www.wesmarkinauthor.com

facebook.com/WesMarkinAuthor

instagram.com/wesmarkinauthor

twitter.com/markinwes

amazon.com/Wes-Markin/e/B07MJP4FXP

REVIEW

If you enjoyed reading *Better The Devil,* please take a few
moments to leave a review on
Amazon, Goodreads or BookBub.

Printed in Great Britain
by Amazon

58867669R00192